MW01487756

ACCIDENTALLY MINE

A Birch Crossing Novel

STEPHANIE ROWE

Authenticity Playground, LLC

COPYRIGHT

For further information, please contact Stephanie@stephanierowe.com

CHAPTER ONE

HE'D MADE A MISTAKE.

A gruesome, life-changing, stupid-as-hell mistake.

Jason Sarantos felt the familiar sense of doom and failure settle over his shoulders as he stood in the doorway of the small Maine cafe he'd bought, sight-unseen, six weeks ago. He'd then promptly dismantled his life and his son's to leave New York and move to Maine to take over the store and open a pizza joint.

The sparkling new key dangled from his fingertips as he took in the magnitude of what he'd chosen in that one, desperate attempt to reclaim a life for his son. The store had once been a cafe, but now it looked like an ancient, long-forgotten tomb of rot and mold.

Not exactly what he'd been anticipating when he'd taken a jackhammer to his life, shredded it, and hauled ass up to Maine for a soul-inspiring new start.

He let out a sigh as he studied what he'd *thought* was going to be a quaint cafe in the center of a charming Maine town. He'd thought maybe there would be a vase of fresh flowers welcoming him, or maybe a little old lady with a plate of cookies would be standing in the doorway with a scruffy dog and an offer to babysit.

Yeah, not so much.

His small town greeting had been a couple of dive-bombing dragonflies, and the only tasty treat was the rotting wood along the top of the doorframe. The old linoleum floors were stained and torn, peeling up at the corners. Water had oozed from the window frames, marking the wood. The tables and chairs that he'd anted up to include in the purchase were nicked and damaged, covered in dust so thick he couldn't even tell what kind of wood they were made of.

Glass display counters were coated with grime, nowhere near large enough for the pizzas he'd planned to showcase to tempt customers into trying a slice, and the "charming light fixtures" were rustic light bulbs dangling from the ceiling. The place was smaller than he'd expected, barely fitting more than ten tables. The walls were once polished wood, but now the varnish was cracked and peeling.

And the stench. The air reeked of pungent decay, as if a rodent had died beneath the floor boards.

This was what it had come to? Two years ago, he'd had a wife, at least in name, two great boys and a career as an ER doc that had consumed him for the last twelve years. Now, it was simply death. Of his wife. Of his son. Of a life he'd thought was doing all right.

And now, today marked the apparent death of a second chance that was nothing but an old store that someone else had been smart enough to abandon.

He glanced over his shoulder at the quaint town center that had felt so charming when he'd driven through thirteen years ago on his honeymoon. An old-fashioned Maine town that had sat in his memory for more than a decade, beck-oning to him until the time was right to claim the dream.

The time had never been right, but he'd always remembered how the town had made him feel, after he'd arrived so strung out from his first year at med school. Relaxed. At peace. At home. He'd never forgotten Birch Crossing, and when he'd seen that ad for the store after another hellish night of pacing the floor to avoid the nightmares, he'd jumped on it and sealed the deal before he had a chance to change his mind.

And now, the fantasy that had nagged at him for more than a decade was a reality of dead rat, mold and dust and a sense of disbelieving failure for what he'd thrust his six-year-old son into.

Noah shifted in his arms, burrowing more deeply against Jason's shoulder. After being too upset about the move to sleep last night or in the car, the boy had finally fallen asleep a half-hour ago. Jason had been planning to wake him up to do the big reveal, but now...

Shit.

He couldn't do that to his son. Not yet. He'd have to find a way to frame it that would somehow, someway, make it okay for Noah.

Maybe he'd play the dead rat angle.

God, was that what he was left with? Trying to restore his son's life with the smell of a decaying rodent? Yeah, okay, so Noah would actually be on board with that, but hell, it wasn't enough.

Jason strode across the room, spread out his sweatshirt as a blanket, and laid Noah on the window seat. Then Jason sat heavily beside him and dropped his head to his hands, digging his fingers into his temples. "Think, Jason," he said aloud, his voice echoing through the abandoned room. "There has to be a way to make this right."

"Of course there is," a woman said, her melodic voice drifting across the dust-filled room. "A fresh coat of lilac paint on the walls and maybe a blue-green turquoise on the ceiling, don't you think?"

Jason jerked his head up at the intrusion, and then froze when he saw who had spoken. It wasn't the old lady with cookies that he'd imagined. He'd been off by several decades and a whole lot of femininity.

A woman was leaning against the doorway to his shop, her brown eyes sparkling with merriment he hadn't felt in years. Her dark brown hair tumbled around her shoulders with a reckless abandon that spoke of a spirit that would never be tamed. Some of the curls had been woven into a yellow and green braided scarf that seemed to disappear into her thick hair. From each earlobe dangled several pairs of earrings, gold wire twisted into designs so intriguing he wanted to stride right over to her and see what they were.

She was wearing a pair of faded jeans that showed womanly curves that he hadn't thought about in way too long. The delicate straps of her pale yellow tank top rested across her collar bones, revealing a smooth expanse of skin that shot right to his core.

But it was her smile that he couldn't look away from. It was so full of life and vitality, that it made him want to grab her and yank her into his store so she could inject the dying place with her energy.

Her eyebrows arched up, and there was no mistaking the glint of interest in her eyes. "You disagree with the lilac paint suggestion but you're too polite to tell me that, or you're just overwhelmed by my mind-numbing beauty and stunned into disbelieving silence?"

Shit. He was staring? Jason swore and quickly stood up, brushing the dust from the store off his jeans. "My name's Jason Sarantos. I bought the place."

Her smile widened, lighting up her eyes even more, like this great gust of relief breaking through the gloom trying to consume him. "Jason, everyone in this entire town knows your name, that you bought the store, and that it was twelve minutes after three when you drove your Mercedes SUV past Wright's General Store when you arrived in town, not to mention the fact you were drinking a Dunkin' Donuts coffee as you went by." She set her hands on her hips and tilted her head, giving him a teasing grin. "Everyone was pretty offended you didn't stop in to buy your coffee at Wright's and introduce yourself."

Jason blinked, suddenly thrust back into the past, into his childhood, into the small town in Minnesota he'd grown up in, where his mother had found out about his first kiss before he'd even lifted his lips from those of Samantha Huckaby. That was why he'd been drawn to Birch Crossing: because it reminded him of everything he liked about his home and his childhood, yet it had the appealing bonus of being two thousand miles away from the sixteen cousins, five aunts and uncles, and four sisters that had driven him east to find his own path. "Shit. Sorry. I wasn't thinking."

The woman laughed, a beautiful, melodic sound that went right to his gut. God, when was the last time he'd seen anyone effuse such life? He was riveted by her, by the irreverence of her smile, by the fire in her eyes. This was a woman who was so damn alive that nothing could bring her down. He wanted that. He needed that. God, he needed that.

"Don't worry about it. The town will have you trained in no time, trust me." She raised her eyebrows. "I don't suppose you're dialed into the gossip chain enough to know my name?" She wrinkled her nose, and he thought he saw a flash of vulnerability in her eyes. "I tend to be fodder for talk in this town. I'm not always a fit."

Yeah, he could imagine. She seemed to carry the kind of spunk that might knock an old New England town on its ass. Jason grinned, and he was almost surprised to realize he still knew how to smile. Felt like a long time since he'd meant it. "Yeah, sorry, I figure I need at least twenty-four hours to recognize everyone in town by sight."

"I'll be back to quiz you in twenty-four hours." She inclined her head and held out her hand. "Astrid Monroe. My brother Harlan is the one who sold you the shop. He's out of town, so he asked me to stop by and see if you needed anything."

Instinctively, Jason reached out to shake her hand. "Nice to meet you. Thanks for the offer." Yeah, he knew what he needed. He needed a damned angel to sweep into his life and fix everything that he'd screwed up, to make this okay for his son. He needed—

Then as he felt the warmth of her palm against his, the light touch of her fingers on the back of his hand, his gut knew what he needed.

He needed *her*.

ASTRID WAS SHOCKED by the burst of electricity that ripped through her as Jason shook her hand. It felt like her entire body had come to life, a reaction she hadn't felt since the day she'd met her ex-fiancé.

Fear rippled through her, and she jerked her hand back.

Jason's eyebrows rose, and she saw a hooded darkness sweep over his face. She was startled by the depths of the shadows in his eyes, shadows that went right to her heart, because she felt those same ones every day. Loss. Grief. Isolation. Pain.

Unsettled, she shoved her hands into her pockets, trying to gather her composure again, unable to stop herself from glancing at his left hand. No wedding ring. Crud! Why was she even looking at his hand? Horrified, she jerked her gaze back to his face just as he pulled his own gaze off her left hand.

Awareness burned through her, and she quickly stepped back, fighting to put distance between them before the roar in her belly could gain traction. "So, we'll expect you at Wright's this afternoon to do your grocery shopping, so you can introduce yourself properly." She swallowed, not liking how quavery her voice sounded. What was wrong with her? He was just a man, another man among the millions that were alive, men that all blended together until they were indistinguishable blurs in life.

Except he wasn't like that.

Jason Sarantos was more. She knew nothing about him. The whole town was in the dark. Harlan had gotten no personal information from Jason during the deal. No one had any idea how long it would take for him to show up and claim his store. She knew only that he was from New York and that he drove a nice car... Something moved behind him and she noticed a young boy sleeping in the window seat. His son? Mixed emotions tumbled through her, feelings so much more complicated than she could begin to cope with.

"I'll be by," Jason said, his voice low and rough, rolling across her skin like the heat from a wood stove on a cold winter night.

"By? By where?" She jerked her gaze to him as chills rippled over her skin.

He raised his brows. "Wright's. Didn't you say I should stop by?"

"Oh, right. Yes." Astrid shivered and hugged herself, trying to regain her equilibrium. "Great." She was used to always being secure and grounded around men, always careful not to make herself vulnerable to a man...*ever*. But her reaction to Jason was so out of her control. She was noticing him as a *man*, and that was terrifying.

7

The silence hung between them. Not awkward. One of intense awareness. He was watching her, those dark brown eyes so full of emotion he wasn't sharing.

His jeans were low and loose across his hips, faded and well-worn, so unlike his shiny Mercedes. His tee shirt was gray and nondescript, but the torn collar spoke of a man who wasn't afraid to get dirty and do hard work. His light brown hair was short and spiky, as if he'd spent the last hour running his hand through it in aggravation. And his body...Astrid couldn't keep herself from noticing his lean torso, his well-muscled arms, and the sculpted chest that the tee shirt didn't hide.

He was all male, all rugged, and affecting her in ways that she hadn't allowed in years. She was so used to being in complete control of her response to men, to keeping them distant, but the way he looked at her...

"Will you be at Wright's later?" he asked, his gaze intent on her. "When I stop by?"

She cleared her throat and quickly shook her head. "No, I'll be working." It was a lie, actually. She couldn't work another moment. Not today. She'd worked the last twenty-one hours without stopping, all the way through the night, and she was exhausted beyond words. The marathon attempt to jumpstart her creativity had resulted only in more failure, and she was terrified that she'd never find her way out of the spiral that had started six months ago.

He raised his brows. "What do you do?"

"I'm an artist. I make jewelry. Not with precious stones. It's more inspirational and personal." She said it almost defensively, knowing that some Mercedes-driving hotshot from New York would disdain that kind of answer.

But he smiled, a knowing, understanding smile of satisfaction, as if he loved her response. "That fits you."

Warmth swelled inside her at his reaction, and she immediately took another step back. "It fits me? You don't even know me."

His gaze flickered to the scarf in her hair, then traveled over her earrings and her outfit, making blood rush to her skin. "No, I don't." He met her gaze. "I still think it fits you."

She pressed her lips together, shocked by how good it felt to have this stranger say that. It was as if he saw the sides of her she showed to no one. Dear God, what was going on with her? Why was she responding to him like this? She had to get out of there and get her composure back. Find her space. Reclaim the persona she'd been clinging to so desperately the last two years. "So, if you're all set, then I'm going to head out—"

"Can I get your number?" Jason touched her arm, the contact sending sparks all the way through her. He studied her with those deep brown eyes, so rich that she felt like she could get lost in them for days. "In case I have any questions about the shop? Or is Harlan coming back soon?" He left the question hovering out there.

She could tell him Harlan was coming back at the end of the week, that he needed to wait until then, but before she could stop herself, her phone number tumbled off her lips.

Jason immediately pulled out his phone and typed it in, and she couldn't stop her heart from pounding. When was the last time she'd given her phone number to a man? She never did. She always kept control. Yes, yes, yes, this was about the store, not a date, but it felt different.

It *was* different.

Jason was a man, pure and elemental in his maleness, and she was noticing it on every level of her being.

"Thanks." Jason shoved his phone into his pocket and studied her again, and this time the shadows in his eyes were so evident that she felt her own throat tighten and a deep ache filled her heart, a pain that she hadn't let herself feel for so long.

Damn him. She never cried anymore. She couldn't afford to. "I have to go." Then, in a move that was so uncharacteristic of what the entire town would expect of her, Astrid fled.

CHAPTER TWO

"CLARE?" Astrid hurried inside Wright and Son, the general store that she'd just told Jason he needed to visit. The store was relatively quiet, but it was only the afternoon lull before the pre-dinnertime rush hit. It would be heating up shortly, as people swung by to pick up takeout or groceries for dinner, or beer for the town softball game later in the evening.

But right now, the wooden tables were empty and the only occupant was Ophelia Wright, the wife of the former owner, Norm Wright, who had been the town's keystone for so many years. Ophelia was humming cheerfully behind her deli counter, her new iPod headphones looking so incongruous with her lavender-tinted gray hair and the wrinkles on her face.

Astrid knew she didn't have long until Jason arrived, but she was so freaked out by her reaction to him that she had to talk to Clare. She'd been in town for almost two years now, but Clare was one of only two people who she felt close enough with to admit she was falling apart.

No one else was allowed to know that Astrid Monroe *ever* fell apart.

"Clare's in the addition." Griffin Friese, the new owner of Wright's and Clare's fiancé, walked in from the back room, carrying a massive cardboard box. Astrid grinned at the sight of his platinum watch. The man might have walked away from a tremendous income in New York for Clare, but he still kept wearing that ridiculously overstated watch. Men and their watches. It was almost as bad as men and their cars. "She's picking paint colors for the walls of her shop," he said.

"Paint colors? Without me?" Astrid frowned as she hurried past Griffin. "Emma was going to come by later, and we were all going to do it together." Emma Larson was the only other person in Birch Crossing who Astrid felt moderately comfortable with, probably because Emma seemed to be carrying even more demons than Astrid was. She'd met Emma through Clare, and although she wasn't as close to Emma as she was with Clare, Emma was tentatively becoming another friend Astrid was almost willing to trust. Clare had become the best friend Astrid had never had as a child, which was why she was so desperate to talk to her *now*.

Before Clare had abandoned her legal career, she and Astrid had shared office space, and had spent as much time chatting as they'd spent working. Once Clare had shut down her shop, however, Astrid hadn't been able to afford the rent, since she'd been paying Clare as subtenant for only the tiny corner of the space that she used for her jewelry making. Now that they weren't working together, quality time had been seriously diminished, and Astrid had been reduced to trying to recapture her creativity while breathing the gasoline fumes at her apartment.

Who knew? Maybe they'd help her.

Astrid ducked under the plastic tarp protecting the main store from the construction. Clare was standing beside her daughter Katie and Griffin's daughter Brooke. The three of them were studying six different paint splotches on the wall, engaged in a spirited discussion about what colors would be most appropriate for the cupcake store that Clare was opening adjacent to Wright's.

Having finally quit the lawyer job that was draining her soul, Clare had ditched her slacks and blouses, and she was now wearing a pair of paint-splattered jeans, a tank top and a ponytail. She looked casual and happy, and a twinge of envy went through Astrid at the glow on Clare's face. What did it feel like to be that happy?

"Hey, girls." Astrid stepped over a stack of two-by-fours and a power saw sitting on the new wood floors. "What's up?"

Clare grinned at her, but the two teens didn't even bother to stop their debate about pale blue versus sea-foam green. "Hey, Astrid. Hope you don't mind, but the girls were really excited to get going on the paint colors."

"No, that's fine." Astrid lifted her chin, trying not to mind that Clare had been spending so much time with her new family. It used to be Clare and Astrid together, along with Emma when she had time, or with Katie showing up when she wasn't in school. But with the teens just out on summer vacation and the whole new family thing starting to develop with Clare, Griffin and their girls, Astrid was beginning to feel like there wasn't so much room for her. "Are you picking the paint colors for our mural?" As creative as Astrid was...or used to be... Emma was the one with the true gift of art, able to create the most beautiful paintings of Maine. Combining their divergent but compatible artistic talents, Astrid and Emma had been working together on the designs for the mural and they'd been planning to unveil their creation to Clare tonight.

Clare shook her head. "We were thinking that a mural might be too busy. I think we're going to go with basic colors for now."

"Oh." Astrid's chest tightened as she thought of the reams

of paper pinned up on her apartment walls with her ideas for the mural. "Do you want me to show you the designs anyway? You might change your mind. I could run home and grab them. Or tonight?"

Clare's eyes sparkled, and she pulled Astrid away from the girls. "I can't tonight," she whispered. "Griffin and I are having a date night."

Astrid raised her brows. "Isn't every night a date night with you two?"

Clare laughed. "Yes, true, but we're going to a show in Portland, and he booked us the presidential suite at The Bungalow."

Astrid blinked. "That new luxury hotel that is by invitation only at this point?"

"Yes!" Clare giggled. "I'm so excited. I haven't been to the theatre in so long. The girls are going to Griffin's ex's for the night, so it's just us." She leaned forward, her face glowing. "This is the first time since Katie was born that I've gone off on vacation without her. I feel a little guilty, but I'm really excited. I know it's only two nights, but still!"

Astrid smiled and threw her arm around her friend's shoulder, her spirits restored by Clare's confession. Even though Clare had this new life, she still had the same vulnerability she always did. She was still Clare, and Astrid still had a place in her life. "Don't feel guilty. Every mom deserves a night off once every fifteen years. You deserve it."

Clare grinned. "Thanks, Astrid." She poked Astrid in the side. "When are you going to stop beating the men off with a club and let one into your life? The right one's not such a bad thing, you know."

Astrid stiffened, immediately thinking of Jason.

Clare stared at her. "Oh my God, what happened? Who is it? Astrid!"

Astrid grimaced. "I'm freaking out," she admitted. "You know that guy who bought—"

"What guy?" The tarp was thrust aside and in strutted Eppie Orlowe, the town's gossip and self-appointed savior of all females she deemed in need of her services. Today she was wearing a violet and fuchsia flowered sundress and a straw hat with a stuffed loon on the left brim. "Are you dating someone, Astrid? How could you keep this from me?"

Astrid grinned as Eppie thrust her way into the conversation. Clare had always been aggravated by Eppie's interference in her life, but honestly, Astrid loved that Eppie seemed to have turned her attentions onto Astrid. It felt good. Not that she was going to tell Eppie that Jason had unsettled her. It would take about two seconds for Eppie to march over to Jason's store, announce he'd upset Astrid, and demand a life-résumé to find out whether he was worthy. She would never let Eppie interfere in her life, but on some levels, it felt good to know Eppie had locked onto her. "No man, Eppie. Sorry to disappoint you."

Eppie peered at Astrid, and her eyes narrowed. "Have you created any new jewelry designs this week?"

Astrid stiffened at the intrusive question. "What?" How did Eppie know that she'd lost her creativity? When she'd first moved here, she'd poured her broken soul into her jewelry, creating so many new designs that almost every piece of jewelry she made had been one of a kind.

But it had been harder and harder lately, and she hadn't crafted a new design in months. She could barely manage to spin the ones she'd already created, let alone think of something new. It was as if the fire that drove her creativity had sputtered out, and her profits were beginning to show the effect of it.

Given that money wasn't exactly flowing in the first place, it was starting to scare Astrid, which had crashed her creativity to the final standstill she hadn't been able to recover from. Hence last night's creativity marathon.

"Jewelry. You know that thing you do that supports you?" Eppie shook her head, and made a tsking sound. "You haven't designed anything new, have you?"

Astrid shifted uncomfortably and glanced at Clare, who was frowning at her. "I'm fine—"

"Bullshit," Eppie said. "You're crashing and burning, Astrid, and you're too damn fool stubborn to admit it."

Astrid pulled her shoulders back. "I'm not crashing and burning—"

"No? Have you even thought about your plans yet for moving?"

"Moving?" A cold chill rippled through Astrid. "Moving where?" She and her mother had moved seventeen times by the time Astrid celebrated her sixteenth birthday at the drive-thru of McDonald's with their entire life packed in the back of yet another run-down jalopy, en route to their next "fresh start." The past two years in Birch Crossing had been the longest Astrid had ever stayed in one place. Even though she still felt like she didn't quite fit, she liked the fact she'd been in the same place long enough for her orchid to go through a full cycle of blooming, instead of having to throw it in the trash on her way out the door to a new life. She knew she didn't quite belong here, but she wasn't ready to move on yet.

"Mom, I think we should go with yellow and green stripes," Katie said, drawing Clare's attention back to the decor.

"Stripes?" Astrid shook her head. "The lines in here are all wrong for stripes. That will be too many geometric shapes—"

"Oh, silly me," Eppie said, tapping Astrid's arm. "I forgot to give it to you, didn't I?"

Astrid frowned at her. "Give me what?" She glanced over

at Clare and the girls, itching to get involved before they went off on some crazy decorating scheme that would be a gross insult to colors everywhere.

"This." Eppie fished into her oversized cotton purse that had a goat-herding mountain scene embroidered on it, and then handed Astrid a thin, white envelope that had already been torn open. "I haven't given this to you yet. Of course you don't know."

Astrid frowned as she took the envelope. On the outside was her name and address. "What is this? Did you read it?" Some of her amusement at Eppie's interference faded at the thought of the older lady reading her mail. Interference was one thing. Finding out Astrid's secrets was not okay.

"It's from Sam." Eppie drew her shoulders back and met Astrid's gaze, blinking her eyes with wide and completely fabricated innocence. "I have no idea how it got opened. It must have caught on my car keys while it was in my purse."

"Sam? Sam who?" Astrid grimaced when Eppie rolled her eyes at Astrid's question. As someone who'd lived in Birch Crossing for two years, Astrid was considered an utter failure in the small town because she didn't know the name and personal life of everyone in town. How could she? She didn't want to invade other people's privacy any more than she wanted hers on display.

It was too hard to forget if she saw her past reflected in everyone's eyes when they looked at her.

"Samuel Melvin White. Your landlord," Eppie said impatiently.

Astrid's heart froze. Her landlord had sent her a letter? She'd seen too many of those in her life, taped up on their door when her mother had stopped paying rent to see how long she could go without paying before they got kicked out. "Why do you have it?"

"I stopped by his house to tell him that his roses needed

pruning. Have you seen them? Beautiful yellow ones, but quite frankly they could be much nicer. Ever since he started dating that artist and spending all that time at her home in New Hampshire, he's just not tending to things here the way he should." Eppie shook her head, clucking her disapproval. "He's just damned lucky that I'm here to keep an eye on him."

Her heart pounding, Astrid folded the envelope without opening it. Her hands were shaking. She knew she'd paid her rent on time. She was never even a day late. She made sure of it. Her studio was tiny, and the stench of gasoline from the mechanic's shop downstairs forced her to sleep with the windows open even during the winter, but it was the only place in the entire town she could afford, and it had been her home for two years. He wasn't going to evict her, was he? What could it be?

Eppie raised her brows. "Aren't you going to read it?"

"Not right now." Astrid's mouth was dry. "I need to help Clare with the mural." But then she realized that Clare and the two teens were gone. She glanced out the window just in time to see Clare and the girls climb into Clare's Subaru and pull out of the small parking lot. What? They'd left without even telling her?

"Well, I'll tell you then." Eppie patted her arm. "Sam's decided that he's madly in love with that artist from New Hampshire, Rosa Stevens, and he's going to spirit his arthritic old self off there to grow even older with her." She beamed at Astrid. "Isn't that sweet? He's going to keep his cabin on the lake because that's where they met, but the old coot is finally going to retire! He's going to give the garage to his son, who is going to tear it down and build a fancy hotel or something. So, you've got three weeks to get yourself out of there, and find a new spot."

Astrid's lungs constricted, and her head started to pound.

"I have to move out? In three weeks?" But that was her home. Her only home. The only one she'd had in her whole life. The one that had been her salvation when she'd thought she was going to die. "I can't—"

"You sure can." Eppie nodded cheerfully and patted her arm. "Now, don't you start getting all mopey, girl. There are millions of homes in this damned country of America. Quite frankly, you deserve more than to live on top of that garage anyway. Use this as a chance to get a fresh start and get a little inspiration into your life."

A fresh start.

The words jabbed at Astrid's heart, words she'd heard so many times in her life. They always signified leaving behind a dog or a new friend or a nice teacher. They always meant being thrust into a stark, lonely hotel and sleeping in the car while her mom drove randomly until she saw a man in a diner who caught her eye, and she decided that was the town that would be their next home.

Stunned, Astrid gripped the letter, crushing it in her hand. "I have to go."

Eppie peered at her. "Sweet Lord, girl. You look like you just ate your mama's big toe. What the hell are you looking so upset for? It's just a damned apartment."

Astrid shook her head. "It's not," she whispered. "It's not." Unable to hold in the surge of panic, she blindly shoved her way through the tarp and into the main section of the store.

"Astrid!" Ophelia shouted at her from the deli. "Get your fanny over here. Your meatloaf and fries are almost ready!"

"I didn't order any food," Astrid hurried toward the door, fighting desperately to keep the tears at bay until she got outside.

"You're too damned skinny," Ophelia shouted. "This meatloaf needs to be eaten, and now."

"I don't have time," she yelled back, as she grabbed for the door—

The door opened, and she leapt back as Griffin stepped into the store. His dark eyes took in her expression, and his face grew concerned. "What's going on, Astrid?" He looked past her. "Did Eppie give you grief?"

"No, I'm fine." Astrid lifted her chin and gave him a cheeky grin. "I just got my period, and it always gets me emotional."

Griffin's eyes widened, and he got a pained look on his face. "Oh, well, yeah, okay, then." He stepped aside. "Clare and the girls went to the hardware store. She told me to tell you to come when you finished up with Eppie."

"Sure, okay." Astrid ducked her head as she raced past him, her throat tight. There was no way she was going to tag along with Clare and the girls. They were clearly on a roll, and Astrid knew that she wasn't a part of their vision. Not anymore.

Tears filled her eyes as she hurried down the steps to her car, and she recognized that aching void of loneliness filling her heart. She pressed her hand to her chest, as she reached her car, her lungs so tight she could barely breathe. "Dammit," she whispered, as she braced her hand on her car and leaned over, trying to catch her breath. "I'm not ready for this." A tear slid down her cheeks, and her hands started to shake. "I can't do this again—"

"Astrid?" The deep rumble of an already familiar male voice shot straight to her core as a strong hand settled on her lower back.

Jason Sarantos.

Dear God. She couldn't let him see her like this. No one got to see her fall apart.

Not ever.

CHAPTER THREE

ASTRID'S BODY went rigid beneath his hand the moment Jason spoke her name. He swore as she quickly moved out of reach, her hands up as if she could hold him at bay. Something dark rippled inside him, that same feeling he'd had so many times when his wife had shut him out.

Scowling, he shoved his hands into his pockets, but his irritation disappeared a moment later when he saw the tears brimming in her eyes. "Shit, Astrid. What happened?" He was instantly on the alert, and he glanced into the store, wondering what had stripped that cocky sparkle out of her eyes. He never would have guessed that she would ever sport a look of such vulnerability on her face. Protectiveness surged through him.

His wife had shut him out constantly, but he'd eventually realized that it was because she had nothing else to give other than to her work. But with Astrid, her emotions were so deep and powerful that he could practically feel them pulsing in the warm afternoon air.

She lifted her chin, her eyes flashing a warning to back off. "I just got my period. I always get emotional during it—"

Her voice faded, and he knew she was lying. He swore, a cold shadow descending over him at her evasiveness. He was all too familiar with lies—

Guilt flashed in her beautiful brown eyes. "I don't want to talk about it," she said quietly, abandoning the lie on her own.

He nodded, his tension easing. "I can respect that." Lies, no way. Privacy? Sure. He took in her pale complexion, the death grip she had on a crumpled letter in her hand, and knew it had been something major.

As much as he'd been compelled by her vivacious spirit, seeing her vulnerability made her suddenly so much more appealing. He was used to women who wanted and needed nothing from anyone, especially him. But Astrid's vulnerability was so raw and evident that it made him want to charge into her life and play the gallant rescuer and—

"Dad! Did you see the sign? They have ice cream in there! Can I get some?" Noah leapt out of the Mercedes, his hair still tousled from sleep.

Astrid jumped as if she'd been struck, and she looked quickly at Noah. Pain flashed in her eyes, pain so deep that Jason felt it in his own gut. He knew that pain, because he'd felt it every time he'd looked at his son for the last two years, and he hated that he saw his son with those eyes. He wanted to look at his son and see the boy that was still living, not the one who had died. He wanted to pulse with the life and the future they had ahead of them, instead of the shadows of his past.

But he couldn't do it. At least in New York he hadn't been able to.

Birch Crossing was his last chance.

"Dad?" Noah slammed the car door shut, his skinny upper arms hanging out of his New York Mets tee shirt. "Can I get some ice cream?" he asked impatiently.

"You bet." Jason was relieved to see his son's excitement.

The unveiling of the store hadn't gone over all that well, but if ice cream could help, then he'd have the boy over here six times a day until he was so sugared up that his life was perfect. "Head on in. I'll catch up."

"Thanks, Dad!" Noah high-fived Jason's raised palm as he raced inside, his untied sneakers thudding on the old wooden steps. The door slammed shut behind him, leaving Jason alone with Astrid.

Jason made no move to go after his son. He knew what that small-town general store was like, and was pretty damn certain his son would be surrounded by love by the time he found the ice cream.

The woman standing before him, however...different story. What exactly her story was, he didn't know, but he wanted to. Hell yeah, he wanted to. He studied her more carefully than he had at the store, and this time he saw not just the flamboyant jewelry and audacious scarf twisted through her hair, but the tiny lines around her eyes and the corners of her mouth. Laugh lines? Or simply the signature of a life well lived? He didn't know, but he had a sudden urge to smooth his thumb over them...maybe feather a light kiss over the corner of her mouth...

Astrid cleared her throat and started to back toward a beat-up Ford sedan parked beneath some trees. "So, I'll see you around—"

"Wait." Jason strode after her and grasped her arm, unable to let her walk away. He was shocked by how soft her skin was, by the delicate curve of her muscle beneath his grip. She was so feminine, so unbelievably female, that it awoke something inside him, something primal and male that hadn't responded to a woman in years. Instinctively, he tightened his hold on her arm, suddenly terrified she would pull away, that he would lose how she made him feel. He hadn't thought of tender kisses and soft skin in so long he'd forgotten what it felt like.

She froze, her wary brown eyes meeting his. "What do you want?" But she didn't pull away.

Dinner. Dessert. You. The words tumbled through his mind, but he shook his head, the thoughts too foreign to him after so long. "I don't know."

Her face softened, and she managed a small smile. "Welcome to Birch Crossing, Jason." She nodded inside the store. "They're waiting for you."

He shrugged. "Yeah, I know they are." He knew how small towns worked. They were probably grilling Noah right now to get as much information about the two of them as possible, and they would hit up Jason the moment he walked inside. He knew that, and that was why he'd brought his son here to live. Maybe the town could give Noah what his own father couldn't. "Who's waiting for you, Astrid?" he asked, the question coming out before it had even fully formed in his mind. But the moment he said it, he knew he wanted to know the answer. Was someone waiting at home for this beautiful, vivacious woman who hid so much inside?

He knew she wasn't wearing a ring on her left hand, but that didn't mean anything these days. Her heart could still be fully claimed.

"Who's waiting for me?" Astrid's face closed up, and he saw her summon that same flirtatious cockiness that she'd shown him before, the one that told the world that she was just fine the way she was. "Everyone and no one," she said. "Isn't that the way it is?"

He narrowed his eyes. "What does that mean?"

She managed a cheeky grin that didn't quite cleanse the pain from her eyes. "It means nothing. Unless you want it to, and then it does." She raised her eyebrows and lightly tugged on her arm, requesting her freedom.

Jason slowly let his fingers drift off her arm, and he saw the goose bumps pop up on her skin at the sliding touch. "It means I get to interpret it myself?"

She hugged her arms to her chest. "It means that I get to learn about you by how you interpret it. It's a trick to manipulate you into showing me what you don't want me to see."

He laughed, a sound that started in his chest and came to life of its own accord, the way it used to do, long ago. "You are trouble, aren't you, Astrid Monroe?"

She grinned, and this time, the smile was real. "I am. You should watch out for me. The town will warn you off me, for sure."

"All the more reason to learn more about you."

She laughed, a cheerful sound so much like the one she'd first gifted upon him at the store. "Well, good luck with that. I'm an enigma, and I like it that way."

He grinned. "I like challenges. I accept."

Her eyebrows shot up, and for a split second, wariness flashed across her face.

He softened his smile, and gave her a cocky grin to lighten the moment. "You should be worried, Astrid. I'm incredibly tenacious."

She smiled then, amusement flashing in her eyes. "You'll never find out my secrets, Sarantos. Even Eppie can't figure them out."

"Eppie?"

She pointed behind him. "Eppie."

Jason turned to see a weathered old lady striding across the porch toward him, a stuffed loon dangling precariously from her tilted hat. Ah...Eppie. There had been an Eppie in the town he'd grown up in. Her name had been Marianne Weddlington, and she probably still knew every detail about Jason's life even though he hadn't lived there since he was seventeen.

Eppie thrust her hand out at him as she neared. Adorning her fingers were an assortment of large rings trapped forever on her fingers by swollen, arthritic knuckles. But the challenge in her eyes told him that she'd probably never even bothered to take time to notice anything as insubordinate as knuckles that wouldn't bend properly. "Eppie Orlowe," she announced. "Welcome to Birch Crossing, Mr. Sarantos. You have a lovely son. Very articulate and charming."

"Thank you. Noah's a good kid." Jason shook Eppie's hand and glanced over his shoulder just as Astrid climbed into her car. She gave him a cheeky wave as she drove away, leaving him stranded with Eppie.

He laughed softly, knowing that she'd intentionally delivered him to Eppie, leaving him trapped.

For now.

But for the first time in years, he felt a surge of life pulsing as he watched Astrid's rusted car rumble out of the parking lot. The woman had spunk, and he liked it.

"Jason." Eppie's hand fell heavily on his shoulder as she turned him back toward her. "Before you go looking all googly-eyed at our Astrid, you'd best be telling me where your son's mama is. Are you married?" She raised her brows. "What kind of a man are you, Mr. Sarantos? I need to know."

Jason's adrenaline faded, and he looked Eppie in the eye and gave her the truth. "Not the kind of man you want in your town, I suspect."

Eppie's eyes narrowed, and for a moment, she stared at him.

He waited.

Then she let out a whoop of laughter and slammed her fist against his shoulder. "Hot damn, boy. I like you already! Come on in."

And just like that, he knew what kind of town this was.

It was the right town.

Which meant he had a chance. Noah had a chance.

A chance was more than he'd had in a long, damned time.

～

THE ORCHID WAS BLOOMING.

Astrid stood in the doorway of her apartment, shocked by the sight of the purple flower on the end of that lonely stalk. A third cycle of blooms? How was that possible? She'd never had three cycles of blooms on an orchid. She hadn't even noticed a bud forming.

Tears filled her eyes as she shut the door and knelt on the ottoman that she used for a window seat. She closed her eyes and pressed her nose against the blossom. The delicate fragrance filled her nose, and she smiled, letting it wash over her. Yes, this was home.

Then her smile faded, and she looked down at the crumpled letter in her hand. After spending four hours at the town library going through art books to try to find something to inspire her, she'd finally read the letter on the way home. Eppie was right about what it said. Astrid had three weeks to find a new place to live. Three damn weeks.

She turned and surveyed the one-room apartment. Now that it was evening, the shadows were thick and long inside. The overhead bulbs and the birch log lamp by her bed would do little to illuminate the place, but the bright desk light over her work station would concentrate enough light to work all through the night if she wanted to. With a sigh, Astrid studied the scarves dangling from the curtain rods above the two windows, providing bright color and privacy at the same time they hung on display for her to select the scarf of choice for the day. Curtains were the sign of someone who was going to stay put for a while.

They'd never had curtains as a kid, and Astrid had hung those scarves up the first day.

They looked good. In fact, the whole place looked good. Her bright quilt was so Maine-esque and cozy with its square patterns. She loved the picture of Wright's General Store that Emma had painted for Astrid as a Christmas present. In the corner stood the apothecary cabinet she'd fished out of the pile at the dump and refinished for storing her jewelry supplies. Her things. Her home. Her life.

Sudden tears filled her eyes, and she sank down on the bed. Dammit. She didn't want to leave. She looked down at the letter, and then frowned. Did she really have to? Was there a way to fight it?

She grabbed her phone and dialed her landlord. The answering machine picked up on the first ring. "I'm off with my girl. If you can find me, you can talk to me. If you can't, then figure your problem out on your own." The message trailed off with the cackling laughter of an old man in love.

Astrid gripped her phone. "Hi, it's Astrid Monroe. I got your notice, and I was hoping there was a way we could work around it. If you could give me a call, that would be great." She left her number, then hung up. There had to be another solution—

"Hey! Open up! I haven't got all night!" Eppie's voice echoed through the apartment as she thudded on the door. It sounded like she was kicking it?

Astrid set her phone down and opened the door. "Eppie—"

The older lady surged past her, almost buried beneath a stack of flattened cardboard boxes. "Griffin was going to toss these," she announced as she dumped them on Astrid's carpet. "Can you imagine? He said he hadn't even realized you were moving. How could he not know?" She set her hands on her hips and glared at Astrid. "The man's been the owner of

Wright's for almost two months now. He has a responsibility to know everything. What are we going to do with him? Seriously?"

Astrid stared past Eppie at the massive pile of boxes at the top of the stairs, her heart sinking at the irrefutable evidence that she had to move. "How much did you bring?"

"All of it." Eppie wiped her forehead with the back of her wrist. "That's all I'm carrying in, though. The rest is up to you. I need to go to Bingo. I heard the chicken buffet was cold last week, so I want to check it out. Just because I skip one week, they think they can slack. Astonishing, really." She set her hands on her hips. "Did they truly believe I wouldn't hear about it? Really?"

"Eppie. No one on this earth would think you wouldn't hear about it. They probably made it cold to force you to come back because they missed you."

"Oh..." Eppie fluffed her hat, a cheerful expression on her face. "I like the way you think, Astrid. You're a good girl."

Astrid was so surprised by Eppie's comment that she almost dropped her phone. "I am?"

Eppie paused, then shook her head. "Yes, you're right. No one would buy into that description of you. It doesn't do you justice." She patted Astrid's arm affectionately. "Do you know where you're moving yet?"

Astrid swallowed, trying not to let Eppie's recant of the compliment hurt. "No, I just found out—"

"Well, don't waste time. The summer help is rolling in and they take all the cheap digs." Eppie sauntered toward the door, her face serious. "How was work today, Astrid?"

Astrid lifted her chin. "Fantastic. I did three new designs."

Eppie narrowed her eyes. "Give it up. No one can lie to me. You let me know what I can do to help you, you hear?" She didn't wait for an answer, letting herself out the door.

Astrid sighed, but before she could begin to deal with the boxes, her phone rang again, and she answered it immediately. "Sam?"

"No, it's Jason Sarantos." His voice was low and deep, rumbling over her the same way it had the first time she'd met him.

"Oh, hi." She swallowed, trying to find her pep again. "How's the new place?" she said, forcing cheerfulness into her voice.

He laughed softly. "It's got some work to be done, I'm afraid, but Noah thinks the decaying rat we found under the sink was awesome."

Astrid chuckled at the vision. "You boys can keep the dead rats for yourself."

"Oh, I don't think Noah's going to be sharing it, so don't worry." He cleared his throat. "Listen, do you know where the key is to the storage room out back? The front door key doesn't work in it, and I need to get in there."

"Oh." Astrid frowned. "Wasn't it unlocked when you arrived?"

"It was. I took my computer in there to do inventory, and then when I left, Noah shut the door. So, yeah, now it's locked, and it has my computer."

Astrid laughed. "I'm sure your computer is having a lovely time."

Jason chuckled. "I doubt it. It's not really a fan of cobwebs and dust. Any chance you have the key?"

"No, but I know where Harlan keeps the keys to the places he represents. I'm sure I can find it." Astrid looked around at her small apartment, and suddenly she wanted to get out. She stood up and grabbed her car keys. "I'll bring it over now. Are you still at the store?"

"Yes, but I'm leaving. Noah's crashing and I need to get him to bed. We're heading home."

"Where's home?" When Griffin answered, Astrid blinked in shock as he gave her the address. She knew exactly the house. A huge Cape on a rolling lawn that went right down to the edge of the lake. It had a charming guesthouse with a widow's walk on the roof that looked out across the mountains. It had been empty for a long time, and she'd spent more than a few hours sitting on the hill beside the house watching the sunset, figuring that someone needed to be appreciating the scenery since no one was living there. And that's where he lived? In her dream house.

Lucky man.

Excitement rippled through her. Maybe she could get inside and see it? She'd peeked in the windows before, but she'd never been inside. "It's no problem to swing by there. I'll be by in an hour or so."

"Really?" Jason sounded distracted, and she could hear Noah chatting at him. "You don't need to do that. Morning is fine."

"No, I want to." She headed for the door, needing to get out of the home that was no longer hers. She stepped over a cardboard box, gave up getting the door shut around the load Eppie had dumped there, and headed down the stairs.

Anything to get out of her life for an hour.

CHAPTER FOUR

JASON LEANED against the doorjamb of Noah's room, watching his son sleep. The boy had passed out on the floor while Jason was still putting his bed together. He hadn't woken up even when Jason had finally transferred him to the mattress, the race car sheets and comforter in place. Of course he wouldn't wake up. Once asleep, Noah would be oblivious to a thunderstorm in his own bedroom, a merciful gift which had kept the youth unaware of the nights Jason spent pacing sleeplessly along the hallways of their condo in New York.

In their new home, a beautiful old lake house with dark wood beams and huge windows, Noah had found sleep again, despite the chaos, for which Jason was grateful. Moving boxes were piled high, and he'd managed to find only one box of Noah's toys. The poor kid had been relegated to playing with toys he hadn't used for two years while Jason had been assembling the bed.

There was nothing to see in the room and hallway but an ocean of cardboard, and a few boxes ripped open in search of basic necessities. Chaos and disorder. Not the home he'd promised his son. Not the new life he'd promised them both.

Instead, it was even worse than New York had been. The house was too silent. With a driveway almost a quarter of a mile long, there was no noise from passing cars. His twelve acres of property, surrounded by lake on one side and forest on the other three, meant there were no neighbors to thud on the walls or play their music too loud. No hum of electronics or even humanity. No light from the street or neighbors. Just darkness. Just emptiness. Just nothing.

It was an empty house without a single memory, which is what he'd wanted. But now...shit...it felt overwhelming, like death itself. He needed to find a way to hold onto the memories that mattered, but he hadn't even been able to find the pictures of Lucas. Jason felt lost without the images of his younger son surrounding him, as if he'd lost hold of the memories of his son once he'd left New York behind.

As if Lucas was fading from his grasp, slipping away like he had that night he'd died—

"Shit!" Jason slammed his palm against the doorway and tore himself away from Noah's room. He shoved his way through the crowded hallway, trying to fight off that same overwhelming sense of loneliness that had consumed him in New York.

Nothing had changed with the move. It was the same. He'd brought it all with him. He'd brought all the hell, the guilt, the inexorable punishment of memories that were eating away at him, stripping him of the ability to function as his son's father.

Swearing, Jason grabbed his utility knife and sliced open another box. No pictures of Lucas. What box had he put them in? He couldn't even remember. He slashed at another, and then another, but all he found were towels and sheets and other crap that didn't matter. "Come on!"

Desperate guilt and loneliness surged through him, and he braced himself on the last box in the hallway, which held only Noah's old stuffed animals. Sweat trickled down his brow as he fought for composure, as he fought to fend off the overriding sense of doom.

In the silence of the night, Noah's breathing was loud and steady, and Jason tensed. What if he failed Noah, too? He'd failed Lucas. He'd failed to keep his marriage intact and his wife alive. He'd completely failed everyone and now...shit...was he finally dragging Noah the rest of the way down as well?

Loneliness surged over him, that same darkness that haunted him every night. Jason knew that there was no point in setting up his own bed. Sleep wouldn't be attainable in Maine any more than it had been in New York—

The loud crunch of tires on his gravel driveway caught his attention, and he jumped to his feet. Who the hell was here?

A car door slammed, and Jason tensed. Shit. He wasn't in the mood to be sociable right now. If the little old lady from his fantasies had finally shown up with a plate of cookies, she was too damn late. She was just going to have to leave them on the porch.

Jason sheathed the blade back into the casing, waiting for that inevitable ring of the doorbell. How many times had he answered his door to find another note of condolence or another casserole after Lucas's death, and then Kate's? Well-meaning acquaintances who thought that a smile and a slab of meatloaf would ease the gaping void in his soul. He'd stopped answering the door, because there was no way to pretend to be appreciative when all the darkness was consuming him.

And now, after fighting like hell to get past that, after scraping his way back into a place from which he could function, all those emotions had returned, brought on by the overwhelming silence of his house. That same silence that had flooded him when he'd come back home after watching his son die at the hospital and felt the gaping absence of Lucas.

Silence fucking sucked, but a doorbell was no better.

But the doorbell didn't ring, and the car didn't drive away.

Scowling, Jason walked across the landing to peer out the back window at the driveway.

Astrid Monroe's rusted junker was in his driveway. *Astrid.* He'd forgotten she was coming.

Adrenaline rushed through him, breaking him free from the tentacles of the past. His heart suddenly began to beat again, thudding back to life with a jolting ache. He tossed the knife aside, spun away from the window and vaulted down the stairs, taking them three at a time, almost desperate for the air he knew Astrid would feed back into his lungs.

He jerked the back door open and stepped out onto the front porch, unable to keep the hum of anticipation from vibrating through him. "Astrid?"

Her car was empty, and she was nowhere in sight.

Trepidation rippled through him. Another woman dead? He immediately shook his head, shutting out the fear that had cropped up out of habit. Instead, he quickly scanned his property, knowing she had to be there somewhere.

But there was no Astrid. Frowning, Jason jogged down the pathway that led around the house toward the lakefront, urgency coursing through him to find the one woman who had brought that brief respite into his life, that flash of sunshine, that gaping moment of relief from all that he carried. Where was she? He had to find her. *Now.*

Jason was almost sprinting by the time he rounded the rear corner of his house and found her. The moment he saw her, he stopped dead, utterly awed by the sight before him.

"Son of a bitch," he whispered under his breath as he

stared at the woman who'd rocked his world only a few hours before.

Astrid was standing on one of the rocks on the edge of the lake, silhouetted by an unbelievable sunset. The sky was vibrating with reds, oranges and a bright violet, casting the passionate array of colors across the lake's surface. Astrid's hands were on her hips, her face tilted up toward the sky, as if she were drinking the beauty of the sunset right through her skin. Her brown hair was framed in the vibrant orange and violet, a wild array of passion that seemed to mesh with the wild woods around her.

Her sandals were on the ground beside the rock, her bare toes gripping the boulder. She was wearing the same jeans and tank top as she had earlier, despite the slight evening coolness cropping up in the air. It was as if she hadn't bothered to notice, as if she couldn't deign to succumb to something so mundane as a cool breeze.

She was above it all, and Jason felt the tightness in his lungs easing simply from being in her presence. *Astrid.*

He knew then that he hadn't come to Birch Crossing for the town, or for the plate of cookies, or even for the damn pizza store he was planning to open. He had come for her. For Astrid. For the sheer, raw passion that she exuded with every breath.

She was the epitome of freedom, of passion, of life. Rightness roared through him at the sight of her on his land, basking in the sunset, breathing in the air that he suddenly noticed. The fresh, clean scent of woods and crystalline water filled him, as if Astrid's reverence of their surroundings had brought his own senses back to life.

She was beautiful. Not simply beautiful. She was beauty itself, the definition of all that it could be in a person's wildest, most desperate imagination.

Yearning crashed through Jason to lose himself in her, to

use her vibrant energy to wipe away the smut covering his soul and give him the chance to breathe again, to find his path in this second chance that he'd tried to give his son. He was captivated by her, even by the way she ignored protocol and had helped herself to his rock and the sunset, not even bothering to ring the doorbell. She was a free spirit, a woman who didn't fit into the town and didn't care.

He wanted that freedom. He needed to get caught up in her spell. He would never survive if he didn't find a way to forget, even for a minute, all the burdens crashing down on him. There was no choice, no other path, no other option, than to lose himself in the aura that was Astrid. To remember that there was something else in life besides the darkness that consumed him.

"It's beautiful, isn't it?" She didn't turn around, but her voice drifted to him, a melody that seemed to crawl under his skin and ignite flames within him.

"Yes, it is." He began to walk toward her, tentative, almost afraid of spooking her and losing the moment. But he couldn't keep from approaching her. He was drawn to her as if she were a magnet, calling to his soul, to the part of him that had once been alive. His need for her was pulsing through every cell of his body, so intense that it almost hurt, as if something inside of him was fighting its way to life after an eternity of being dead.

"This is the best place in town to watch the sunset. Is that why you bought it?" She spoke softly, almost as if she were afraid to disturb the beauty of the sunset.

"I haven't noticed a sunset in years," he admitted as he reached her. He stopped beside the rock, suddenly uncertain of how to approach her. Of what to do next. Of how to get closer. "I bought the house because it has lakefront, and I thought Noah would like it."

Astrid turned her head slightly to look at him, and he

caught his breath at the sight of her face. The sun was casting a soft glow, illuminating her face so that her eyes seemed to vibrate with depth and passion... He realized suddenly that there was none of the levity in her expression that he'd seen before. Just pain and emotion, fighting to be free. His chest tightened for the agony he saw in her face, for the depth of trauma that seemed to echo what beat so mercilessly in his own soul. Outrage suddenly exploded through him, fury that someone had inflicted such damage on this angel that she could harbor such pain. Astrid was so free, so untamed, that she should be gallivanting across the surface of the lake, not looking at him as if her heart had been carved right out of her chest.

"You don't notice sunsets?" she asked.

He barely heard her words or registered his response to her. All he could think about was the woman before him, the depth of her spirit, his need to somehow chase away the shadows and bring back the spirit that he knew was coursing through her veins. "No. I wouldn't have noticed this one if you weren't out here."

She shook her head, and that teasing glint sparkled in her eyes again, making his stomach leap. *Yes, Astrid. Come back to me.* He moved closer to the rock, ruthlessly drawn toward her.

She grinned at him. "Well, you've got some learnin' to do, Sarantos, if you're going to be living in this here town. Sunset appreciation is mandatory for all residents, and you'll be quizzed every morning at Wright's when you show up for your coffee." She held out her hand and beckoned with her fingers. "Up," she ordered.

Jason grinned at her bold command, and he immediately set his hand in hers. Electricity leapt through him as his skin touched hers, and she sucked in her breath at the contact. Wariness flashed in her eyes, and Jason sensed she was about to retreat.

No chance.

He wasn't missing this moment.

He immediately tightened his grip on her hand and hauled himself up onto the rock beside her. The peak of the boulder was smaller than he'd expected, bringing them dangerously close to each other. For a moment, neither of them moved. He just stared down at her, and she gazed at him, her brown eyes wide and nervous. Her pulse was hammering in her throat, and he instinctively pressed his index finger on it, trying to ease it down. "Your heart is racing."

Those dark, expressive eyebrows of hers shot up, and she lifted her chin. "Beautiful sunsets get my adrenaline going."

"Do they?" They were so close to each other that he could feel the heat from her body. "Shouldn't they calm your soul and ease the stress from your body?" He moved closer, easing across the boulder. "Are you afraid of me, Astrid? I won't hurt you."

She blinked, and he saw doubt flicker across her face again. "Don't touch me," she whispered.

Instead of moving his fingers away from her throat, he traced her collarbone. Goose bumps popped up on her skin, and she sucked in her breath.

Awareness leapt through him at her transparent response, at the realization she was as affected by the touch as he was. Sudden desire blasted through him, along with raw, physical need that leapt straight to his loins. Jason froze, shocked by the pulse of desire that shot through him. Son of a bitch. He hadn't responded to a woman in years. *Years.* "Jesus, Astrid," he whispered. "What is it about you?"

She shook her head once, her eyes so wide that he could read every nuance of her emotions. Unexpected, powerful desire, coupled with a fear so deep that it came from her soul.

Excitement. Anticipation. Uncertainty. Vulnerability. "It's not me," she whispered. "It's you."

He spread his hand over the back of her neck, basking in the sensation of her skin beneath his palm. She felt so alive, vibrating with life, and yet at the same time, her skin was so delicate and soft that protectiveness surged through him. A need to be the strong male and take care of her, in the way that his former wife had never allowed him to do. His fingers tightened on her neck and he drew her closer. "No. It's both of us."

Astrid braced her palm on his chest, blocking him. "Don't," she said. "Please, don't."

"I can't help it." He couldn't tear his gaze off her eyes, off the myriad of expressions racing through them. He couldn't breathe. He felt like his soul was screaming with desperation, frantic for one chance, one moment, one kiss with this woman. As if the brush of her lips could save him from the free fall threatening to consume him. "I need to kiss you, Astrid. Now."

IT FELT SO good to be touched.

Astrid had forgotten what it felt like to have a man's hand on her skin. To feel the warmth of another human touch. To feel the sensual caress of his fingers across her skin. To stare into the eyes of a man who was looking at her as if she was the only thing on the entire earth that mattered to him.

She'd never belonged. She'd never fit in. She'd spent a lifetime on the fringe, trying desperately to find that niche that felt right, struggling to figure out what she had to do to become accepted, to be admitted into the club of belonging. She'd thought she was on her way in this town, but the eviction had changed everything.

Home was an illusion. A sense of place that was an elusive illusion that never came true. And yet, standing there on her favorite rock, beside her favorite house, under the glow of a beautiful sunset, she'd always found peace and solace.

But to be here, with Jason's fingers caressing her neck, his body so close against hers, and to see such desperate need in his dark eyes...she felt like she'd finally come home, as if this were the moment she'd been running desperately toward her whole life.

"Kiss me, Astrid," he whispered, his voice deep and rough as it rolled through her. "I need it."

I need it. The raw truth of his words plunged past her defenses, and tears filled her eyes. The depth of his pain was so evident, a reflection of the constant ache in her own soul. They were the same, this flashy doctor from New York and the transient from a thousand different towns. He understood her, and she understood him, because they were the same.

Yearning swelled through her, a need to fall into his spell and let him sweep her away from her life, from the memories, from the terrifying thought of losing her home. For a minute, for a day, for however long it lasted, she knew that Jason could fill that emptiness inside her, and she knew she could fill his.

His hand grew heavy around the back of her neck, asking her to yield, to allow him to pull them together.

"I can't," she whispered, even as her body succumbed to his unspoken request, letting him tug her against him. Her breasts touched his chest, and electricity leapt through her, a sudden pulse of desire so intense she felt her blood burn through her veins.

Jason's eyes darkened, and she could feel the steady beat of his heart against her chest. "I came here to find you," he said, his voice rough with emotion that plunged straight into her heart. "I knew it the moment you walked into my restaurant."

Astrid swallowed, fighting to stay above the swell of desire and need trying to consume her. "I don't even know you. You're a stranger—"

He brushed his lips across the corner of her mouth, and Astrid closed her eyes, her body soaring at the tender intimacy of the touch. Dear God, how long had it been since a man had kissed her like that? As if she were a treasure that he planned to spend the entire night cherishing, inch by inch by inch?

"We're not strangers," he whispered as he kissed the other side of her mouth. "Can't you feel the connection of our souls? As if an invisible thread has been pulling us together and we finally were able to find each other? It's like our souls have been incomplete, and now they've found the part that was missing."

Astrid squeezed her eyes shut and gripped Jason's shoulders as he trailed a row of the most delicate kisses along her jaw. "I don't believe in that kind of thing," she whispered, unable to keep the emotion out of her voice. Dear God, the words he was saying were so beautiful, she wanted to cry. How could there be someone saying those kinds of things to her? And sounding like he meant it? She wanted it to be real, to be able to open her eyes and discover that this man, with all his depth and his passion and his fire, really meant it, that something had happened to her to make this really be true. But it wasn't. She knew it wasn't. She didn't live in a fantasy world anymore. She knew better than to delude herself. "Life is just a series of incidents you survive—"

"Fuck that." Jason pulled back, and she opened her eyes to see fire blazing in his. "I won't live like that anymore. I fucking won't. And you shouldn't either."

She stared at him, and for the first time in forever, she felt a breath of hope. "I don't want to," she whispered. "I want the magic and the fairytale."

He grinned, a wicked smile that plunged right to her soul, and she knew in that moment that Jason was her magic. He was her fairytale. He was her moment.

His smile faded, and raw desire flashed in his eyes at her expression. His fingers tightened on the back of her neck, and his other hand slid down her back and wrapped around her lower back. One quick tug, and her hips were against his, the hardness of his erection pressing into her belly.

She swallowed, and she knew this time, she wasn't going to stop him. She needed this man. She needed to be touched by a man who saw her pain and answered it with his own. She needed to be kissed by this tormented male who was so desperate for what she could give him.

He wanted nothing from her, nothing but to find relief from his demons, which was exactly what she needed too.

This time, he didn't ask. This time, when he lowered his head, she knew it wasn't going to be a demure kiss on the corner of her mouth. This time, he was going to unleash all that depth inside of him into the kind of kiss she'd been waiting for.

And she was ready.

CHAPTER FIVE

THE MOMENT his lips touched hers, Jason knew he was lost to Astrid, to the kiss, to the passion that exuded from her.

He couldn't keep the kiss gentle. He couldn't be the refined suitor. He couldn't offer the restraint he'd always shown when he kissed a woman. Everything was lost the moment he kissed Astrid, everything that had defined him his entire life. Gone was the discipline, the focus, the dignity. In its place was a raw, untamed passion that tore through him like an inferno gone mad, and it felt unbelievable.

Astrid's body was warm and soft against his, her breasts crushed against his chest, her kiss just as fervent as his. He could taste her need, and he knew that she burned for it as much as he did, as if he was the very same relief for her that she was for him.

Lust raced through him at the realization that she needed him, that the kiss wasn't a one-sided, empty routine offered only to appease him. God, no, Astrid's fingers were clenched in his hair, her mouth as desperate as his, her body burning with the same heat that was searing his veins.

He slipped his hand beneath her tank top and spread his

palm over the bare skin of her back. Electricity seemed to burn his palm, and Astrid trembled against him. Her response was intoxicating, the way she welcomed his touch and deepened her kiss when he gripped her hips, the way she whispered his name so frantically against his lips, the way she tore his shirt out of his jeans and slipped her hands beneath the fabric.

"Jesus, Astrid," he almost lost his footing on the rock at the feel of her hands on his bare chest. God, it had been so long since he'd been touched like that, since a woman had run her hands over his skin as if she couldn't get enough. She was the light that he'd been searching for, the one that would tear through the blackness trying to consume him. She was the passion that had died from his soul so long ago, before Lucas had died, back when his marriage had started to decay, before his wife had died while he stood there and let her go—

"Shit!" The guilt and the loneliness flooded back over Jason, tearing him away from the respite Astrid had given him. Son of a bitch. He didn't want to go back there. He couldn't go back there. He wouldn't survive it.

Suddenly, the kiss with Astrid wasn't enough. The kiss, the clothes, the skin. He needed more. He needed all of Astrid. He needed to bury himself so deeply in her that the past wouldn't be able to destroy him. She was his beacon, his guide to get where he was struggling so hard to go, and he was losing his grip on her.

With a growl, Jason scooped her up in his arms and tumbled them both off the rock onto his lawn. He didn't let them land on their feet. He took them all the way down to the earth, trapping Astrid beneath him without even breaking the kiss.

The grass was cool and damp on Astrid's back, the soft blades like nature's blanket cradling her as Jason lowered himself on top of her. His body was heavy and hard, his kiss relentless and intoxicating, his shoulders rippling with muscle beneath her fingers. He was all male, so strong and powerful, and he seemed to know exactly how to kiss her, how to touch her, how to ignite the part of her that made her a woman.

It had been so long since she'd been with a man, and it felt so unbelievable to be held and kissed with such passion, as if his entire soul was burning for her. And she knew it was. Maybe it was just for this moment, for this connection that had brought them together, but she had felt the depth of his pain and his need for her, and she knew that every kiss and every touch was real, that his need wasn't a lie, that Jason was as desperate for her as she was for him.

Not just for sex. But for *her*.

Tears filled her eyes, and warmth seemed to blossom in her chest, chasing away years of aching loneliness, loss and guilt.

"God, Astrid. I need more." He broke the kiss, his dark eyes riveted to her face as he tugged her tank over her head. "I feel like I can't breathe without you." Then he was on her again, tearing off her bra between kisses, as if he couldn't stay off her long enough to disrobe her.

Then his mouth closed on her breast, and she gasped, shocked at how amazing it felt, by the intensity of her body's response to him. It was as if he had the magic key to her soul, and his every touch and every kiss triggered another level of response from her. Her body felt out of control, twisting and writhing as he grazed his teeth over her nipple. Never had it been like this before. She'd always been in control with a man, too much control. Never had anyone been able to wrest her away from her mind and thrust her into a haze of desire and lust, of feeling so intense that reality seemed to disappear, until all that was left was skin and desire and passion and *him*.

This wasn't sex. This was *Jason*. Somehow, someway, this

stranger from New York had reached into her soul and found a way to call to the depth of who she was. He'd taken her away from the noise of her mind, from the ache of her heart, and carried her into a world of magic and passion.

Need pulsed at her, a need so deep she couldn't even name it, but Jason seemed to understand. Without words, without an acknowledgment of what they both needed, he unfastened her jeans and tugged them off, his dark eyes fastened on her as he ditched his own pants.

Astrid caught her breath as she watched him. His body was lean and well-muscled, no wasted fat, just raw, hard male. His chest was dappled with hair, his quads rippling with muscle. Jason grinned as he lowered himself back onto her. "Every man dreams of being looked at the way you just looked at me." He cupped her face, and she saw something flash in his eyes. Vulnerability. Naked, agonizing vulnerability. "Thank you, Astrid."

And this time, when he kissed her, it was more than passion. It was more than lust. There was a tenderness that made her throat tighten. How could this man feel as empty as she did? How was it possible there was someone else who seemed to understand how she felt, who seemed to need her as much as she needed him? She didn't understand how she could have found the man who understood, who lived in the same hell she lived in.

"Kiss me," Jason said, his mouth hovering over hers. "Kiss me, sweet Astrid. Let me take away your shadows."

She couldn't stop the tears this time as she wrapped her arms around his neck. "Damn you, Jason. No one is supposed to notice my shadows." And no one had ever offered to take them away.

"Kindred spirits, my angel. We're kindred spirits." Then he shifted his hips, sliding his knee between her legs, and she knew he was going to make love to her. Right then. In the grass, beneath the setting sun, on the shore of the lake that had saved her spirit so many times.

"Look at me," Jason whispered as he slid his arms beneath her shoulders, bracing himself on his elbows so he wasn't crushing her, but so his weight was heavy and protective. "I need to see into your eyes."

Astrid met his gaze, and her heart tore at the depth of pain she saw in Jason's eyes. "Yes," she whispered.

"Yes," he agreed, his words still hovering in the air as he slid inside her, an effortless entry that was so perfect, so amazing, so *right*. Jason swore under his breath as he began to move. "God, Astrid," he said. "How is it that this can feel so right?"

"I don't know," she gasped. Ripples of desire spread through her belly, cascading along her limbs as he thrust again. "But please don't stop."

He laughed, a deep, throaty sound that brought a surprised smile to her face. "Hell, no, woman. No chance of that." And then he thrust again, and again, moving faster and faster until she couldn't think of anything but Jason, of how he was everything she'd needed for so long. Until her body was screaming with need, and still she wanted more.

He kissed her again, so deeply it felt as if he were trying to bind them together forever. Astrid held onto him fiercely, losing herself in all that he was, in how he made her feel, in the desire and need racing through her. In the depth of the connection to this man in her arms, in the gift of this moment that he'd given her.

Then he thrust again, and the orgasm exploded through her, seizing her in a relentless spiral so intense she screamed.

"God, Astrid." Jason lurched on top of her, his body going rigid as he came with her, joining her as the orgasm consumed them both, tearing them from the shadows that haunted them and catapulting them both over a precipice into a place of safety, of connection, of life.

TRAPPED IN JASON'S ARMS, cradled against his chest, buried in the strength of his body, Astrid was afraid to move. She was terrified that she would never feel this way again.

Never had she felt safe in a man's arms. Content, yes. Sated, sure. But never safe.

But as they lay together, their hearts slowly easing back to their normal rhythms, the sounds of nightfall beginning to come alive in the woods around them, Astrid felt like the world couldn't hurt her anymore. She felt like she didn't need to pretend to be strong or funny when all she wanted to do was cry. Jason had somehow sensed her pain, and that had brought them together.

But at the same time, she'd seen the appreciation in his eyes when she'd first appeared in his store armed with her outrageous scarf and flippant attitude. He'd seen all the facets of who she was, and he'd still craved her so badly that she'd felt his need all the way in her soul.

Jason Sarantos made her feel safe. For the first time in her life, she knew what it felt like to *really* trust a man all the way down to his soul, and it was unbelievable. She tightened her arms around him and pressed her face against his shoulder. "Thank you," she whispered. "That was beautiful."

"Astrid." Jason propped himself up on his elbow, his dark hair tousled as he peered down at her. His face was shadowed now, the sun almost set completely behind the mountains on the other side of the lake.

She smiled and smoothed his hair, the intimate gesture coming naturally before she had time to question whether she had the right to do it.

He leaned his head into her touch, as if he wanted it as much as she did. "Come inside," he said. "Let me make you dinner. Stay the night."

She blinked, startled by the offer. "What?"

"Stay with me tonight." His gaze searched hers, and she saw such yearning in his eyes that her heart tightened.

She realized she wanted to say yes. She wanted to pretend that this was forever, that she'd found her way to this beautiful life and this perfect man...

"I want to get to know every inch of you." He touched her cheek. "I want to know the secrets hiding in your eyes. I want to hold you until dawn—" Then he grinned slightly sheepishly. "Or maybe until just before dawn. Noah wakes up at seven, so it's probably best if I'm done ravishing you by then."

"Noah?" Astrid said blankly, coldness creeping over her limbs as reality began to intrude.

"My son." He raised his brows. "He's a good kid, Astrid. You'd like him."

"Your son." Anguish suddenly coursed through her, the pain of memories she'd tried to forget. She pressed her hand to her eyes, fighting off the surge of tears, the sudden onslaught of grief so intense that it seemed to wrest her breath right from her lungs, her heart from her chest. The surge of emotions was so sudden and unexpected that she had no time to brace herself against it, to head it off before it consumed her, sucking her down into the abyss.

"Astrid?" Jason caught her wrist, his fingers closing around her arm. "What's wrong? What did I say?"

"Nothing. God, nothing." She struggled out from under him, suddenly feeling so raw and exposed. How had she fallen into the trap of deluding herself that this was more than a dream, even for a moment? It wasn't. His son. *His son.* Tears blinded her as she lunged for her clothes, yanking them back on frantically, desperate to get away from Jason and his son, and the dreams that he'd reawakened inside her.

"Astrid!" He leapt to his feet and grabbed her arm, concern etched on his face. "Talk to me. What's going on? What upset you? Did I do something?"

"No, it's not you. It's—" She looked up at the house looming behind Jason, and suddenly the truth seemed to hit her in the face. The Mercedes. The beautiful house. His son. This wasn't her world. This wasn't her man. Of course he didn't love her, not on any level, and the magnitude of their incompatibility would become all too vivid if they tried to pretend that there was something more between them.

He'd needed her in that moment, as she'd needed him. To take it further would be to strip the moment of meaning, to tarnish it before it had even settled. She needed what he'd given her, and she had to pull herself together before the costs of their moment crushed the respite it had given her. "I can't do this."

"Do what?" His fingers tightened on her arms almost desperately. "You can't stay with me tonight? See me in the morning? Is it my son? Is that the problem? That I have a kid?"

She stared at him, so much emotion welling in her throat that she couldn't risk speaking, or she would snap. All she could do was shake her head. "I can't," she managed to say, her voice cracking with the strain.

"You can't." Slowly, Jason released her arm, and his face became shuttered. Gone was the warmth, the openness of his pain, the genuineness of who he was. In its place was cool reserve, that same distant expression she remembered so well from her ex-fiancé when he'd walked into her hospital room while she was fighting for her life and told her that since their son had been still-born, there was no reason for him to marry her.

The utter lack of emotion on Jason's face was exactly the same as Paul's expression when he'd told her that since he didn't have a son to protect, there was no way he would burden his family with the ignominy of who Astrid was and the legacy she brought with her. He'd turned and walked out, and his expensive cologne had been the last she'd ever seen of the first and only man she'd ever managed to trust.

And suddenly, here, with Jason, the shields protecting her heart were cracking, and it was too much. She had to survive, and feeling this kind of pain would never let that happen. "I can't do this."

Jason's face hardened. "I can see that."

"I—" Guilt coursed through her for causing him distress, and she touched his arm. "It was beautiful, Jason. Truly beautiful." She stood on her tiptoes and pressed a kiss to his whiskered cheek. "I wish I was the woman who could have that forever," she whispered.

His eyes narrowed, and suddenly the coldness was gone, replaced by a thoughtfulness that sent trepidation through her. "Why aren't you?"

"I—" She hesitated, hating the yearning pulsing inside her, the wish to fall into his arms and forget the world. She pushed him away. "Damn you, Jason. I can't do this."

"But you want to."

She glanced up at him, saw satisfied conviction on his face, and realized that he wasn't going to let her go. He didn't want the moment to end, and he was prepared to make her stay. Fear rippled through her, and she took a step back. She lifted her chin and gave him a defiant glare. "No, I don't," she said, managing to keep her voice steady. "If you ask around town, you'll find out I'm not that kind of girl. I'm not the kind of woman for a man with a son."

For a long moment, he simply studied her, and then finally, he nodded. "Okay."

Regret coursed through her at his easy acceptance, but she also felt a relief so vast that her body began to tremble. "Okay, then." She managed a smile and hurried back to her car, suddenly desperate to get away from him and everything that had happened. She had just slid into her seat and was closing the door when Jason grabbed the window frame. Astrid caught her breath in anticipation. "What?"

He held out his hand, his dark eyes unreadable in the dim light. "The key to my storage shed."

"Oh, right." She let out a breath, fighting off the disappointment, and grabbed the key from the console. She dropped it into his hand so she didn't have to touch him. "Here. Harlan will be back in a couple days. Call him if you need anything."

"Thanks." Jason stepped back as she started the car. "Just so you know, Astrid..."

She hesitated at his serious tone. "What?"

"When I said 'okay,' I didn't mean that I accepted your claim that you weren't the kind of woman for a man with a kid."

She swallowed, her skin suddenly hot. "You didn't? What did you mean?"

He grinned. "I meant, okay, I'll ask around town and find out exactly what kind of girl you are, and then, I'm going to make my own damn decision." He slammed the door before she could argue, turned and walked back into the house, abandoning her in his own driveway.

She should be terrified at the thought of what the rumor mill might say about her, but instead, she felt laughter bubbling up in her throat.

Jason Sarantos was trouble, and trouble was her kind of world.

But that didn't mean she was going to sleep with him again. She couldn't afford it.

Because it was the God's honest truth that she wasn't the kind of woman for a man with a child. Her ex-fiancé may have been a bastard, but he had been absolutely right about her when he'd referenced the ignominy of her past and her background.

As horrible as it had been to lose her son, she knew that it had been the world's greatest gift to her son that he had been spared having her as his mother.

CHAPTER SIX

IT WAS time for her power outfit.

Astrid was wearing her most cheerful scarf, half-woven into a thick French braid, as she trotted up the steps of Wright's the next morning for her daily coffee ritual with Emma and Clare. Clare was off in Portland with Griffin, but at least Emma would be there.

Astrid had selected her favorite pair of jeans, a hot pink tank top with sparkles, and four different earrings from her inspirational collection adorned her earlobes: love, peace, hope and "girls kick ass," which was her personal favorite at the moment.

She'd put on enough makeup to hide the fact she'd spent the night alternating between failing to create a new design and looking up apartment rentals on the internet. She'd failed at both of them, and was now so tired she could barely even think.

Good. If she was too tired to think, maybe she'd be able to get Jason out of her mind. Jason and his unbelievable love-making. Jason and her dream house. Jason and his shadows.

Jason and his son.

Argh! Why couldn't she control her mind? She needed to be a creative, problem-solving genius, not some pathetic female sobbing over dreams and fantasies that were not her life. She was not a dreamer. She was a practical girl, and she knew how to survive.

Jason simply needed to get out of her mind, and now. Seriously.

Shoulders back, chin up, Astrid threw open the door to Wright's and strode into the store. She tossed her hair, shooting her trademark grin at the patrons who were strolling about with their morning coffee, pancakes and Ophelia's famous muffins, getting their morning dose of gossip before heading out for the day. She was rewarded with a few smiles and a couple of shout-outs about her new scarves, the welcome easing some of the tension in her chest.

Determined to feel better, Astrid gave Ophelia a cheerful greeting as she picked up the coffee that Ophelia had waiting for her. "Morning, Ophelia."

"Wait." Wearing a red plaid shirt and a pair of jeans that had seen years of washings, Ophelia slapped a tray of scrambled eggs, bacon and a spinach quiche on the counter. "Here's your breakfast."

Astrid's stomach turned at the sight of all that food. "You know I don't eat breakfast."

"And you know I don't care. Eat it." Ophelia held up her hand to stop her. "Wait." She pulled out a box of Clare's cupcakes and set a double chocolate fudge with M&Ms on the tray. "You need one of these today. I can tell."

"Chocolate?" Well, that was different. She always had room for chocolate. She would have asked how Ophelia had known today was a chocolate day, but there was no point. Ophelia always knew, and that was the way it was. "Okay, thanks." Astrid picked up the tray and headed across the store toward the corner table, where Emma was already sitting.

She slid down across from Emma, who was hunched over the table, busily sketching on a small pad with colored pencils. "Hi."

Emma looked up from her sketchbook. "Hi—" Her eyes widened as she looked at Astrid, and then her eyebrows shot up. "What happened to you?"

Astrid grimaced. What was up with Ophelia and Emma's intuition this morning? Did she have a sticker on her forehead announcing that she'd had sex by the lake yesterday? "Nothing, I—"

"That's a total lie." Emma set her sketchbook down. Her blond hair was up in a loose ponytail, and her white blouse meant she was heading into Portland for work at the museum today. As usual, her only jewelry was a thin silver chain with a tiny emerald on it, and a ring on her right hand that was a simple silver band with a turquoise stone. Her only capitulation to spunk were the triple gold hoops in her ears that had crystal teardrops hanging from them. "Spill, girlfriend. What's up?"

Astrid shifted in her chair. A part of her wanted so desperately to tell Emma what had happened with Jason, but she didn't know how to confess. She was so used to being on her own and pretending to be fine, that she didn't have any clue how to open the female bonding door. Plus, what would Emma think if Astrid told her she had slept with a total stranger? She still couldn't believe it. She hadn't been with a man since Paul. To fall into Jason's arms was so not in her character, despite what people might think. She sighed, and decided not to broach the topic. "You don't know of any rentals in town, do you? Super cheap."

Emma gave her a sympathetic grimace. "I heard about you

being evicted. That's a total bummer, but at the same time, you do deserve better than living over a mechanic's shop."

Astrid raised her brows. "You've been talking to Eppie?"

"Who hasn't been talking to Eppie?" Emma closed her sketchbook and leaned back in her chair. She folded her arms over her chest and gave Astrid a thoughtful look. "Seriously, Astrid, what are you going to do? Did you find anything?"

"No, but I'm sure I will. I have three weeks." But she knew it would be difficult. Her budget was almost nothing, and the only reason she'd been able to snag her current place was because the ancient landlord was still charging the same rent that he'd been charging since he'd bought the place thirty-five years ago.

"Well, you have a little extra money, right? Since you're not leasing workspace from Clare?"

"Yes, sure." Astrid didn't feel like explaining to Emma that with the decline in her jewelry business lately, she would have had to cut that expense from her budget anyway. There was no sense in dwelling. The only logical thing to do was to figure out how to fix her situation, hence her all night party with her jewelry and apartment listings. Yes, total failure so far, but she still had three weeks. And honestly, the whole thing with Jason was seriously distracting her from her work and living crisis. She was so undone by what had happened, and had no clue how to go forward. She cocked her head and looked at Emma. "Can I ask you something?"

"Sure." Emma plucked an M&M off Astrid's cupcake. "What's up?"

"Would you ever consider dating again?" Astrid didn't know the exact details of Emma's past, but she knew that something had gone horribly wrong with her marriage before she'd returned to Birch Crossing, where she'd grown up with Clare.

Emma's face paled, and she shook her head. "No way. I'm

done." She held up her sketchbook. "This is who I sleep with at night, and that's the way it's going to be."

A book? Really? Astrid leaned forward. "But, don't you ever miss being held by a man? Don't you ever have moments when you wonder what it would be like if you met the right guy?" She hadn't thought she longed for intimacy, and she'd never spent nights imagining what it would be like to find a knight in shining armor. She'd been at peace with her life...until yesterday. Until Jason had reminded her of how beautiful it could be to feel cherished by a man. Was she wrong thinking that she could go through the rest of her life alone?

Emma sighed and set down her notebook. "I used to have that dream, and that's why I made the mistake I did when I got married. I wanted to be loved and taken care of so badly, Astrid. I wanted a family so desperately that I made myself blind to the truth and convinced myself that marrying Howard was the right choice. I'll never make that mistake again. Ever."

Astrid bit her lip and leaned back in her seat, knowing that was exactly what she'd done with Paul. She'd wanted the fairy tale. She'd wanted to be rescued from her life, and because of that, she'd made herself vulnerable to the wrong man and been burned terribly. She'd thought she'd learned her lesson, but even after all that, she'd almost made the same mistake again. For that brief moment with Jason, she'd almost let that same fantasy trick her into wanting too much, into allowing herself to feel the need for a man and a connection. With a sigh, she raised her coffee mug. "Some of us are just destined to be independent goddesses, don't you think?"

Emma grinned and tapped her coffee against Astrid's. "Amen, sistah. Listen, when we're both old and doddery, we'll be the ones running around taking cruises in the Bahamas, while Clare will be stuck taking care of Griffin and pushing him around in his wheelchair so he can stock the shelves at Wright's."

Astrid laughed at the image of Griffin, who was a total male specimen, in a wheelchair. "So true. We have the freedom to live our lives the way we want without being accountable to anyone."

"Exactly." Emma grinned. "After all, just look at Eppie. After her husband died thirty-five years ago, she took over the whole damn town. The woman vibrates with life, right?"

"This is true." Astrid took a deep breath, feeling better. Emma was right. She was just fine on her own, and she had the freedom to take her life in any direction. She could go live in a hovel if she wanted to, because she didn't have to worry about taking care of a child or impressing a man. There had to be some condemned rental somewhere that she could live in, right? She didn't need much. Just a bathroom and enough light to work on her jewelry. "Total freedom."

"Of course." Emma grinned. "So, did I tell you what I decided last night?"

Astrid shook her head. "That you're going to quit that tour guide job you hate in Portland and start trying to sell your amazing artwork?"

"God, no. My creativity would dry up if I had the pressure of supporting myself with it."

Um...yeah...Astrid could relate to that. "But it's worth it—"

"I have to tell you what I decided." Emma leaned forward, her eyes glistening. "I can't believe I'm going to do this, but I'm going to—"

"Good morning, ladies." Eppie pulled up a chair and plunked herself down between them. "You two are just the women I wanted to see." Eppie was wearing a lavender and pale yellow sundress with a matching necklace, each bead almost as large as her fist. Her bright yellow and red polka dotted hat should have been a gross insult to the dress, but somehow, she made it work. She set a digital camera on the table. "You girls know how to work one of these, right?"

"Of course." Astrid chuckled and picked it up. "Eppie has gone digital. I love it."

"Yes, well, a woman must evolve if she's going to stay current." Eppie set her hand on the back of Emma's chair and gave the camera a seductive smile, tossing her head so that her loon earrings banged gently against her wrinkled cheek. "Take a picture, Astrid."

Astrid raised her brows at Emma, but obligingly took a picture of the seventy-something woman.

"And another." Eppie changed her pose, lifting her chin and giving the camera a haughty look.

Astrid took another one, and then six more while Eppie went through an assortment of poses. "What's this for, Eppie?"

"Online dating."

Emma burst out laughing, and Astrid almost dropped the camera. "What? Seriously?"

"Of course." Eppie shot them both looks of disdain. "What? You think that just because I'm seventy-two I don't have a need for some hot loving? A girl can be independent for only so long." She stretched back in her seat, giving both younger women a satisfied smile. "I've had my fun, girls, and it's time to get a younger man to take care of me as I start to get older. A woman has to plan for these things, you know."

Astrid frowned. "But I thought you loved being single."

"There's a time and place for everything, Astrid, and the time has come for this sexpot to settle down." Eppie picked up the camera. "So, which one of you sparkling young things is going to meet me here at four o'clock today to show me how to use my new computer and get this loveforever.com thing started?"

Emma grinned cheerfully. "I have to be at work until six. Astrid? Are you around?"

As if she could deal with trying to get Eppie dating. She needed to get away from that scene, not involved in it. "I'm trying to find a place to live—"

"Nonsense. You can't do that all damn day." Eppie nodded. "It's a date. Four o'clock. I'll bring the beer. All you have to do is show up. Got it?" Before Astrid could reply, Eppie snapped her fingers. "I almost forgot, Astrid. I talked to Sam today, your landlord, in case you failed to retain that information. He said he got your message about wanting to stay in the apartment."

Astrid sat up, her heart racing. "He did? What did he say?"

"That you need to get a life. Living in his apartment is not the life for a sweet young thing like you."

Astrid stared at Eppie, her heart sinking. "Sam would never say that."

Eppie laughed and slapped her thigh. "Okay, you got me, I talked him into it, but he agreed it sounded good." She pushed back from the table. "Get a new place, Astrid. Live a little. You're turning into a shriveled old prune and that would just be a terrible shame for a gal with your zest."

"A prune?" Astrid stared at Eppie. "I'm not a prune." Yes, she might be creatively drained and sleeping alone every night, but she worked extremely hard to stay fired up about life. A prune was something that was shriveling and dying. Not her!

"Actually, it's not a bad analogy," Emma said. "Compared to when I met you a year ago, you're a little prunish."

"What?" Astrid sat up straighter, shocked by their comments. "How can you say that?"

"Ophelia!" Eppie shouted across the store. "Is Astrid turning into a prune?"

"She wouldn't if she'd eat some damn breakfast once in a while," Ophelia yelled back.

Eppie shrugged. "See? Prune." Then her eyes gleamed and she turned on her camera. "Oh, I just had the most brilliant stroke of genius. Let's both go on loveforever.com. I'll spring for your membership fee. That'll be your payment for helping me."

"Oh, no—" Astrid winced as Eppie took a picture. "Eppie, stop!"

"One more. Smile," Eppie commanded. "Men prefer a woman who looks happy."

Happy? She was supposed to put on a show to attract a man? Not that Jason had needed fake happy. She'd been overwhelmed with her life when he'd come out to see her on that rock, and she knew it was their shadows that had brought them together. Not all men were so superficial that they needed some woman who was so shallow that all she could do was giggle. Jason had appreciated her. Not that she wanted him. Or anyone. "Dammit, Eppie. I'm not going to fake it for a man."

"Faking it? Who said anything about faking it?" Eppie's well-plucked eyebrows shot up. "Hell, Astrid, if a man isn't good enough to give you a real one, he doesn't deserve to have his ego stoked with a faked orgasm. Make him earn every compliment he gets."

Emma almost snorted her coffee, and Astrid would have laughed at the irony of a senior citizen lecturing her about faking orgasms if she weren't so strung out. "Eppie, please leave me out of this." Astrid shoved back from the table. "I don't want anyone. I'm just done. I'm not ready."

"Ready?" Eppie leapt on the word. "Ready since what? What did a man do to you, Astrid? What are you so afraid of?"

Astrid met Emma's gaze, and saw an empathy so deep it

made her throat tighten. Emma understood. They didn't know each other's pasts, but Emma understood. For a moment, a real smile flashed on Astrid's face, and she suddenly didn't feel so alone.

"Astrid," Eppie interrupted. "Sit your butt back in that chair and have some girl chat. It's time to stop being an outsider and let it all hang out."

Fear rippled through Astrid and she looked at Eppie. Those old violet eyes were so vibrant and alive, so full of gossip and intrigue that Astrid knew she couldn't tell the truth. It would be all over town within minutes, and then she would never be able to move past it. She would see her past reflected in everyone's faces whenever they looked at her. "Let it go, Eppie," she said quietly. "Just let it go."

Then, with a brief smile of understanding at Emma, Astrid turned and walked out, needing her space. She didn't look back as she heard Eppie calling after her. She just wanted to get away. Loveforever.com? Dating again? She felt like choking as she hurried down the steps toward her car. Maybe getting evicted was a sign. Maybe it was time to move on. Maybe it was time to move to a new place where people didn't know her well enough to start to figure out that she was really a complete wreck, or to decide to interfere in her life.

But as she pulled open the door to her old car, she glanced down Main Street at her old office, which now had a For Lease sign on the door. She smiled as she remembered the hours of conversation she and Clare had enjoyed once she'd moved in as a sublessor into Clare's space. Her best creative work had been there, when she'd first moved into town. She took a deep breath and looked around the tree-lined street, at all the little shops that were so quaint and small. People who lived here stayed forever. This wasn't a town of transients.

She didn't want to be a transient anymore. She wanted to be a forever—

Then she saw a shiny black Mercedes rolling toward her, and her belly tightened. *Jason.* She swallowed as longing rushed over her, and she seemed to be stuck to the ground, unable to dive into the car and hide from him.

His car slowed down as his tinted window opened. Her heart racing, Astrid lifted her chin and turned to face him. He leaned out the window and grinned, that same magnetizing smile that she'd succumbed to yesterday. "Good morning, Astrid."

"Hi." Warmth flooded her at his warm tone, at the possessive way he looked at her. This wasn't a man who was going to pretend yesterday hadn't happened. This was a man who was fully engaged and ready to claim her, and it felt incredible.

Dammit. Why couldn't she resist him?

"Hi!" Noah piped up from the back seat. "I'm Noah!"

She glanced past Jason into the backseat, and saw Noah sitting on his booster. He grinned at her with the effervescence of a boy who thought the world was his playground. "Hi, Noah. My name is Astrid."

He waved. "I'm going to my new camp today. They have swimming, soccer and they even have archery!" He made a shooting motion with his arms. "And guess what! They have a huge playground there. Bigger than the one at my old school in New York."

Astrid's chest tightened at his tremendous blue eyes and long black eyelashes. He was so adorable, so engaging, and so open. "How old are you, Noah?"

"Six."

"Six." Her son would have been three. Riding in her backseat just like Noah... Astrid's heart ached, and she tore her gaze off Noah, struggling to tamp down the emotions she usually had locked away. She focused on Jason, who was studying her so thoughtfully that chills ran down her spine. "What?"

"Dinner tonight?"

"No." God, no. Not when every fiber of her being was screaming at her to accept his invitation and fall into his spell, to allow him to sweep her up into his life and help her forget everything she was dealing with. She couldn't do it, because it was so much easier to be alone, than to trust and then be destroyed again. She couldn't recover again. It would be too much.

"Tomorrow?"

"No, I—"

"Friday?"

Jason's eyes were flashing with challenge, and Astrid suddenly realized that he wasn't going to give up. For some asinine reason, she had become a challenge that he wasn't going to abandon. As much as she wanted to believe it, she knew it wasn't because she was so special that he wanted to sweep her into his life and give her the fantasy. She wasn't the naïve girl who thought she was enough for a man like Jason Sarantos. He didn't want *her.* He wanted something *from* her, and once he got it, he would no longer want her or need her. She stepped up to the window and lowered her voice. "Why, Jason? Why me?"

Those same shadows flashed in his eyes, and she remembered the depths of his pain last night when they'd met under the sunset. "Because you make me smile," he said.

And then she knew. Jason wanted her because he was hurting so deeply inside and he felt like she was his gasp of relief. It was just like how she'd met Paul on the heels of his breakup with his girlfriend of seven years. She was the relief, the rebirth, the desperate grasp at survival. What would happen when Jason got his feet under him again? When he didn't need a hand to hold him up, and then he realized what kind of woman he'd brought into his life?

She already knew.

She would not make the same mistake again of trusting a man's beautiful words and believing that he meant them forever. Jason was a single dad with an impressionable son. He might want an angel to breathe life into him now, but ultimately, he would want a mother for his son, a beacon of domesticity to flood their home with security and love, and that was one thing she couldn't offer. Not *ever*. Thanks, but no thanks. She wasn't going to throw herself out there and get crushed again. "I'm sorry, Jason, but not Friday, not Saturday, not ever." She stepped back from the car. "Good-bye, Jason. Have a good day at camp, Noah."

"Bye!" Noah shouted from the back.

For a long moment, Jason didn't drive. He simply stared at her, and after a moment, his expression began to cool, and she knew that he'd finally accepted her rejection. It was done.

She felt no relief. She simply felt the painful ache of loss, even though she knew it was the only way it could be. Damn him for reminding her of all the things she used to dream of, for showing her how alone she really was.

"As you wish, Astrid." Then, without another word, he took his foot off the brake and let his car coast away from her.

And with that, it was done.

But as he rounded the corner, Astrid knew that it wasn't. Not really. Because this was a small town and she would see him all the time. And every time she saw him, it would remind her of what it had felt like to be needed, even if it had been only for a moment. He would make it impossible to forget all that had nearly destroyed her before.

Could she survive being constantly reminded of that?

As she got into the car, she knew what the answer was. No, she couldn't. The only way she could survive was to not feel that kind of pain, and she simply wasn't strong enough to see Jason every day and not feel anything. It was time to move on.

It was time to leave her home.

It was time to find a new place.

It was time for another fresh start.

The mere thought of leaving Birch Crossing brought a swell of anguish to her chest, and she was already crying by the time her wheels started to roll.

But by the time she reached the one stoplight in town, her eyes were dry, and her shoulders were back.

Another adventure meant another beginning. One of these times she was going to get it right. There was simply no other option.

CHAPTER SEVEN

"HERE'S TO ASTRID! The coolest chick ever to live over a mechanic's shop!"

Astrid grinned as Clare raised her beer in yet another toast to her. After three weeks of packing and avoiding questions, this morning Astrid had finally told Clare and Emma during their daily morning coffee that she was leaving town the next day. Clare and Emma's shock and outrage had been so genuine that Astrid had almost considered changing her mind, but she hadn't.

She wasn't a "forever" kind of person, and it was time to move on. She'd thought they'd accepted that, until they'd showed up at seven o'clock this evening while she was packing the last of her things and kidnapped her for a going away party of booze, sex and roasting. In Birch Crossing, that kind of party involved a corner table at Johnny's Grill and Swill, a couple pitchers of beer, and too many platters of nachos. The sex part involved making raunchy suggestions about the well-muscled bartender with a military buzz cut and a healthy dose of tattoos.

"We have presents," Emma announced, holding up a blue

and yellow sparkly gift bag and setting it on the table, almost on top of the third platter of nachos. "We can't send you off without being properly gift-laden."

Astrid laughed, touched by the gesture. Of all the times she'd moved, no one had ever given her a going away party. She and her mom had just slipped away, because good-bye hurt too much. She'd considered going that route this time, but she hadn't been able to do it. Clare and Emma simply meant too much to her. "You guys are crazy."

"Not crazy," Clare said as she took a drink of the beer. "Just totally devastated that you're really moving away. I have a guest room. Please live there."

"And listen to you and Griffin have crazy monkey sex all night while I'm sitting there by myself?" Astrid snorted. "That is cruel and unusual punishment for a single girl."

"Amen, sistah," Emma said. "No secondhand sex necessary." She grinned as she picked up another nacho laden with cheese, chili and olives. "Sleep on my couch. There will be none of that to bother you. In fact..." She dug into the bag and pulled out a small box wrapped in blue foil. "Here you go. This should help you sleep."

Astrid grinned as she started to unwrap it. "I must admit, I've never felt so loved. I really appreciate it."

"Is it enough to keep you here?" Clare said hopefully. "I mean it, Astrid, I don't think you should go—"

"You're kidding!" Astrid burst out laughing when she saw what was in the box. "A vibrator?"

"Yeah." Emma leaned forward and pointed at the box. "The guy at the store in Portland said this is their best seller. It's got this dual action thing with the penetration and stimulator—"

"Perfect." Astrid grinned. "And it's in pink. My favorite color."

Emma nodded. "I thought you'd like the pink." Then she

winked. "I bought one for myself, too. I figured why not, right?"

"You got it, girl." Astrid tapped her beer against Emma's, exchanging knowing glances with her. It was such a thoughtful gift, actually. It could keep a girl out of trouble...

"What about me?" Clare picked up the box and studied it. "Why didn't you get me one? This actually looks kind of interesting."

"Because you have Griffin. Women who have real men have to buy their own sex toys," Emma said.

"What is that?" Eppie plunked herself down at the table and yanked the box out of Clare's hands. "Good lord, Almighty, is that really supposed to fit inside a woman? They didn't have things like this when I was your age. We had to make do with a—"

"So glad you could make it," Clare quickly interrupted, mercifully sparing them from whatever Eppie was about to describe. "Have a beer."

"I want one of these." Eppie flipped the black box over, tugging at the corners. "How do I get this open? I want to check it out—"

"Can I get you anything—" Their waitress stuttered in surprise when she saw what was in Eppie's hand. "Oh, how cool! I've heard about those. They're supposed to be great."

"I know," Emma said. "That's why I got it—"

Eppie started to tear at the box, and Astrid plucked it out of the old lady's hands. "Get your own, thank you very much. That's mine." And she truthfully was kind of excited about it. Maybe it would keep her from making insane choices like sleeping with Jason Sarantos twelve hours after meeting him just because it felt so damn good to have someone look at her the way he had...

"Okay, well, I have a different theory about how you should be living your life." Clare pulled a twelve-inch wooden box out of the gift bag. "This is my going away present."

Astrid took the box, marveling at the intricacies of the wood overlays. The wood was beautiful, and it was hand-carved with dozens of beautiful flowers that had once been painted. The colors had faded now to a bare hint of rose and green, which made it almost even more stunning. "That's beautiful."

"I thought you'd like it." Clare smiled. "It was my mother's jewelry box. I want you to have it."

"Your mother's?" Astrid immediately shook her head and set the box on the table. Clare's mother had died several years ago, and Astrid knew how much Clare still missed her. "I can't take a memento of your mother, Clare. There's no way."

"I want you to have it." Clare picked it up and put it in Astrid's hands. "When I see it, it reminds me of when she and I used to sit at her dresser and model her jewelry. They were beautiful memories I had with her, and I cherish them."

"That's why—"

"But you are all about jewelry, too, Astrid," Clare said. "That's how we met, with you sitting there in the alcove in my office, making these amazing designs while I wrote out wills. Use this box for your most special pieces and think of me. There's so much love in that box, and I want you to have it with you, so that you always have a piece of me with you, so you always remember that you are loved."

Tears filled Astrid's eyes, and she started to cry. "How am I supposed to leave when you say things like that?"

"That's my hope," Clare said with a misty grin. "By the end of tonight, you'll be so weepy that you'll decide to sleep in my bed between me and Griffin because you love us so much."

Astrid managed to laugh through her tears. "God, no,

that's just creepy." Then she opened the box and started laughing again. "How many boxes of condoms are in here?"

"Twenty. It was all that would fit." Clare grinned. "When you gave me that box of condoms last spring, it changed the entire direction of my life, so I thought I'd return the favor."

"With twenty boxes?"

Clare grinned. "Well, maybe your life needs a big change."

"That it does." Astrid flipped through the boxes. "You've got every type in here. Even flavored? Cinnamon? Really? That just doesn't sound appealing——" Then she uncovered what was at the bottom and her stomach dropped. "A pregnancy test?"

"Two!" Clare laughed. "You know, condoms are only about ninety-seven percent effective, so I figured if I was encouraging you to have sex more than a hundred times, I should at least give you a couple tests."

"That's why the vibrator is better," Emma announced cheerfully as she refilled her beer from the pitcher. "No risk there."

Astrid suddenly felt sick, and she pushed the beer away from her. "Thanks," she said, suddenly not able to stop thinking about the fact that she and Jason had not used a condom.

How long had it been since they'd been together? She quickly counted off the days. It had been over three weeks. Her period had been due last week, but she hadn't even thought about the fact she was late because she often missed her period when she was stressed. She was accustomed to missing it, and had not given it a thought since her stress level was off the charts. She was exhausted. She hadn't slept more than two hours a night due to worry and working on her jewelry. So it made complete sense that she'd miss her period. It happened often, and she was never pregnant.

Except that this time, there had been sex involved, so that

changed everything. This time, there was a possibility that it wasn't the stress or lack of sleep... "Oh, shit." She gripped the edge of the table, suddenly having trouble breathing.

"Here's my gift," Eppie said, as the girls chatted about condoms and vibrators, clearly not noticing Astrid's sudden panic. She handed a small envelope to Astrid. "For you."

Her fingers shaking, Astrid took the envelope and opened it. Inside was a small pink notecard with two words written on it: "Angel27" and "beli3ve4u." "What is this?"

"Your loveforever.com profile name and password," Eppie said. "I bought you a year's subscription and put together a lovely profile for you after you showed me how to work it. You already have sixteen messages, and some of the men are quite lovely. I screened out a couple who were clearly no-good-womanizing bastards, but left the ones you might be interested in."

Astrid stared at Eppie, fear wrapping its cold tentacles around her heart. "But I told you—"

"I know, sweetie." Eppie reached across the table and squeezed Astrid's hand with surprising strength. "But no matter how much you claim you want that pink vibrator as your bedmate, the truth is that we're women. We don't want to be alone. We all want to find that true partner who will love, honor and cherish us even on our worst days."

The table fell silent as all three women stared at Eppie in surprise. Clare had a soft mushy look on her face, but Emma's expression was as stark as Astrid felt. "But you've been single for years, Eppie," Astrid managed to say. "You've been happy being single." Eppie had been part of her inspiration that it was okay to resign herself to a life of being alone. Eppie was her reassurance that it was okay.

"I was happy being single because I already found my true love and had almost forty amazing years with him. I don't need another true love." Eppie grinned and leaned back in her chair, clasping her arms behind her head like she was basking on the beach in the hot sun. "But I do want someone to wait on me hand and foot as I get older, so I need to snag myself a young buck. I'll be competing for the men with you, darling, so don't hate me when I steal one away from you."

Astrid swallowed and looked at Emma, who was pressing her lips together tightly. Emma glanced at her and managed a stiff smile. "So if Eppie's right and we are secretly craving a man, then I apologize for getting you the vibrator, Astrid. I'll return it—"

"Return it?" Astrid grabbed the gift bag off the table. "No—"

"And exchange it for the one that comes attached to the blow up doll that says "I love you" in six different languages when you lick his nipple. That way you can have romance and sex at the same time, just like Eppie says we all want."

Astrid stared at Emma, and then the whole table burst out laughing.

"That's where I draw the line," Eppie declared. "I won't be licking any plastic nipples no matter how good the man may be at being my serving boy when I get old."

"I don't know, plastic nipples might be like the new way of safe sex," Emma said.

The three women launched into a discussion of plastic nipples and what languages were the most romantic to be wooed in, but Astrid couldn't stop thinking about the pregnancy kits in Clare's mom's jewelry box.

She and Jason had made love one time. The odds were almost infinitesimal. Seriously.

Everything was going to be okay. Really. *Really.* She took a deep breath as Eppie raised her glass to Astrid to give another toast. "Astrid, good luck with your new venture, and always remember that this town is here for you. When you realize that it's time for you to come back, we'll all be here, ready to welcome you home."

Astrid managed a smile. "Thanks," she said, looking around the table at the three women who had gathered to see her off. She'd never had friends before, not like this. "I can't tell you all how much it means to me to have your friendship. I treasure it."

"We treasure you," Clare said. "Are you sure you need to go?"

"She does," Eppie interrupted. "Can't you see it in her eyes? Astrid's not ready to settle yet. She's still running from the shadows of her past." She leaned forward. "Don't you worry, Astrid. Your time will come, and you'll know when it does. You'll find your place."

Astrid bit her lip against the sudden swell of hope. "You really think so?"

"Of course. That's what we women do." Eppie gestured at the table. "We survive until we finally find the place we were meant to settle in. Clare found hers, and the rest of yours are still coming." She nodded at Astrid. "You're next, my dear. I feel it in my old bones. Your world is about to be shaken up, but good."

Astrid thought of the pregnancy kit and almost hoped Eppie was wrong.

She knew what she would be doing when she got home tonight.

◦⌇◦

SON OF A BITCH. He'd forgotten how beautiful she was.

Jason leaned on the bar at Johnny's Grill and Swill, waiting for his takeout order while he watched Astrid laughing with Eppie, Clare and another woman whose name he couldn't quite remember.

Her brown hair had a vibrant auburn glow beneath the bar lights, and she looked sexy as hell in a loose-fitting blouse that had slipped off one shoulder, making her appear soft and vulnerable. Her feet were tucked behind the rung on her tall chair, her sandals on the floor beneath her. She was wearing at least ten silver bracelets on her left wrist, and her earrings caught the light as they twirled. Her face was somewhat shadowed, but he could see the relaxed lines of her body as she laughed with her friends.

Damn, she was so alive. So fucking alive. Suddenly, Jason regretted his decision to give her the space she wanted. It had seemed to make sense at the time, and the last damn thing he had time for was a woman who wasn't interested in what he had to offer. He'd been married to that kind of woman for far too long, and he'd received that same message from Astrid loud and clear. Cold. Distant. Aloof. Independent.

He hadn't come to Maine to indulge his fantasies with a woman who got under his skin. He'd come to Maine to build a home and family for Noah, and that meant finding a mother for his son. A real mother, not a ruthless, cold workaholic who was more interested in accumulating fame and fortune than her own kids. Or, in Astrid's case, a fluttering free spirit who couldn't come down to earth long enough to connect with anyone. Different women, but same end result.

Astrid had made it clear that she wasn't the mothering type, and that ended the deal for him right then, no matter how alive she made him feel.

But as he watched her now, there was none of that cool distance she'd shown him. Her laugh was warm and engaging, and the way she leaned in toward her friends spoke of genuine affection and connection. Suddenly, he was back in that moment on the rock, when she'd looked up at him with all the pain and vulnerability in her eyes. He'd fallen for her instantly, and suddenly, all that was back.

He wanted her, every bit as much as he had that first moment he'd seen her. Yeah, she was irreverent. Yes, she walked her own path and didn't let anyone else on it. Granted, she wasn't the woman he'd come up here to find, a doting, domestic woman who would be the mom Noah had never had. But Astrid had *something,* and it wasn't letting him go.

Shit. He couldn't afford this. He'd made a mistake once, and he wouldn't do it again.

"Clare's mine, so don't be checking her out," Griffin warned as he walked up to the bar.

Jerking his gaze off Astrid, Jason glanced over at the owner of Wright's. "Hey, Griffin. I didn't think you ever got sprung from that place."

"It's almost eleven. I got out for good behavior. I came by to give Clare a ride home when she gets finished here." Griffin leaned on the bar as he studied Jason. "Seriously, man. Which one of the women over there put that look on your face?"

Jason cleared his throat and turned his back on the women. "No one in particular."

Griffin snorted as he gestured for a beer. "I'll tell you a few things. Eppie's a hot ticket, but she's too much woman for you."

Jason grinned. "Yeah, I got that figured out."

The bartender set two beers down in front of them, shrugging when Jason said he hadn't ordered one. "Drink it. It's on the house. Welcome to Birch Crossing. Your dinner's going to take a few minutes anyway."

Griffin grinned and raised his beer as Jason gave up the protest and accepted the beverage. He'd told the sitter that he'd be home by midnight, so he still had time. With Noah already asleep, Jason had no reason to rush home. He wanted out of Astrid's influence, but he was hungry after working at the shop all night, and he had nothing in his fridge.

Griffin nodded his approval as Jason sat down. "Emma was royally messed up in a prior relationship, and she's got the whole damn town protecting her. Don't mess with that woman unless you're prepared to escort her to the altar and sacrifice your soul to take care of her."

Jason rubbed his jaw as he contemplated that. "That's what I'm looking for, actually." He glanced over at the table again, and studied Emma. She was attractive enough, but there was nothing about her that made his soul ignite. Astrid wasn't there, and he glanced quickly around the restaurant. Bathroom? Yeah, probably in the ladies room.

"Yeah?" Griffin looked surprised. "Emma's the one who caught your eye? I thought you were checking out Astrid. That's what I heard."

Jason didn't even bother to get surprised by Griffin's insight. It was a small town. News traveled, even if it was by magic, apparently. "Astrid's not my type."

"Astrid is no man's type," Griffin agreed. "Clare says that Astrid hasn't even looked at a guy twice since she's been here. She goes on an occasional date, but no second dates. Ever. No matter who it is. And even the first dates have stopped. The woman is untouchable."

Jason stiffened at Griffin's description of Astrid's modus operandi. That sounded all too familiar to what she'd done with him: one first date, no second one. Shit. He'd been just one in a long line of men? "Does she sleep with them all?" He couldn't quite keep the bitterness out of his voice.

Griffin narrowed his eyes. "Never, so don't waste your time thinking she's easy prey. You fuck with her, and you have the town to answer to. Including me."

Never. Relief coursed through Jason. Astrid never slept with any of the men she dated. Except him. What the fuck was different about him? Why had he broken through her barriers? He glanced again at the table and saw the women were beginning to pack up. Astrid still wasn't there. Where the hell was she?

When he turned back to the bar, Griffin was glaring at him. "You're a fucking liar," Griffin said under his breath. "You're looking for Astrid." He leaned forward. "I swear to you, Sarantos, you mess with her, and I will run you out of town so fast you won't have time to breathe. She's Clare's best friend, and I'll protect her like she's my own."

Jason tightened his fingers around his beer and turned his back on the table again, willing himself not to look for her. "Nothing to worry about, Griffin. She's not my type. I'm looking for a mother for my son."

Something flashed in Griffin's eyes. "She doesn't do men with kids. Ever."

"Yeah, she told me." Jason ground his jaw as he took another swig of his beer, shifting restlessly. He needed to get out of there. There was no point in thinking about Astrid. Their incompatibility went far too deep. He'd focus on his shop. Yeah, that was it. He'd engage in some man talk about woodworking. "Hey, you know anyone who can do a little construction work? The cafe needs more work than I thought, and I want to hire someone to help me out."

Griffin nodded. "I got a guy. Jackson will stop by tomorrow and see what you've got." Griffin raised his brows. "Emma could use a good man interested in settling down. She needs someone to take care of her."

Shit. Jason wasn't sure he was up to the challenge of taking care of someone who was broken. He'd already failed too many times at that. Or maybe it was just that Astrid had him so thoroughly captivated that he couldn't even consider another woman. For the last three and a half weeks, every time he'd seen her around town, every cell in his body had gone on high alert, and the desire and compulsion to be with her had almost knocked him on his ass. After almost a month, it hadn't decreased, and it was getting tough as hell to resist. Astrid had never looked his way, almost like she didn't notice him. How could that be? They'd been mere yards apart a dozen times at Wright's, and yet she had never made eye contact. That should have cured him of his attraction to her, but it hadn't.

Seemed like nothing could, and he had no idea how the hell to deal with it. "Yeah, well, I'll keep that in mind about Emma." The bartender came by with Jason's food. Relieved, Jason grabbed the bag and tossed cash on the bar. "So, I'll catch you later—"

"Griffin!" Clare hurried up and threw her arms around Griffin's neck, giving the store owner a kiss that was so intimate and personal, it made Jason want to look away. Shit. He wasn't sure he'd ever seen a kiss like that before, and he couldn't stop the twinge of envy as Griffin wrapped his arm around Clare's waist and pulled her close. "Labor day weekend," Griffin said. "Come to the wedding. Everyone in town is invited."

Clare beamed at Jason, and he was startled by the intensity of her happiness and love. Shit. Griffin was a lucky man to have a woman look at him like that. "Yeah, thanks for the invite."

"Bring Noah," Clare said. "Kids are welcome, of course."

Jason grinned at Clare's obvious warmth toward his son, who she'd gotten to know on Jason's morning visits to Wright's on his way to dropping Noah off at camp. "Yeah, okay, thanks." He glanced over at the table again and saw it was empty. Emma and Eppie were walking out the door, but Astrid was nowhere to be seen. "Astrid left?"

Clare sighed, and genuine sadness flickered across her

face. "Yes, she didn't even stay until the end of her own party."

Jason frowned. "Her party? Was it her birthday?" He recalled now seeing the gift bag on the table.

"No, she's moving." Clare's smile faded as she turned back to Griffin. "I couldn't talk her into staying. I'm so bummed."

"Astrid's moving?" Jason grabbed her arm, turning Clare back toward him. "Moving where?"

Clare frowned at him, as if annoyed that he was interrupting her moment with Griffin. "To northern Vermont. She leaves in the morning." She gave him a sad smile. "I can't believe she's really going."

"Of course you couldn't talk her into staying, sweetheart," Griffin said to Clare. "Astrid is a free spirit. She needs to move on."

Jason gritted his teeth at the thought of Astrid disappearing from town. Free spirit or not, how could she take off without telling him? "Moving to *Vermont?* In the *morning?* As in, nine hours from now?"

"Yeah, Jackson and I are going over in the morning to load up the U-Haul for her," Griffin said.

"I'm afraid I'm never going to see her again," Clare said softly, leaning on Griffin in a way that made real jealousy ricochet through Jason. So, there were women who would turn to their man for support, and not kick him in his ass on their way out the door to work?

"There was something about her tonight that felt final," Clare said as Griffin trailed his fingers through her hair. "I don't think she's going to come back."

"Not coming back? Son of a bitch." Jason didn't miss Griffin's narrowed eyes, but he didn't care. Astrid was bailing on him? Disappearing without even telling him? Never coming back? Shit, he was not okay with that. He'd been giving her space, not planning to never see her again. What if she disappeared from his life entirely?

No way. Unacceptable. He grabbed his bag of takeout off the counter, suddenly burning with the need to see her one more time. It didn't matter that they were incompatible in the long term. That night had been some sort of amazing connection, and he couldn't let her walk out of his life without acknowledging it. "Where does she live?"

Clare raised her eyebrows at his demanding tone. "She lives down the street. Over Mack's Garage."

"Mack's Garage?" Jason knew where that was. It was beside the old train tracks on the south side of town. All he could remember was the service station. He didn't remember seeing any apartments over there. "Is she there now?"

Clare nodded. "She left about twenty minutes ago. She had to finish packing—"

"Packing." Son of a bitch. Urgency coursed through Jason, and he spun toward the door.

Griffin's hand came down heavily on his arm. "Sarantos," he said quietly. "Astrid seems tough, but she's not. Don't hurt her."

Jason met his gaze. "I know exactly how tough she is," he said. "That's why I'm going after her."

For a long moment, the men simply stared at each other, then Griffin nodded and released him.

Jason didn't waste time. He simply sprinted for the door, urgency coursing through him. Astrid Monroe wasn't bailing on him. Not yet.

CHAPTER EIGHT

Jason swore as he got out of his car at Mack's Garage. The place reeked of gasoline and oil fumes, and it was stacked with at least twenty beater cars, as well as an assortment of well-used foreign luxury models that seemed to be finding a second life in the woods of Maine. The garage was a shuddering wooden building with siding falling off in places, and a couple of the windows were held together by duct tape.

Above the south side of the garage was a second floor alcove, with two small dormers. The double hung windows were open wide, and a small, faint glow came from within. This was where Astrid lived? This shit hole?

Outrage burned through him, and he strode toward the building, searching for a way to the second floor. He jogged around the perimeter, and finally saw Astrid's junker car parked behind the shop, beside a faded red door that didn't quite close all the way. This was her home? A place where the exterior door didn't shut, let alone lock?

Shit. He hoped she had a badass dog living with her, or he was going to be in an even worse mood.

Remembering too clearly the way she'd shut him down so

completely the last time he'd reached out to her, Jason didn't bother to knock or give her a chance to tell him to take a hike. He just pushed open the door and vaulted up the narrow, steep stairwell, scowling at the cracks in the plaster. He couldn't even imagine Astrid cloistering herself in this hellhole, cutting off her vibrancy and life before it had a chance to blossom.

He reached the landing, which was piled high with cardboard boxes. The reality of her move hit him hard, and he sobered. She had really been planning to leave town without telling him, despite the unbelievable connection they'd had? The thought passed through his mind that maybe the intensity of their connection had been one-sided, that it had been only him who'd felt the world shift when they'd made love.

Then he thought of her passion and the way she'd embraced him, and he knew that she'd felt the same thing. Regardless of what had happened to make her pull back, he was dead certain that she'd been as affected by their lovemaking as he had been, at least in that moment.

He navigated around the towers of boxes and walked over to the one door at the top of the stairs. He knocked lightly, frowning when he saw it open slightly from his touch. No security whatsoever. Did she have no idea of her vulnerability?

There was no answer from within, and Jason was about to raise his hand to knock again, when he heard a low moan from the other side of the door. A moan of pain. "Astrid!" Adrenaline rushed through him. He immediately shoved open the door and bolted into the apartment.

Astrid was sitting on the edge of a bed, hunched over in a ball. She looked up sharply at his entrance, and her face went ashen. Tears were streaming down her cheeks, and the raw terror in her eyes made him clench his fist and do a quick recon of the place to see if anything was in there threatening her. The place was stripped of everything but piles of boxes, a couple pieces of furniture and an outfit folded neatly on a box.

No one was there, but as he turned back to Astrid's face, there was no mistaking the depth of fear in her brown eyes.

There was nothing arrogant and flippant about her now. Just the raw agony of a woman freefalling into hell. Protectiveness surged through Jason, and he shut the door behind him, locking out the world as he walked into her space.

"No," she whispered. "Go away." She moved her hand quickly, and Jason saw a flash of white in her grasp before she hid it behind her back.

For a long second, his mind went blank with shock as he struggled to process what he'd just seen. The white stick? He felt his throat close up and he stared at her. "Astrid?"

"No. Go away." She scrambled to her feet and stumbled over a box.

Jason leapt across the tiny room and caught her before she fell. Her body felt too bony and frail beneath his hands, and her skin was icy cold. She sucked in her breath and pulled back, and as she did, something fell from her hand.

He caught it before it hit the ground, and the moment his fingers closed around the hard plastic, he knew what it was. Slowly, he looked down at it and saw a white window.

In the window was a blue plus sign.

Griffin's words leapt into Jason's mind. *Never.* Astrid *never* slept with anyone.

Except Jason.

He was the only one she'd been with, and he was holding a positive result pregnancy test in his hand.

Son of a bitch. She was pregnant with his child.

ASTRID SAW the shock on Jason's features. She knew that he'd realized what was in his hand, and what it meant. She went still, her body going numb as she waited for the inevitable words, the same ones that Paul had given her when he'd realized she was pregnant with his child. The demand for ownership and control. The offer of marriage. All of it meaningless, using her as a pawn for him to get what he wanted: his child.

She lifted her chin and faced Jason, preparing for the battle.

But Jason didn't say anything. He just stood there staring at the test for what felt like forever. Finally he looked up, and she saw the stunned expression on his face. It was so stark, so surprised, so at a loss, that she started laughing. Not a laugh of joy and bliss. The laughter of shared pain and shock, which was yet another connection between them that seemed to close the chasm she'd tried so hard to create. "I know," she said softly. "That's exactly how I feel."

"Jesus, Astrid." Jason ran his hand through his hair, and suddenly he didn't look like a threatening male who would prey on her. He looked like a guy who was standing on quicksand and had no idea which way led to safety.

Slowly, some of her fear began to ease. She sat back down on the bed, her legs still trembling from the shock of finding out. She'd read the results only minutes before Jason had walked in, and she was still shaken, still trying to grasp the enormity of the situation. "Aren't you going to ask if it's yours?"

"No." Jason shoved the stick in his back pocket and clasped his hands on top of his head, his biceps bunching. His tee shirt was covered in white splotches that matched the streaks on his jeans, and she knew he'd been at the cafe working. "Of course it's mine."

"Oh." Something warm fluttered in Astrid's chest, something that made her feel good. Based on what he'd seen of her, making love with a stranger on the day she'd met him, he'd have been justified in wondering whether he was part of a long line of one night stands.

But she could tell the thought hadn't even occurred to him. He'd absolutely, instantly, without a moment's hesitation, believed that she had been with no one else.

Paul had insisted on a paternity test before he'd been willing to accept that the woman he'd been dating for over a year hadn't been sleeping around on him.

Jason hadn't even hesitated, and the thought made her throat tighten. No one saw her in that kind of light, a woman so honorable that he would trust her automatically, despite all evidence to the contrary. It felt so incredible, this gift that made her heart actually ache, his absolute belief in who she was. It made her want to ask him to wrap her up in his arms and hold her so tightly that she'd never have to breathe on her own again.

Which of course she couldn't do. She had learned her lesson about relying on anyone else, and she thought she was used to it. Until Jason made her want more by being so damned nice to her.

Damn him for having faith in her.

With a muttered curse, Jason turned away and walked over to the window. He braced his hands on the window frame and looked out over the garage, his body rigid with tension. Saying nothing. Giving away nothing. Astrid's initial relief that he hadn't launched into a series of threats began to fade, replaced by increasing trepidation. What was he thinking? What was he going to do? She couldn't tell at all.

The silence loomed threateningly in the small room, and Astrid's heart began to pound again as the reality of her situation began to descend upon her. *She was pregnant.* Sweat broke out on her skin, and suddenly she felt hot. Her head began to buzz, and the room began to spin. Her mouth was pasty dry, and suddenly she started to pant, unable to get her breath. *It's going to be okay. It's going to be okay.* But she couldn't stop the growing panic, the terror trying to take her. She waved her hand at her face, trying to cool herself, trying to ground herself.

"Shit, Astrid. Lie down." Jason was suddenly beside her, his hands on her shoulders, supporting her.

"No." She tried to brush his hands off, feeling trapped by his touch. "Let go of me."

"Hey, I'm not going to hurt you." His voice was gentle, but his grip was unrelenting. "You're going to pass out if you don't lie down."

"I'm fine." She bent forward, putting her head between her knees, as she fought for breath, trying not to think, trying to blank her mind so she couldn't process anything that was happening. But the room began to spin more, and suddenly she felt herself falling forward. The floor rushed up toward her, and she tried to brace herself as Jason swept her up in his arms, catching her before she face planted onto the stained floorboards.

He deposited her on the bed before she could protest, pinning her shoulders to the mattress when she fought to get up. "Stay," he ordered. "For two minutes. Just stay."

"Let me go," she gasped, panicking at his grip. "I can't do this——"

"Astrid." He leaned over her and caught her chin, forcing her to look at him. "It's me," he said softly. "You're safe. Just take a deep breath. I'm not going to hurt you. No one is. Okay?"

His voice was so gentle, his touch so soothing, that it broke through the panic threatening to consume her. She stared at him and saw only genuine concern in his dark eyes. His brow was furrowed, and he was gently stroking her hair.

There was no threat from him, no domination. He wasn't going to hurt her.

"Yeah, see? It's all good. Can you lie still for a couple minutes?"

His voice was so kind that Astrid's fear finally slid away, and she sagged into the mattress, her body too exhausted to hold on anymore. "Okay." She closed her eyes and tried to take a deep breath, concentrating on the feel of his hands caressing her shoulders. His touch was warm and strong, and some of the panic began to ease from her.

For a long moment, neither of them spoke, and the only sound Astrid could hear was the pounding of her heart and her own breathing. She concentrated on each breath and on Jason's soothing touch. Eventually, her breathing slowed and the trembling eased. She opened her eyes, and saw Jason sitting beside her. He was watching her carefully, his dark eyes hooded with resolve. It was the expression of a man who had decided to take what he deemed to be his.

A new fear rippled through her, and she sat up abruptly, suddenly needing to be on her feet, not sprawled helplessly in a bed beside him. He didn't stop her, but he caught her hips as she scooted past him, helping her to her feet. Her skin seemed to burn from his touch, and she quickly moved away from him to perch on the trunk she used as a window seat.

Jason didn't take his gaze off her, and she met his stare. "I don't want anything from you," she said. "I'm leaving in the morning. This isn't your problem."

"My *problem?*" Anger suddenly flashed across his face, and his jaw jutted out. "Is that what you consider a child? A *problem?*"

She froze, shocked by the hostility in his voice. "No, I—"

"You will *not* have an abortion," he growled. "That's not an option."

"What? I didn't say—"

"Son of a bitch, Astrid," he said, suddenly leaping to his feet. "Don't you understand that this is a gift? A fucking gift, not some *problem* that will get in the way of your career or your need to blow town and—"

"Stop it!" She jumped up, shocked by his venom. "What's wrong with you? I didn't say any of that—"

He strode across the room and grabbed her by her upper arms, his grip unyielding, but he was careful not to hurt her, even in his fury. "I saw the look of horror on your face, Astrid. You called it a *problem*. This baby deserves more, Astrid—"

"I know it deserves more," she shouted at him. "For God's sake, don't you think I know that? I drank beer tonight, Jason. *Beer!* How long do you think it will take before I lose this baby, too? Did I already destroy it with that stupid beer tonight?" Her voice broke, and she clutched her stomach as all the memories flooded her, as she stared at him in horror. "Dear God, Jason, what if I somehow make this one die, too?"

The anguish in Astrid's voice broke through the haze threatening to consume Jason, jerking him back to the present. He suddenly realized how tightly he was gripping her, and he swore when he realized that he'd shouted at her. Son of a bitch. This was *Astrid*. Not his former wife, telling him that she was going to abort their son because it would interfere with her career. "Shit, Astrid." He immediately softened his grip, swearing at the pain in her eyes. "I'm sorry."

"Let go of me," she said, her voice rough and unsettled. "Now."

He immediately dropped his hands and jammed them in his pockets as she stepped back. Her face was ashen, but her body language was furious as she stalked over to the door and pulled it open. "Get out," she said. "Just get out."

Jason stared at all the moving boxes on the landing, and

something seemed to freeze in his soul. If he left, Astrid would be gone, along with his child. "I can't," he said quietly.

"You don't have a choice," she said, her voice steely. "It's my house."

He let out his breath, aware of the raw pain in her eyes. Her hand was trembling where she was holding onto the door, and her face was stark and haunted. He couldn't leave. Not this woman. Not his child. He had to find a way to bridge the chasm he'd just created between them by being such an ass.

Swearing, he paced away from her and ran his hand through his hair. Shit. There was no other way. He had to tell her the truth, a truth that hurt every time he spoke of it, or even thought of it. A truth that was better off being buried deep than being laid out in the open to flay him raw.

"Jason. I mean it. Leave." Her voice was unyielding and hard, and he knew he'd crossed the line to the unforgivable.

Fuck that. He had to fix this. Gritting his teeth in resolution, Jason spun toward her, fixing his gaze on her hard face, banking on the fact that the depth and emotion he'd sensed in her so many times was really there, that he could reach that side of her with the truth. "A few years after Noah was born, my wife became pregnant again. She didn't tell me, and by sheer coincidence, I ran into her at the hospital when she was on her way in for an abortion."

Astrid blanched. "What?"

"Shit, Astrid." He strode over to her, desperate for her to understand. "I'm sorry I reacted the way I did just now. I was suddenly back in that moment with Kate, and I panicked." Jesus. He would never forget the raw terror he'd felt when he'd realized what she was going to do, when he'd thought he wouldn't be able to stop her. The complete powerlessness coursing through him. "She used the same words with me. 'It's not your problem.' That's all I could think of when you said it." He met her gaze. "I already lost one son. I can't lose another child."

She stared at him, her beautiful brown eyes searching for understanding. "What do you mean?"

"Kate didn't abort our son that day, and he was born eight months later." Jason steeled himself against the pain and grief that always accompanied the memory of his second child. "His name was Lucas Jonathan Sarantos. He was four years younger than Noah. He was born early with a heart condition and required constant medical supervision."

Astrid heard the pain in Jason's voice, and her heart tightened. God, she knew that pain of losing a child. It was so devastating. She touched his arm lightly, and he immediately flipped his wrist and caught her hand, gripping it tightly.

"I was on call at the hospital, and my wife was supposed to be home that night. She was a doctor as well, so we didn't have the nurse on duty when one of us was home. Kate got an invitation to a high profile fundraiser, so she left Lucas with a sitter, because the nurse wasn't available for another two hours. Lucas died before the ambulance even got to the house." He met her gaze. "He wouldn't have died if one of us had been home. He was ten months old."

Tears filled Astrid's eyes at the self-recrimination in his voice, at the weight he was carrying. God, she knew that, she knew what it was like. "I'm so sorry, Jason."

"Yeah, me, too," he muttered, fighting to keep his composure. Every time he thought of that night, he felt like it was going to break him again. "I'm sorry I overreacted just now with you. I'm an ass, and you didn't deserve it."

A faint smile flicked at the corners of her mouth. "No, I didn't. But thank you for the apology."

He didn't ask if he was forgiven. He didn't want to hear it if he wasn't. He needed Astrid's faith, he needed to connect with her. So, instead, he took her hand and raised it to his mouth, pressing his lips against her knuckles. "Tell me about your baby, Astrid. The one you lost. Help me understand why you're so afraid."

The gentleness of his tone nearly undid Astrid, and she fought for control of her emotions. Dammit. She couldn't tell him. No one knew about her past. She couldn't let herself lean on anyone again. It had been so hard to get back onto her feet and learn how to stand alone. She couldn't get caught up in Jason's spell. "I'm not afraid."

He raised his brows at her. "Tell me why you're afraid, Astrid," he repeated. "My son died. I understand."

Tears suddenly filled her eyes, and the effort of holding it in seemed too much. No one knew. Not even her brother or her mother, but suddenly, with this stranger, this man who carried the same grief she did, she didn't want to be alone with her memories again. "His name was Justin. He was stillborn at eight months."

"Hell," he said quietly. "There's no other word for the experience of having your child die."

She nodded, biting her lip. "I know."

Jason tugged on her hand, pulling her toward him. She was too drained to argue or to resist when he wrapped his arms around her and tucked her against him. She pressed her face to his chest, accepting his warmth, the shared understanding of a burden almost too great to bear. His body was like a great shield of protection surrounding her. Strength and understanding, a bond that they shared. She closed her eyes as she felt him press his lips to her hair. It wasn't sexual. It was comforting and beautiful, without judgment, and somehow, it eased some of the pain from her soul.

"You can't leave town," Jason said softly. "You have to stay."

Astrid stiffened. She'd forgotten about the fact she was losing her home. How was she going to support a child?

"Astrid." Jason pulled back to look at her. "I have an empty carriage house. It's yours."

She stared at him, shocked by his offer. That carriage house was beautiful. Her dream. Yearning rushed through her...and then she saw the expression on Jason's face. Determined. Protective. There wasn't love on his face. It was the male instinct to protect a child.

Jason didn't want her to stay for herself. He wanted to protect the baby.

Just like before. Just like with Paul. It wasn't about her. Even though she knew that, she realized he was so tempting that she knew she wouldn't be able to stop herself from falling under his spell or from opening her heart to him...and then what? He would break it, and there would be nothing left. She couldn't recover from that kind of devastation again. She knew it.

She shook her head. "I can't." She pulled away. "I'll be fine. I'll think of something." She would get a job. A real job. Someplace that had health insurance. Clare had been able to be a single mom. She could do it, too...assuming she could carry the baby full term...Fear rippled over her again, and she felt light-headed. What if she failed the baby again?

"What other choices do you have, Astrid?" Jason's gentle intrusion slashed through her fear, yanking her back to the present.

No choices. She had no options. Time would run out tomorrow morning. Then what? Where would she go? How would she manage? Nausea churned through her, and her head began to pound. "I can't—"

He caught her chin, gently asking her to look at him. "I can give you a home and security." His voice was earnest and gentle. Kind. Not dominating and threatening. It was as if he sensed she was treading on the edge of terror and was ready to bolt, and he knew he had to ease her down from her fear.

"I'm a doctor, for hell's sake. You've got me twenty-four/seven. I'll be there if anything goes wrong."

Astrid stared at him, the truth of his words sinking in. Could she really risk the baby by going off and living in some shithole while she was pregnant? No, no, no, of course she couldn't. She couldn't do that to her child. But to put herself under Jason's influence? And what if she stayed in town and people found out she was pregnant? There was no way to keep that a secret. They would judge her and—

"Astrid." Jason turned her toward him. "We'll work it out. We'll find a way. I just want you and the baby safe. At least stay there for now, until we figure things out."

His voice was gentle, but there was no mistaking the steeliness beneath, the male protectiveness he was trying to hide from her. Jason Sarantos was staking claim to his child, regardless of the cost to her. Dammit. She couldn't let herself fall victim to him. She couldn't endure another repeat of trusting the wrong man, like she had with Paul, not again. But what other options did she have? None, right now. She had nowhere to live, and no source of income. She needed help right now. But just for now. What if she took his offer for just a few days, while she tried to get things organized? Yes, that would be okay. She could resist his charms and the feelings he stirred up in her for a short time. He would keep her safe for now, and then she could take her life back, but on solid ground because he'd given her time to figure it out.

She set her hand on her belly and made her decision. She'd take this gift and use it to give herself time, but she would be gone long before Jason Sarantos could start to destroy what was left of her heart. "Okay. For a couple weeks. No longer."

Relief washed over Jason's face, making him look ten years younger. She was shocked by how handsome he was, and her heart softened at the expression of raw relief on his face, by the realization of how much tension he'd been holding.

"You can stay as long as you want," he said. "There's no limit."

"Two weeks," she said firmly. "I just need a little time to get things organized."

He met her gaze. "Two weeks, then." But there was no mistaking the determination in his eyes. Jason Sarantos had a plan, and it didn't involve Astrid leaving his carriage house in two weeks.

Damn men and their plans.

CHAPTER NINE

JASON SPRINTED up the stairs to Astrid's old apartment. Dawn had barely hit, but he'd still driven like a madman to get over there, terrified Astrid had changed her mind and taken off during the night. He'd managed to get the sitter to come back at six in the morning, and he'd bolted the moment she'd arrived.

It had been a fucking night from hell. He'd dreamed of Lucas dying, the dreams so vivid he'd woken up drenched in sweat, his body trembling with grief. It was the worst the nightmares had been in years. He'd dreamed of Kate dying. He'd dreamed of Noah dying, dreams so intense he'd wound up sleeping on Noah's floor so he could keep waking himself up to check that his son was alive and safe. And he'd been haunted by his growing terror that Astrid would cut out during the night, and he'd never find her again.

Raw terror had churned through him as he'd raced up Astrid's steps at six-fifteen, and his relief had been astronomical when he'd shoved open the unlocked door to her apartment and seen her asleep in her bed.

Still there.

But shit, she looked so vulnerable while sleeping. Her dark hair spread out on the pillow, she was curled into a ball. Her hands were tucked under her chin as if she were trying to protect herself even in sleep. In that moment, she wasn't the independent woman who had reminded him of Kate. She was a vulnerable woman struggling to survive, to hang on and make it one more day. He wanted to pick her up right then and carry her out, take her away from the shithole she was living in.

Instead, he sank down on the edge of her bed and forced himself to wait. He knew he should give her privacy and wait outside in his car, but the thought of being away from her was unacceptable. Just as he'd had to sleep on Noah's floor to ensure he didn't lose his son during the night, he couldn't tear himself away from her. There had simply been too much loss in his life, and he couldn't handle another. He had to protect what little he had left, and right now, that meant Astrid.

Jason braced his elbows on his knees and rested his forehead in his palms, trying to get a handle on his tension. Now that he was back in her apartment and knew Astrid was still here, he had to pull his shit together and calm down.

Astrid was his second chance.

He'd come to Maine for a second chance for Noah, and as God was his witness, this was a hell of a second chance. He didn't even know what the hell to do with it, or with Astrid. All he knew was that he couldn't let her go. Not yet. Not with his child.

A light knock sounded on the door, and Jason stood up as Griffin opened the door. Both men froze at the sight of each other in Astrid's space.

"What are you doing here?" Griffin asked, his gaze shooting suspiciously to Astrid and back to Jason.

"There's been a change of plans," Jason said, ignoring the question. "Astrid's moving into my carriage house."

Griffin's eyes narrowed. "Is she? How'd you manage that?"

Jason moved in front of Astrid, blocking Griffin's view of her. She was wearing a skimpy camisole and he didn't want any other men seeing her in that vulnerable state. "It's cool, Griffin. I've got it covered."

Astrid mumbled something, and Jason glanced over his shoulder at her. Her eyes were still closed, but she'd rolled onto her back and flung her arm over her head. The sunlight was streaming across her, kissing her skin with golden warmth and casting shimmering highlights in her hair. In that moment, Jason knew she'd been sent from heaven for him. She was his. And he was keeping her.

He had to find a way to keep her.

He'd failed too many times already, and Astrid and the child she carried were his chance to do it right this time. *I will not let you down*, he promised. *I swear it.*

But as Griffin moved toward Jason and Astrid, he knew that this small town was not going to let him do it that easily. The town felt like it had a claim on Astrid as well, and they were going to make damn sure she was safe. "Back off, Griffin," he said. "I'm on this."

"I'm sure you are," Griffin said quietly. "Did you sleep with her last night?"

"No." Jason met his gaze, but Griffin clearly knew that he wasn't being entirely forthright. Yes, he wasn't lying. He hadn't slept with her last night, but there was more shit going on. Griffin's tense shoulders indicated he was well aware that Jason wasn't telling the entire truth.

"You bastard," Griffin growled. "You don't get to come in here and abuse her—"

"I'm not. Jesus, I'm not." Jason swore as Astrid mumbled in her sleep. "Let's take it outside, Griffin," he said quietly. "Astrid needs her sleep."

"Does she?" Griffin didn't move and didn't back down

"And why is she so tired? Did you have a private going away party for her? Did you take advantage of her emotional vulnerability because she was so sad to be leaving town?"

Jason's adrenaline was raging. "Is that what you think of her? That someone can take advantage of Astrid? She's stronger than that."

"She's not as strong as she likes people to think."

"Shit, I know that. You don't think I know that?" He looked over at Astrid and saw she had moved her hand over her face, as if she were trying to block out the sound. Vibrant energy raced through him, and he was suddenly jazzed almost out of his skin. She was waking up. His woman was waking up.

He couldn't keep the shit-eating grin off his face, even as Griffin continued to harass him. All he could do was wait for the woman who carried his child to open her eyes.

Anticipation was a killer.

ASTRID SCRUNCHED her eyes shut against the low murmur of voices. God, she was tired. So tired... Then she jerked awake as reality set in. There were voices in her apartment? She sat up abruptly and saw Jason in the doorway, talking in low voices with Griffin. For a moment, all she could do was stare blankly at them, trying to figure out why they were there.

Then she noticed Griffin's jeans, tee shirt and heavy boots, and realized that he was ready for heavy lifting. Her things! Today was moving day. Last night's events came rushing back to her, and she jerked her gaze to Jason. Was she really going to move into his carriage house? Or was he there to retract his offer?

To her surprise, Jason wasn't watching Griffin. His gaze was fixed on hers, and heat flushed through her at the intense expression on his face. He was watching her as if he owned the very air in her lungs, and he treasured every last bit of it.

A slow grin spread across his face, a smile meant only for her, and anticipation rushed through her. "Morning, Astrid." His voice was a low rumble, rolling through her like a sensual caress.

She swallowed. "Hi," she managed.

Griffin turned around, and she saw he looked furious. His eyes were dark, and his hands were bunched by his side. "Jason says you're moving in with him."

Excitement leapt through Astrid. "He did?" He wasn't changing his mind? He was claiming her publicly, admitting to Griffin that she was staying with him? Paul had never claimed her, not even when he'd put the ring on her finger. She'd always felt like he wanted her to walk a step behind him and sit at the other end of the table...which he always had when they'd been at his family's house for dinner.

Determination flashed across Jason's face, and she realized that he half expected her to change her mind, to jump in her barely functioning car and run for the Vermont border.

He wasn't going to let her do that, was he?

She smiled, new power rushing through her. Suddenly, Jason didn't seem like a threat to her independence, or a danger to her heart. In the light of day, in the glare of her dire circumstances, he was her influx of strength, the temporary support system that would keep her afloat while she got her life together.

She wasn't the naïve girl who'd let Paul decimate her heart. She wasn't the innocent romantic who thought getting an engagement ring because she was pregnant meant the fairytale would come true. Nope. She was now a survivor who knew a brass ring when she saw it, and she knew exactly what it meant.

Jason's offer meant a chance. It didn't mean love, romance

and forever. It meant she finally had an opportunity to start her life over the way she wanted it.

Griffin's eyes narrowed. "Astrid," he said softly, moving closer and blocking Jason with his shoulders. "You are *always* welcome to move in with me and Clare. There's plenty of room, and you're part of our family. If you're staying in town, and by God, I hope you are, stay with us."

Astrid saw the genuineness in Griffin's eyes, and her throat tightened. He really meant it. He and Clare were barely started in their relationship, still trying to learn about each other and find private time around all the craziness of two teenage girls and two businesses, and yet he was willing to dump her in the middle of it. She smiled, the day suddenly feeling even brighter. "Thank you, Griffin. That means a lot. I appreciate it."

He nodded. "So, you'll come?"

She looked past him at Jason, who was leaning against the door jamb, his arms folded over his chest. He met her gaze, and the intensity of his expression said it all. This man she barely knew had one goal, and that was to protect her and keep her safe. It didn't matter that it was because of the baby she carried. What mattered was that she had been given that gift. She wasn't naïve enough to think she could fix her life without help right now, and she wasn't going to turn down what Jason was offering her. "No," she said, not taking her gaze off Jason. "I'm staying in Jason's carriage house." She finally looked at Griffin. "Not in his *house*, Griffin. His carriage house. Just for two weeks while I get things sorted out."

Griffin's eyes narrowed, and he looked back and forth between them. "You're sure you're okay, Astrid?"

Well, she was pretty damn sure she was far from okay, but right now, Jason had given her a breather to get it figured out. Dear God, she was *pregnant*.

No, no, no, she could not think about that.

Denial was the only order of the day. So she cast Griffin one of her trademark smiles. "I am fantastic," she said. Then she threw the covers back, revealing the fact she'd been sleeping in only very short shorts. Griffin immediately looked away, but Jason's eyes heated up as they traveled down her legs.

He didn't even pretend not to stare, and awareness rippled over her at the realization that although Jason had made the offer last night because of the baby, he absolutely had not forgotten she was a woman. So, that was something at least. At least she existed as her own being.

Grinning, feeling optimistic and happy for the first time in months, she stood up. "Thanks so much for helping me move, Griffin—"

"Astrid." Griffin took her arm and moved her to the side. "This isn't like you to move in with him. I'm not blind. I can see the way he looks at you. What are you doing?"

She grinned at him, unable to keep her newly surging energy at bay. "Griffin. It wasn't easy to manipulate an almost stranger into allowing me to move into the house of my dreams at a price I can afford, so don't mess with it, okay? I'm the one in control here." Which, weirdly, she felt like she was. Yes, Jason was doing his man thing, but at the same time, it was his protectiveness and ownership that was empowering her and giving her the freedom to breathe deeply again and the respite to think clearly. "It's all good."

Griffin studied her, and then he finally grinned. "You astound me, Astrid."

She smiled. "I will take that as a compliment." She squeezed his arm. "Thanks for helping me today, Griffin. I appreciate it."

"It's what we do in this town." He winked. "Or so Eppie made sure to tell me fifteen times." There was a loud roar of trucks outside, and then the sound of slamming doors and male voices.

Astrid frowned and peeked out the window. There were three pickup trucks parked beside Griffin's, and seven men were climbing out of them. She recognized Jackson and a couple of the men from the softball team. Three of them she thought were from Jackson's construction crew, because she'd seen them at the store with him. One man with short blond hair and a massive build she didn't recognize, but he seemed to be hanging back by Jackson as well. "Who are they?"

"Your moving crew." Griffin leaned past her and stuck his head out the window. "Around back, and up the stairs," he shouted.

As the men hollered back and she heard the thud of boots heading up her stairs, Astrid began to smile, truly smile. So many people there to help her? She'd never had that happen before. It was such a treat, a delicious feeling. She looked across the room at Jason, who was already discussing with Griffin the order they would move things out, and a sense of immense peace settled over her.

Maybe she had no money, no creativity and no future, but right now, in that moment, she had a team helping her. She'd never been the recipient of that kind of support before, and it felt amazing—

Jason suddenly turned away from Griffin and strode across the room toward her. Her heart began to race as he approached, and anticipation swept through her. "Sweetheart," he said as he reached her, sliding his arm down her bare skin as he brushed his lips against her ear. "I'm not going to pretend I don't love seeing you dressed in almost nothing, but I'll tell you right now that if I have to deal with seven other men checking you out in that outfit, it's not going to be pretty."

Heat flushed Astrid at the raw desire in his voice, and she

swallowed. Paul had never been possessive of her. Not even for one minute. It was intoxicating to see the turmoil in Jason's eyes. "I'm not yours," she told him, unable to keep the tremble of awareness from her voice. "I'm just going to live in your carriage house."

"Yeah, I know that." He trailed his finger possessively down her arm in direct contradiction of his words, sending goose bumps shooting across her flesh. "But it's not going to matter when the guys walk in here. I'm feeling possessive, jealous and ready to kick some ass in defense of you."

Okay, wow, so there was no way to ignore how incredibly hot that was. His words went straight to her belly, to the part of her that was pure female. "You are a caveman," she said, unable to keep the grin off her face.

Jason's eyebrows shot up. "A caveman? Damn, woman, you keep giving me compliments like that, and I'll have you pinned against the wall and naked in less than a second."

Heat flushed through her as she grabbed for a sweatshirt. "I'm not moving into your carriage house to become your concubine," she snapped as she quickly pulled it over her arms and zipped it, all too aware of the men thudding up her stairs.

"You're not?" The disappointment in Jason's face was so comical she burst out laughing. "We're going to have to renegotiate." He grabbed the zipper of her sweatshirt and yanked it up to her chin. "You are going to be trouble, woman." Then, in front of all the men who had just arrived, and before she had a chance to react, Jason had the audacity to grab her around the waist, haul her against him and plant one on her.

This kiss was hard and fast, in full view of the others, making it absolutely clear to everyone that there wasn't anything the least bit platonic about Astrid moving into Jason's carriage house. Jason grinned smugly as he released

ent. She was pulsing with emotion and passion. There was so much to Astrid. He couldn't lose her as well, and yet here he was, on the same path as before. Kate had left him emotionally, and Astrid could walk out physically.

Or she would try. He couldn't allow it to happen. He couldn't allow Astrid to shut him out the way Kate had.

This time, it was going to turn out differently.

~

JASON WAS BEAT.

He pulled his car into his driveway, tired as hell after another sixteen hours of manual labor on the cafe. It was almost one in the morning, and the place still looked like it had been upended by a front end loader and torn to shreds.

The new chairs were arriving tomorrow, supplies for his pizzas were coming on Friday, and his "Grand Opening July 4th" banner had been waiting for him when he'd gotten back from lunch. July 4th was less than a week away.

He shoved the gearshift into park and leaned his head back against the seat. A cold pizza sat on the seat beside him, uneaten even though he'd picked it up at Wright's almost four hours ago. He hadn't taken time to eat, and he was ravenous now.

He'd eat, take a twenty-minute nap and a shower, and then be back at work before two. He could lay the last six yards of floorboard by the time the wood guys arrived to refinish the cabinets and do the floor. Thankfully, Noah had already found a best friend at camp, and the boys were having a sleepover tonight.

Jason had taken advantage by working late on the cafe, but now that he was home and looking at his empty house, a deep sense of regret filled him. It wasn't supposed to be like this up here, with Noah being taken care of by other people. It was supposed to be all about time for Noah, but Jason hadn't counted on the cafe being in such bad shape. He'd had to invest a lot more money than he'd planned into refurbishing it. The money he'd had to put in had increased the urgency of getting the store open so that the cash could start flowing in the other direction.

Groaning, Jason rested his forearms on the steering wheel and stared at the massive house he'd bought for his son. Huge yard. Massive windows. Lakefront. His new boat was supposed to arrive this weekend. When was he going to get time to take it out? When was he going to take Noah up on his offer to hit some baseballs in the backyard? Or order a basketball hoop for the driveway?

Shit. He was beat. Which was the only way to live, his only chance at getting any sleep. It was what he was used to and how he'd operated in New York: burn himself out until sleep came. It was, however, exactly what he'd promised Noah would change when he got to Maine. "Shit!" Frustration rumbled through him, and he rubbed the back of his neck. "I swear this will change, Noah. This is going to work. I promise you."

With a groan, he hauled himself out of his car, noting the multitude of sawdust shavings on his luxurious seats. Sawdust. How many years had he lived in sawdust, helping out his dad with assorted home projects?

He'd intentionally left sawdust and pizza dough behind years ago, and now it was back? It was supposed to fix their life, but it wasn't. It just wasn't fucking helping.

Jason grabbed the pizza off the seat and kicked the door shut with his foot. He was just turning to go into the house when he saw a glow emanating from the carriage house. Astrid was still up? At this hour? In her condition?

Scowling, Jason headed toward her place, knowing he shouldn't bother her. He was too tired to be polite, and the last thing he could afford to do was drive her away.

He was going anyway.

She was the one glow of hope in his damn life, and he needed a dose of her.

ASTRID HELD up the bracelet and studied it in the light. It was the first piece of jewelry she'd ever designed for men, and she examined it with her usual critical eye. It was a black leather cord with a metal plate on it that was just a little wider and thicker than she ones she used for her regular designs. She'd stumbled across the larger plate when she'd been unpacking, and had stopped unpacking to play with it.

The engraving was bold and stark, with none of the artistic curls she usually used. There was one word blazed across the plaque: FIRE.

She didn't know why she'd picked that word, but she'd had Jason in mind from the moment she'd seen the piece. Frowning, she studied it, her eyes bleary from spending hours engraving it by hand. As she inspected the bracelet, her excitement began to fade.

There was something missing from it. The piece felt incomplete. Empty. Wasted. She didn't know what exactly was wrong with it, but there was a distinct lack of urgency and passion in the item. It was simply flat and uninspired.

Just like all the other designs she'd tried over the last six months.

"Dammit," she muttered, dropping it on her table. It landed with a small clink, and she leaned back, pressing her hands to her eyes. Why had she thought that moving into the carriage house and breathing in fresh air would suddenly bring her creativity back? If she didn't start designing new pieces, or at least find the ability to craft the ones she'd already designed that were for sale on her website, she would soon be truly broke.

The one thing she enjoyed was her jewelry-making, and now she was failing utterly at it. She gritted her teeth as she stared at her inbox on her computer. There were so many orders waiting to be filled. And yet, as hard as she worked, she didn't seem to be making any progress on filling them. She'd had to throw away so many pieces of jewelry because they hadn't come out well enough to send to her clients. Orders were dwindling. Her reputation was falling. Dammit! How hard could it be to do that which she loved?

It shouldn't be hard. It should be easy. But it wasn't. Not anymore. Not even in this beautiful home with so much natural light and inspiration.

The problem hadn't been with where she was living. It had been with her.

Frustrated, she pushed back from the table, then froze as she heard a light knock at the door. "Astrid? It's Jason."

Her heart began to race, and she went still, utterly quiet.

After helping unload all her belongings from the trucks, he'd taken off to work at the store. He'd been gone all day, leaving her alone to pretend that he didn't exist. That the reality between them didn't exist. But it did. He did.

Emma and Clare had both called to tell her how happy they were that she was staying in town, but the two women had been in Portland for the day on a girl bonding trip and hadn't gotten back in time to stop by.

Which was fine with Astrid. She was restless and moody, not at peace the way she'd been when she'd first arrived. She knew it was because it wasn't *her* place. She was staying here on Jason's goodwill, which meant it was nothing more than a fragile ground that could shatter beneath her feet at any moment.

As beautiful as it was, she wished she were back in her studio apartment over the gas station, because at least that had been hers and no one could take it away...except they had. Even the security of that place had been an illusion. Paying her rent on time religiously hadn't been enough to keep her home. What else was she supposed to do?

"Astrid?" He knocked again. "Are you up?"

She bit her lip, not wanting to deal with him.

There was a small thump, as if he'd tapped his fist against the door in frustration. "I have food."

Food? Astrid's stomach growled immediately, and she glanced over at her bare kitchen. She hadn't felt like dealing with town, so she'd made do with the few staples that she'd packed from her old house. Food or privacy?

Food.

With a nervous sigh, she walked over to the door and opened it.

There, on her front step, was the man she'd been unable to get out of her mind all day, despite her best efforts.

And he was even better in person. Yes, his hair was disheveled and there was sawdust on his shoulder. His jeans were covered in paint and his boots were tracking sawdust. His eyes were dark and there was stubble on his jaw that made him look like a weary warrior stumbling home after a hard day in battle.

He was raw male. Total testosterone. And she responded to him exactly the same way as she had every time she'd seen him. With pure, unbridled longing and desire that reverberated through every cell of her body. She sighed. Why did he affect her so intensely? "What is it with you?"

He raised his brows, and propped his shoulder against the door jamb. "What exactly are you referring to? My boyish good looks? My rugged manly appeal? Or my sense of timing with food?"

Astrid's stomach fluttered at the hint of weary humor in his voice. "Food. It's all about the food," she lied, not really wanting to launch into a detailed explanation about how he made her want to strip naked and throw herself at him.

"Then I'm here to deliver." He raised the pizza. "It's cold, but I hear you've got an oven. I haven't figured out how to turn mine on yet, so I was hoping you had."

She laughed and took the box, his lighthearted banter making her feel more at ease. "You're such a guy. You can't turn on your oven? Really?"

"I can't find the damned thing," he said. "Too many boxes still in the kitchen. There aren't as many takeout options here as there are in New York, so Noah and I have been living on Wright's pizza for the last month. We usually eat it cold, though I have recently located the microwave." He walked inside and shut the door behind him, making himself at home in her space.

As she headed toward the kitchen, Astrid glanced over her shoulder at him. He seemed to fill the room with his strength and power, with the way he strode across the floor behind her and seemed to own the very space around him. He was so very male, in a place that was so female, with her colored scarves, throws and jewelry supplies.

She swallowed as she set the pizza on the stovetop and turned on the oven. She made herself busy getting the pizza out of the box and onto the tray to give herself a moment to regroup from her reaction to Jason. In a state so foreign to her, she felt awkward with him, not sure what to say, so she gave herself the excuse of the pizza.

But once it was in the oven, there was no more distraction.

She took a deep breath, and then turned to face the man who had turned her life so upside down.

Jason was leaning against the kitchen counter, his arms folded as he watched her. For a moment, she was startled with how close he was, and then she realized there was nowhere else for him to be in the room. She had no kitchen table, no couch, no chairs. Her old studio had barely been big enough for a bed, the dresser she'd found at the garage sale, and her design center.

Her belongings had felt full and complete in her old place, but in this place, her life felt woefully inadequate. She swallowed nervously. "Do you want a drink?"

"Sure. What do you have?"

She pressed her lips together, suddenly embarrassed. "Tap water. I haven't gone shopping yet, and I used up everything when I thought I was going to move."

One slow eyebrow went up. "Tap water is fine. Do you have glasses?"

"Of course I do." She quickly turned and opened the cabinet to grab her glasses, but as she looked at them, suddenly she saw them for the first time. Four mismatched, scratched glasses, scavenged at the same garage sale that had provided her bedframe. They were beautifully engraved, full of interesting curves, which is why she'd loved them, but they were old and well-used. Suddenly she wished she had a set of beautiful, pristine matching glasses, ones that would be good enough for a wealthy doctor from New York.

She snuck a peek at Jason, and this time, she didn't see the sawdust and the paint. She saw jeans that fit him perfectly, boots of high quality leather, and the sculpted cheekbones of a beautiful man. She thought of his luxurious, expensive car. Of the fact he'd been able to afford this amazing property even after walking away from his career and any steady source of income. How did she look to a man like him? How did her little world look to a man like him?

"I'll take the one on the right," Jason said, reaching past her to pluck her favorite glass off the shelf. He held it up, inspecting it. "This is incredibly cool. Are these hand blown? I've never seen designs like this."

She swallowed. "I don't know. I found them at a garage sale."

"Yeah, I would bet you'd have to. I doubt anyone takes the time to make things this beautiful anymore." He grabbed another one. "This one good for you?"

She stared at him, a warm feeling suffusing her as he filled their glasses. "You like the glasses?"

"Hell, yeah," he said as he handed her one. "My mom used to collect glasses and plates," he said. "Every single thing in our kitchen was one of a kind. Coffee cups, plates, silverware, you name it. She had an incredible knack for finding this stuff." He ran his hand over the glass, turning it to watch the light refract. "I forgot how she used to do that," he said. "It's cool."

A slow smile spread across Astrid's face, and the tension eased from her. "My mom used to steal glasses from whatever man she was walking out on," she said. "Not quite the same thing—" Oh...crap. Had she just said that aloud?

"Yeah?" Jason raised his eyebrows at her as he settled back against the counter, holding his glass loosely between his fingers. "Tell me about your mom."

"Um, no." She turned and walked away, sitting down on one of the smaller boxes that she was using for a seat. It was beside a larger box that had become her table. "So, the pizza will be ready in a couple minutes. How's the cafe coming along?" She smiled at him, trying to give her most charming grin to distract him from asking any more questions about her mother.

Jason narrowed his eyes as he studied Astrid. She had such a wall around her, just like his former wife had. But he'd seen past Astrid's defenses before. He knew there was more to her. There was softness, passion, vibrant energy and warmth. How did he get to it?

This woman, this mysterious, aloof woman was carrying his child. He had to know more. He had to find out what she was like, what he was facing with her.

He walked across the room and sat on another box. It sagged beneath his weight, but he didn't get up. If Astrid wanted to sit on boxes, he'd sit on boxes. "The store is not going well," he admitted, trying to get comfortable on the box that was sinking lower and lower beneath him. "It's in bad shape, and I'm scheduled to open on the Fourth. I haven't even found my recipes yet."

"Recipes?" She narrowed her eyes suspiciously. "Wait a second. Don't you have a chef you're planning to hire?"

"Nope. I'm the chef." He moved his box against the wall and leaned back against it. Ah...better.

"How does that figure?" She studied him with eyes that were clearly trying to ferret out his secrets, and he grinned, realizing he was enjoying her scrutiny, her need for answers about who he was. "You're planning to open a pizza shop with homemade pies, and yet you can't reheat one in your own kitchen?"

"Yeah, well, I lied about not being able to find my stove." He stretched his legs out, trying to uncramp them after being on his knees all day. "I wanted company. I saw your light on, and I figured I'd use the pizza as an excuse to get you to let me in."

"Oh." A pleased smile flitted at the corners of her mouth, and anticipation rolled through him as he realized she wasn't as detached from him as she'd tried to act. "You could have just asked."

"I did. You didn't answer the door until I said I had food." He narrowed his eyes, studying her. "How are you feeling? Have you made a doctor's appointment yet?"

Her cheeks immediately turned bright red. "I'm fine. I will handle the medical side of things. You don't need to concern yourself."

"But I do." He sat up and leaned forward. "Do you have medical insurance, Astrid? Can you afford a doctor?"

She leapt to her feet and paced restlessly away from him. "Stop it," she said. "Just because I live here doesn't mean you can control me."

"I'm not trying to control you." Jason stood up, energy coursing through him at Astrid's resistance. "But that's my child you're carrying, and I want to make sure you both are safe."

"We're fine—"

He caught her arm, turning her toward him. "Astrid, the fact you lost a baby before might mean that it could happen again. You need to get to a doctor who can run tests to find out whether there is any preventative treatment that you need to have."

"Stop it!" She pulled her arm out of his grip, her eyes blazing. "I know that! Don't you think I know that? It's my problem. I'll deal with it."

"Shit, Astrid, it's not your issue alone. I'm in this with you. Together. As a team, not as someone trying to control you." He saw her composure unraveling and he didn't know how to help her. "Talk to me, Astrid. What did I do? Why are you freaking out on me?"

She slipped out the window onto the deck and leaned on the railing, staring out into the night. Jason ground his jaw and followed her, easing out onto the narrow deck behind her. For a long moment, neither of them spoke, and the night was filled with the sounds of nature, sounds that Jason hadn't heard since he'd left Minnesota for school.

Astrid wrapped her arms around herself, hugging her arms to her chest as she faced the lake.

After a moment, Jason set his hands on either side of her hips and leaned forward, trapping her between his body and the railing.

She stiffened, but she didn't move away, and Jason became increasingly aware of the intimacy of their position. It was altogether too much like when they'd been on the rock. That moment had led to lovemaking, which meant he should back off now and make sure that didn't happen.

But he didn't. Instead, he leaned forward and rested his chin on her shoulder. "Astrid," he said quietly. "We've got to work through this together. Don't shut me out. Talk to me. What's going on?"

God, it felt amazing the way Jason was holding her. Barely touching her, not trapping her, just feeding her his strength and warmth. Astrid bit her lip, struggling to hold her composure. "I'm scared," she finally whispered.

"Me, too, sweetheart," he said. "Me, too."

"You are?" She hadn't expected that response. Jason was all about strength and power.

"Yeah." His hands slipped off the railing. He wrapped his arms around her waist, easing her back against his chest. She knew she should pull away, but she couldn't make herself do it. It just felt too good to be held. "What are you afraid of?"

"Everything."

"Such as?"

"God, everything." She leaned her head back against his shoulder and closed her eyes, focusing on the strength of his body against hers. "I failed last time, Jason. So completely. In every way."

Jason rubbed his jaw against her cheek, his whiskers

bristling against her skin. "Were you married before? What happened with the baby's father?"

Astrid bit her lip. How could she tell him what happened? She looked like such a fool. A pathetic victim. She didn't want anyone to look at her like that anymore. She wanted to be strong, and to have Jason see her as a woman who could stand on her own. "I'd rather not talk about it." She tensed, expecting him to push, but he didn't.

He was just quiet, and she began to relax.

"My wife's name was Kate," he said, resting his cheek against hers. "She was a dermatologist who specialized in cosmetic treatments. She had pioneered some new treatments that were all the rage in Hollywood, and celebrities were constantly flying out to New York to get treated by her. She was a star, and she loved it."

Astrid bit her lip against the wave of inadequacy. Jason's former wife was a famous and ground-breaking doctor with celebrity clients? As opposed to Astrid, who was a broke, creatively-challenged artist with a stained childhood and tainted family history. The difference was grim and depressing, a bleak stamp of reality on any fantasies about her and Jason.

Suddenly, Astrid wanted out of his arms, away from the façade that he was concerned about her as a woman. How could he possibly be interested in her romantically, after being married to a woman like that? She was nothing compared to that, and she knew it. "I need to go check the pizza." She pushed at him, but his grip tightened in unspoken refusal.

"Kate didn't want to be burdened with a family and kids," he said. "When Noah was born, she barely even acknowledged him. As I told you, she wanted to abort Lucas." There was bitterness in his voice now, anger and guilt, emotions that touched her heart, because she knew what it was like to love someone who didn't have any love to give.

Instinctively, she put her hand over his and squeezed lightly.

Jason flipped his hand over to hold hers, needing her touch as he re-opened memories that bit so deeply. "There was very little left in our marriage," he said, recalling the silence of their condo when he'd get home late. The closed door to their bedroom telling him to sleep in the guest bedroom. The coolness of his wife's body language when they ran into each other in the mornings. "And when Lucas died, there was nothing left between us. Kate disassociated herself from me and Noah. The marriage became in name only, if that."

Astrid turned to face him, and he saw compassion in her eyes, true understanding. He cupped her face and bent his head, brushing his lips over hers, needing the touch of someone so emotional and alive.

"Did you divorce her?" There was an edge to Astrid's voice, a ripple of judgment and fear.

"No." Shit, he should have. He should have had that mercy. "I decided that I couldn't live like that anymore. I was reeling from Lucas's death, and I wanted to try to hold onto the family. I rented a place on Nantucket for a week, and I ordered her to take the week off from work."

Astrid studied him. "Really?"

"Yeah. She showed up two days late, on the eve of a huge storm, and I was pissed." He ran his hands through Astrid's hair, using the silkiness of the strands to ground him, to keep that night at bay. "It was bad shit, what went down between us that night. Things you don't say to the person you're married to." Guilt burned in him for the blame he'd thrown at her for Lucas's death in his attempt to breach that cold wall of emotional distance she'd erected around herself. "She got angry and walked out. She said she was going back to New York. She wanted to get out before the storm stranded her there, because she couldn't abide being with me another moment."

Suddenly, Jason was back there in that night, standing there in the doorway of the cottage, watching Kate stalk down to the car she'd rented. The wind had been raging, the rain wild, the seas high and relentless, and he'd stood there and watched her go. He hadn't tried to stop her. "The storm was closing in fast, but she bribed one of the pilots to take her anyway, and I didn't stop her. I was just fucking tired of fighting with her, and I let her go." He met Astrid's gaze. "The plane crashed less than a half mile offshore. Both she and the pilot were dead."

"Oh." Astrid's hand went to her mouth. "I'm so sorry."

Jason gave her a grim smile. "See, that's the thing, Astrid. I wasn't sorry. Not the way I should have been. When the cops came and told me what had happened, all I felt was this huge sense of relief. Relief. *Relief.*" He met her gaze, baring the truth to the woman who needed to know what he was like, because she was stuck with him in her life, at least on some level. "My own wife had died in a tragic accident, and I didn't feel even one moment of grief. I just sat there and thanked God that Noah would not have to grow up realizing he was stuck with a mother who didn't love him. My son had lost his mother, and all I felt was relief."

That was it. That was all he had to say. That was who he was.

Astrid stared at him, but he couldn't read her expression. "What?" he urged. "Talk to me."

"And now," she asked. "Do you feel sadness now?"

He grimaced. "No, and I know I'm a total bastard for the fact I don't. I know I betrayed Kate by letting her get on that plane when I knew how bad the weather was. I feel guilty about that, and every day I look at my son, I know that I'm responsible for the fact he doesn't have a little brother or a mother. I fucked up his life, Astrid, and I'm making it worse with every choice I make, but no, I still don't grieve Kate's death, not the way I should. I grieve the fact that I don't, and for what kind of a person that makes me."

Astrid couldn't believe it, but she knew Jason was telling her the truth. He truly did not grieve the loss of his wife. "I don't understand. How could you not care about her?"

He shook his head. "I ask myself that every day." His voice was anguished, tormented, but Astrid could barely register it, she was so consumed by his confession. How could he not care about the woman he'd made so many promises to? "It was my job to find a way to connect us. If I'd tried harder, if I'd cared about my marriage and my kids enough, there must have been a way to salvage everything. But I was working almost as hard as she was, and I didn't do shit to make it happen."

"Wow." She pulled away, staggered by the enormity of his confession. Was that what Paul had thought of her? Had a part of him been glad when she lost the baby, freeing him to move on and find the right woman? "Jason, I need to go—"

"Don't!" He grabbed her arms. "I'm trying to fix it," he said urgently. "That's why I moved to Maine. I quit my damn job. I'm not going to repeat that mistake. I'm going to do it right this time." His grip softened on her arms. "I'm not going to walk away from you, Astrid. I lost everything before, and I won't lose it again. That means you, and it means our child."

"No," she shook her head, trying to pull away from him.

Jason felt his heart split when Astrid rejected him. "Astrid!" He grabbed her hand, catching her as she tried to climb over the windowsill back into the carriage house.

She spun back toward him, her eyes blazing. "Did you tell

her that you loved her, Jason? When you asked her to marry you, did you promise forever? Did you?"

He swore at the agony on her face. "Shit, yeah, Astrid. I meant it, too. I had no idea things would disintegrate the way they did—"

"You couldn't have meant it! If you love someone like that, you don't have the right to stop loving them, to walk away from them—"

"I didn't walk away from her." He leapt over the windowsill, grabbing her as she stumbled away from him. "I tried to save the marriage. I made her come to Nantucket. I didn't walk away—"

"You let her get on that plane!"

"I know I did, but as God is my witness, I didn't know she was going to die when she got on that plane! I'm not that much of a bastard, Astrid!" He yanked her over to him, refusing to let her retreat. "Don't you get what I'm trying to tell you? I'm trying to show you that I fucking blew it before, and I know it, and I'm willing to do *anything* to make it work this time." He gripped her shoulders. "I won't let you down, and I won't let our child down. No matter what. *Ever*."

"Isn't that what you said to Kate when you proposed?" Tears were streaming down Astrid's face. "Didn't you make that promise before? How can men do that? How can men make those promises and then betray them?"

And that's when he knew. Astrid wasn't talking about him anymore. She was talking about her own past. "Shit, Astrid, what did he do to you?" Jason didn't even know who the "he" was, but there was no doubt that there was a man who had eviscerated the woman in his arms.

"He left," she said. "He promised me forever. But when our son was stillborn, he left me that same day."

Jason swore, his soul breaking for the pain in Astrid's voice. "He left you in the hospital?"

She nodded. "The doctor came into my room and told us that I'd lost the baby, and he said I was still in danger. I was devastated. I was terrified I was going to die right then."

"Shit, Astrid." He started to reach for her, but she held up her hands to block him.

"The minute the doctor left, my fiancé looked at me and said that since there was no baby, he wouldn't burden his family by making me a part of it. Then he dropped five thousand dollars in cash on the bed to pay for my medical bills and walked out. I never heard from him again." She met his gaze. "I've never told anyone that before," she whispered.

"Thank you for trusting me." But even as he spoke the words, a dark, deep fury began to roil through Jason, a primal anger that seemed to lash through his veins. "Astrid."

She lifted her chin, her eyes glittering with tears she was fighting so hard to control. "Why?" she asked. "Why do men make promises of forever and love, and then turn it off and stop caring?"

As he looked at her ashen face, Jason had no answers to give her. "There are no excuses," he told her. "Your ex-fiancé was a bastard beyond words, there's no doubt about that. My guess is that he never loved you the way you deserved to be loved, and he knew he could never deliver what he promised."

She stared at him. "That's no excuse."

"No, it's not." Jason took a deep breath and reached for her hand, sliding his fingers through her cold ones. "But I'll tell you one thing. I spent thirteen years married to a woman who never loved me, not even for a minute. She married me because she wanted to marry a doctor, like her, and that never changed. I was the one who changed. When we got married, all we wanted was to be doctors. I wanted away from my past, from the burdens of family. We promised each other a dual career marriage, and I changed the rules."

Astrid frowned at him, but he could tell she was listening.

"I decided I wanted kids. I wanted a wife, not a business associate who shared my bed. I changed the rules, and she didn't want it." He gripped her hand. "This time, I know what I want, and I'm going to make it happen."

She searched his face. "What is it that you want, Jason? Our child? A woman who will be a perfect, loving mother and doting wife?"

He knew the answer should be yes, that he wanted the family, the whole package, and the scene of domestic tranquility that were the stuff of his fantasies. But as he looked at the woman standing before him and he saw the conviction in her eyes that she could not offer him any of that, he knew what answer he was going to give her. He was going to tell her the truth that she needed to hear.

"You, Astrid." He traced his finger along her hairline, brushing her hair back from her face. "You're what I want."

She closed her eyes, and he felt her body shudder in response. "How can you say that?" Her voice trembled. "You don't even know me."

"I know you're a woman who carries so much weight in her heart. You're courageous and brave, even though inside you're so soft and vulnerable that I want to cradle your heart in my hands and protect it from all the world." Astrid opened her eyes, searching his face, but he didn't stop.

"You're the woman who breathes life into my soul," he said softly as he framed her face with his hands. "You force me to step up and be the man I want to be, because you deserve no less." He pressed his lips to the corner of her mouth, smiling when she closed her eyes, losing herself in the intimacy. "Your love for your friends is so deep, but you don't know how to trust anymore." He kissed the other side of her mouth. "You make me want to lose myself in your soul, and to make the world a better place so that you can thrive and come back to life."

Her eyes fluttered open, and there was so much yearning in them that he smiled. "Plus," he whispered, "You're the sexiest woman I've ever encountered in my life. If I could make love to you every night until the end of time, it still wouldn't be enough." And then he kissed her, showing her that he meant every damn word of it.

CHAPTER ELEVEN

HIS KISS BREATHED life into her very soul.

Astrid went still under Jason's kisses, almost undone by the intensity of her response to him. Dear God, it felt so amazing to be kissed by him. His lovely, heartfelt words were still reverberating through her. So many beautiful sentiments, the kind she'd dreamed of someone saying to her.

Somehow, despite her best efforts to the contrary, Jason saw her as she really was. He saw every inch of her. He'd broken through her artificially glowing exterior, delving right into the pain in her soul, just as he had that very first time they'd kissed.

He didn't care that she was scarred and damaged. He really didn't care. He still wanted her, even though he knew she wasn't all roses and flippant attitude. *See, Eppie? Not all men only want happy women.*

"Kiss me, Astrid," he whispered against her lips, nudging her for a response.

Desire rolled through her, fierce longing to connect with him physically. She wanted to succumb to his demands and lose herself in his affections. God, she wanted to. But how could she expose herself to him like that? How could she make herself vulnerable? She was too caught up in him, and she knew there was no going partway. She would be head over heels in an instant, and with that she would lose all ability to protect herself from him. No matter how hard she tried to remind herself not to count on him, to prepare herself for him to leave, she knew she wouldn't be able to do it. He simply touched her soul too deeply.

She shook her head, unable to keep her breath from shuddering as he kissed her again. "It's not me that makes you feel like that," she whispered, gripping his wrists, trying to hold him at bay, at the same time she was clinging to him, afraid to let him go. "You want the baby. It's the baby. You're just trying to convince yourself you want me because you want the fairytale, and I come with it."

Anger blazed in Jason's eyes. "Fuck that, Astrid. I was in a loveless marriage for thirteen years. I was in a marriage where my soul fucking died because there was nothing to keep it alive, until my kids were born. There's no chance in hell that I'd get involved with a woman who didn't fit me. Not again. I don't have to be romantically involved with you to be a dad to our child." He laughed softly. "In fact, it would probably be a hell of a lot easier to co-parent with a woman that I was simply friends with, but that's not what I want." He pulled her close, so close that they were sharing the same breath. "No, Astrid, your appeal is all your own, and has nothing to do with the baby."

God, she wanted to believe it, but she couldn't be a fool. Not again. Yes, she felt that same connection to Jason, but they barely knew each other. It wouldn't last. It couldn't be real. She couldn't hold him to promises that he'd want to retract in a day or a week or a month. "You don't know that," she said, struggling to keep her distance, not to fall into the magical words he was weaving. "You lost your son, and because of me, you have a chance for another. There's no way to think clearly through that—"

"The night we made love there was no child at stake." He grasped her wrists and locked her hands together behind his neck. "There was simply an incredible woman, so full of pain, and yet so full of vibrancy and life." He met her gaze, letting her see the truth blazing in his eyes. "I've been dead for so many years, and moving up here was my last-ditch effort to save myself and my son. When I first saw the cafe, I thought I'd blown it. It wasn't my finest moment." He smiled, a genuine, beautiful smile that lit up his handsome face. "And then you walked in, and my heart began to beat again. You, Astrid. Nothing but you made my heart come to life again."

Tears filled her eyes, and hope leapt through her. "You make it sound so logical, like you really can feel that way about me even though we don't know each other."

"We know enough." He tangled his fingers in her hair and tugged her toward him. "Unless I'm the only one feeling this way, but I don't think I am. I feel like there's hope for the first time in a long, long time." His mouth hovered over hers, not kissing her, but so close. "Do you feel the hope, Astrid? Do you?"

She closed her eyes for a brief moment, her body trembling. "I do," she whispered. "You're a bastard for making me feel it, but I do."

A grin flashed across Jason's face, a heart-melting smile that touched her very soul. "Why thank you, my dear. I appreciate the compliment." Then his grip tightened on her hair, his arm locked around her waist, and he kissed her.

The kiss was possessive, controlling, and desperate, nothing like the kind, gentle words he'd been whispering to her. It was as if all the emotions buried inside him after the death of his wife and son had come to life, tearing through his shields and flooding them both, igniting the same intensity of need that had raged inside her for so long, desperate for an outlet.

There was no way she could stop, no chance of resistance. He simply gave her too much of what she'd craved for so long. It simply felt too right: his words, his touch, his emotions, his values. So, tentatively, carefully, she gripped the front of his shirt and kissed him back.

The moment she accepted the kiss and leaned into him, Jason gave a growl of pleasure that sent chills rushing through her. His kisses were fierce and relentless, as if he were calling to her soul and bringing it to the light.

"No making love on the grass this time," he whispered as he slid his hands down her hips and lifted her against his chest, never breaking the kiss. "Tonight, we will inaugurate your bed—"

"My bed?" Astrid had sudden panic as he carried her toward it. She'd never allowed a man in her bed before, not even Paul. She had always stayed at his place, always protected the sanctity of her bed. She'd spent too long watching the parade of men through her mother's bed, and it was the one thing she swore to always hold sacred. "No, not the bed. I—" She hesitated, frantically trying to think of an excuse that would make sense, but before she did, Jason grabbed the comforter off the bed and flung it on the floor.

He didn't ask any questions. He didn't demand answers. He didn't look at her like she was insane. He simply accepted the urgency he'd heard in her voice and gave her the space she needed, as he lowered them both toward the floor, cradling her against him.

The sense of relief was heady, rushing through her like a burst of light. Suddenly, there was no more fear, no more hesitation. For some crazy reason, Jason really did accept her for who she was, and it felt amazing. Grinning, she braced herself back on her elbows as Jason set her on the comforter. "Kiss me, you fool," she teased, relishing the lightness of her heart. "I think I've been waiting my whole life for you."

"Or at least since you met me." He moved over her with a growl, shoving her on her back with a rough kiss that made her giggle. "It's been what, a month since I ravished you? How have you been able to hold out for so long?" He bit her collarbone, making her shriek and scramble to get away.

"Stop," she laughed, almost giddy with relief that she didn't need to impress him, that she didn't need to pretend to be more together than she was.

"Never, woman." He grabbed her by the ankle and dragged her back across the blanket, a wicked grin on his face. "You're not escaping. You may not have been fantasizing about my naked body for the last month, but I've been tormented every minute of every day, reliving your kisses—" He paused to kiss her, a decadent seduction that made her body sing with need. "And wondering whether your stomach is as soft as I remembered—" He yanked up her shirt and pressed his lips to her belly, suckling and running his tongue in tantalizing circles over her skin.

"Did you do that before?" she gasped, writhing beneath him as she buried her fingers in his hair. "Because I don't remember that. It was kind of quick last time—"

"Quick?" He shoved her shirt out of his way and cupped her breast with his hand. "Hell, yeah, it was too quick, but you turned down my offer for an entire night of lovemaking." He lifted his head and palmed the floor on either side of her shoulders, holding himself above her. "But this time, I've got the night, and you're not getting away from me."

Hot anticipation and raw desire pulsed through Astrid, and she knew that she was about to find out exactly what true passion was. The kind of lovemaking where there were no secrets, just pure acceptance and honesty. She smiled and tugged his shirt out of his jeans. "Bring it on, Sarantos," she whispered. "Bring it on."

Surprise flickered in his eyes, and then raw lust. "Damn, woman," he said. "You don't know what you just asked for." Then he lowered himself on top of her and kissed her as if she were his last breath of air, the light that kept his soul alive, the force that made his heart beat.

It was the kiss she'd dreamed of her whole life, and they were just getting started...

Hot damn. This was going to be good.

JASON COULDN'T GET ENOUGH of Astrid. It felt so amazing to kiss her, to feel the silkiness of her skin beneath his palms, to hear her whisper his name as if he were this great gift the universe had dropped into her lap.

He slid his hand across the nape of her neck, holding her more tightly as he deepened the kiss. He needed more of her. More of this woman who carried so much depth in her soul. She was so alive, the antithesis of how he had lived for so long. Yes, she did have a streak of independence, but she was nothing like Kate had been with her cold reserve, her irritation with anything that took her away from her career. Astrid was warmth and passion, and he knew her walls were self-defense to protect her vulnerable interior. Protectiveness surged through him, a need to safeguard this woman in his arms, to make sure that the world inflicted no more pain upon her.

He caught Astrid's lower lip with his teeth, tugging gently as he eased her shirt over her shoulders and down her wrists. He unhooked the front clasp of her bra, and anticipation rippled through him as he eased her bra off her shoulders, releasing her full breasts. As he trailed the straps down her arms, he circled her nipple with his tongue, immense satisfaction roaring through him as her nipple puckered and she gasped. "Jason," she whispered. "That feels amazing."

"Good." He moved to the other nipple, relishing the intimacy of their connection. "You deserve to feel good."

"I want to touch you." She pulled his shirt over his head with a fumbling need that struck him in his core. Her desperation, her need for him was contagious, igniting a fire within him.

This time, when he lowered himself on top her, it was skin-to-skin, the most incredible sensation of her flesh sliding against his. Her breasts rubbed against his chest. Her mouth tasted like sunshine and passion mixed together. Her tongue danced with his, drawing him deeper as he ran his hands over her sides.

She shuddered beneath him as he cupped her breasts, flicking the nipple, teasing it, flirting with her, even as his kiss deepened, consuming them both.

Astrid arched beneath him, whispering his name as she slid her hands down his back, past the waistband of his jeans. Jason almost swore at her touch, astonished by what it felt like to have a woman initiating a caress. It had been so long since a woman had wanted him. It had been years since he'd felt the amazing sensation of a woman *wanting* to touch him, asking for more, taking more. "God, Astrid. That feels incredible."

She smiled then, a nervous smile hazy with desire. "You don't mind if I touch you? It's okay?"

"Hell, yes, it's okay. Do anything you want. I mean it." How could she even ask? Didn't she understand the power she had over him? Had she no sense of how badly he wanted her?

"Like this?" She slid her palms over his hips and swirled

her fingertips beneath his waistband, brushing against the tip of his cock.

A tremor rippled through him and he caught his breath. "Yeah, that's okay," he managed. "As long as it's okay if I do this." He grabbed the waistband of her pajama bottoms and swept them off her hips in a single fluid motion. He ditched his own jeans and then returned to her side, marveling at her perfection. Her skin was flawless, decadently tempting in its soft golden hues and silky softness. "You're like an angel," he whispered as he went down between her knees and kissed her belly button, then lower...and lower...until he reached her core and began to kiss her—

But Astrid pushed at him, trying to get away. "I'm not an angel, Jason." Astrid arched back, moving her hips as he wrapped his arms around her thighs, locking her down. "Please don't say that. I'm not—"

"Shit, Astrid." He slid up her body and cupped her face, staring intently into her eyes. His heart softened at the fear he saw etched on her face, and he realized instantly what had happened. "You need to understand something, Monroe. When I say you're an angel, I don't mean that you're perfect, and I'm not casting any unrealistic expectations on you."

She searched his face, so much vulnerability in her eyes that his heart ached for her. "You're not?"

He smiled and stroked the damp tendrils away from her cheeks. "Sweetheart, all I mean is that you're *my* angel, the bright light that has swept into my life and granted me hope. Your imperfections, your emotional baggage, your laughter...it all combines to make you into an angel. I want you exactly as you are."

Tears filled her eyes, and she grinned. "Now, see? How can I resist you when you say things like that? You're the stuff women fantasize about."

"I am?" He slid his knee between hers, moving her leg to

the side. "Then you women need to raise your standards." He began to move his hips, nudging against her, teasing them both...and shit...it felt incredible.

"I have no standards," she said as she gripped his shoulders, her eyes going hazy with desire as she moved her hips against him. "I don't get involved with men anymore. Ever."

"Until me." He stilled his hips, poised on the precipice, while he waited for her answer. For her confirmation that she had truly let him past the gates, not just physically, but emotionally. He needed it all from her. Every last bit.

She smiled at him. "Until you."

Yes. He swept her up in a kiss at the same moment that he plunged inside her. They both gasped at the connection, and desire raged through him. For a moment, he didn't move, letting her adjust to his invasion, teasing them both with anticipation as he kissed her.

Then she began to move her hips, sliding beneath him, sending fire racing through his veins. No more slow seduction. No more teasing restraint. The need for Astrid exploded within him, as he thrust deeper, then withdrew, then thrust again, driven by a force so powerful he couldn't stop it.

Astrid gripped his shoulders, her eyes searching his as they connected. He swore, at the depth of emotion in her eyes, at the way her gaze was riveted to his face, at the desperate way her hands were moving all over his back and his shoulders, as if she couldn't get enough of him.

"I need more," she whispered.

"Me too, sweetheart." He bowed his head and caught her mouth in another kiss as he moved his hips again and again, until the fire was raging in both of them, until Astrid was writhing beneath him. Their bodies were slick with perspiration, his blood on fire, desire and need so intense that he felt like his soul was going to explode right out of his body and consume them both.

"Jason!" His name tore from Astrid's lips at the same moment that her body convulsed. She threw back her head, gripping his shoulders as she went rigid beneath him, whispering his name again and again.

His name. *His name.* It was such a beautiful sound to hear her saying his name with such passion and longing. With such desire. This woman he craved so badly actually wanted him, too. It was fucking unbelievable that it could really be this way. A damned miracle. No wonder she made his heart beat. She was more than an angel. She was *everything.*

"Astrid," he managed, just as his own orgasm took him, blasting through him so powerfully he bellowed. Together, they clung to each other while the orgasm carried them both, sweeping them away from their realities and into a place of sheer, raw magic.

Jason knew he'd found what he'd been looking for.

Maine had been worth the trip.

ASTRID AWOKE HAPPY.

She hadn't woken up happy in a long, long time.

Jason was wrapped around her, his legs tangled in hers. His forearm was slanted over her chest, nestled between her breasts, tucking her tightly against him, so her back was against his chest. His face was nuzzled in her hair, and his body was heavy the way it was draped over her.

He'd been like that all night, or at least every time she'd woken up. He hadn't taken personal space during the night and drifted away from her. He'd actually locked her down against him, keeping her in the shield of his body.

Astrid smiled, wriggling deeper against him. His body was

so warm, his muscles powerful even when relaxed in sleep. She felt safe and protected in his arms. Cherished even. And utterly, completely content.

The morning sun was drifting through the front windows, casting rainbows across her work station. Rainbows. In her house. How was that possible?

Jason mumbled something in his sleep, and he moved his hand to her belly, flattening his palm across her stomach. It was a possessive move, a protective one. It should have scared her. It should have reminded her that they were being held together by the baby, just like she and Paul had been.

But instead, an immense feeling of satisfaction filled Astrid. Jason had convinced her last night with his words and his intimate lovemaking that he saw her for who she was. He didn't simply see her, he accepted her. No, not just accepted, he *cherished* who she was, with all her ridiculous flaws.

She'd seen his pain, she'd felt his agony, she knew his burdens. He had suffered so much loss and guilt, just like her, which was part of what brought them together. Their connection went beyond the physical, far beyond. She knew that was why she had made love with him twice after being celibate for so many years.

Because Jason was different. He was the man she'd thought Paul was. Everything was going to be okay now. She could simply relax and enjoy the magnificence of the man who'd gifted her with such kindness, love and—

She suddenly heard the loud crunching of car tires on gravel, and she tensed. It was too soon for anyone to find them together. As wonderful as it was to wake up in Jason's arms, she wasn't ready to test their fragile connections by exposing them to the world. "Jason," she whispered, trying to wiggle out from his unyielding grasp. "Someone's here."

"Not ready to get up," he mumbled as he began to kiss the back of her neck. "Stay with me, Astrid."

A car door slammed, and then another. How many people were here? "Jason!" She hit her palm against his forearm. "Get up!"

"No." His voice still groggy from sleep, he rolled on top of her and kissed her. His erection pressed against her belly, making desire ricochet through her. For a split second, she was tempted to succumb to his amorous and tempting advances. Her door was locked, right? It wasn't as if she had to answer if someone came knocking...

Someone shouted his name.

A woman.

Jason's eyes opened, and his head jerked up. "What the hell?"

"Jason Sarantos! Where the hell are you, boy?" A man's voice bellowed.

"Shit!" Jason rolled off Astrid, grabbed his jeans and scrambled to his feet.

Astrid followed suit, grabbing for her clothes, feeling exposed and raw. The nakedness that had felt so beautiful in Jason's arms suddenly felt threatening and embarrassing. "Who is it?"

He yanked his shirt over his head as the voices continued to shout for him. "My parents."

Her stomach dropped. "What?"

"Yeah. I didn't invite them. I don't know why they're here." He caught her wrist and pulled her close, his eyes blazing fiercely. "Don't tell them about the baby, Astrid. It's too soon."

She stared at him, dread curling in her stomach. It was just like Paul, who hadn't introduced her to his parents until she was seven months along. He'd always had excuses, always reasons, but after he ended it, she'd realized the real explanation, the truth he'd always hid so well. He'd been ashamed of her, and he hadn't wanted to admit to the world he was engaged to her until he knew the baby was going to make it. "Too soon," she echoed faintly. "It's too soon to tell your parents about us?"

"Yeah." Jason grabbed her and kissed her hard, then sprinted for the door. "I need to head them off. They'll come in here if they don't find me in the main house." Without even looking back at her, or shooting her a smile of reassurance, he sprinted out the door, paused long enough to make sure it was securely closed, then leapt down the steps of the carriage house.

Astrid moved to the window, watching him silently race up behind them, not calling to them. Her stomach dropped ever further when she realized he was doing it so they wouldn't see where he was coming from. He didn't want them to track him back to the carriage house. To Astrid.

Oh, wow. Again? Hope began to fade, replaced with the rising heat of embarrassment. Was he really not going to admit she existed to his parents? Was he really going to deny it all?

As Jason jogged toward them, the couple had their backs toward her, so she couldn't see their faces. They were holding hands. A marriage based on love, for sure.

So Jason had family who valued that kind of thing. Not a family that would approve of her past.

"Dad." Jason finally caught up to them and set his hand on the man's shoulder.

His dad let out whoop and spun around, immediately wrapping Jason up in a massive hug. His mom did the same thing, so the three of them were caught up in a huge, fierce hug.

Longing pierced Astrid's heart as she watched them, leaning on the windowsill. They looked like the perfect family, a family who loved each other and dropped in for surprise visits.

"Where did you come from?" his dad asked. "We didn't see you when you drove up."

Astrid held her breath, hoping Jason would tell the truth. Hoping that she was wrong that he was trying to hide her. *Tell them, Jason.*

Jason hesitated for a split second, then he shrugged. "I was at the lake, checking things out. I think I'm going to buy a couple kayaks for me and Noah."

Disappointment sank in her gut like lead. She couldn't believe it. He'd told them he was going to buy kayaks? He was going to have a baby, and he'd told them *kayaks?* Astrid slumped onto a cardboard box, her heart aching at his answer. Not even one mention of her? Not a one?

"Damn nice place you got here," his dad said. "We're impressed."

Jason opened the front door, not even looking back over his shoulder at the carriage house. "Why are you here?"

His dad grinned. "You're finally going into the family business, son. We knew you'd fail miserably without our help, so we came to the rescue."

Jason herded them into the house, his urgency obvious from a distance. "I don't need help—"

Then the door closed, shutting them off from her.

CHAPTER TWELVE

"Astrid!" The sound of Clare's voice jerked Astrid out of her stupor, and she turned as Clare and Emma threw open the door to the carriage house and walked in. Their arms were full of flowers, groceries, and a large number of shopping bags.

Shoving herself away from the window and her pathetic gaping at Jason's house, Astrid managed a smile at the sight of her friends. "What's all that?"

"Well," Clare said as she strode past Astrid toward the kitchen, "Emma and I decided that we blew it, and we're going to do it right this time."

Astrid grabbed a shopping bag that was slipping from Clare's arms, peeking inside to see fresh peaches and two pineapples. "What are you talking about?"

"You!" Emma announced as she set three massive shopping bags on the floor beside a stack of boxes. She set her hands on her hips, glaring at Astrid. "We thought you were dead set on moving out of town—"

"And then you wind up staying here just because some hot guy offers you his carriage house," Clare announced as she set the six bags onto the counter with a loud thump. "Both of us find that completely unacceptable."

Astrid felt her cheeks flush. "It's not because he was hot—"

"It doesn't matter *why* he managed to convince you to stay." Emma set her hands on her hips. "The thing is that we thought there was no chance for you to stay, and clearly there was. Therefore, we've concluded that if we'd just figured out the right angle—"

"Then we could have gotten you to stay without having to rely on some sexy New Yorker to jump in at the last minute. So, we're not going to take any chances this time," Clare announced as she began unpacking assorted groceries onto the counter. Pasta, milk, cereal, oatmeal, everything that Astrid usually had in her cabinet. "When you called us yesterday, you said you were staying for two weeks and then leaving—"

"Which is entirely impermissible," Emma declared as she pulled a massive floor pillow out of one of the bags. It was a twirl of blues, greens and pinks, like the sunset on the most beautiful day. The pillow was almost three feet across, huge, and puffy, and Astrid felt a flash of yearning to curl up in her window on the pillow. "We know you love to curl up, so we picked up some comfy furnishings for you when we were downtown yesterday after you called."

Astrid jerked her gaze to Emma's face, startled by her warm smile. "That's for me? But you didn't need to—"

"Of course we did." Clare pulled out a box of strawberries and several liters of bubbly water. "Now that we know you can be manipulated into staying in town, we are going to make ourselves and this town so invaluable that it becomes absolutely impossible for you to leave."

Astrid started to laugh when she saw Clare set three cans of frosting on the counter. "Frosting?"

"Not just frosting." Clare held it up. "Creamy deluxe chocolate frosting. What girl doesn't want to have chocolate frosting around to snack on when she's feeling cranky? I would have made you homemade frosting, but I didn't have time." She grinned. "Whenever you eat this, you'll think, 'Wow, Clare and Emma take care of all my needs. What if I leave town, and I need a late night chocolate fix, and they aren't around to hook me up?'"

"Exactly." Emma took out another floor pillow, this one assorted shades of pale pink and magenta, with tassels on the corners. "We feed your addictions and become indispensable, rendering you completely incapable of functioning without us. It's really basic stuff, you know, creating a dependent and needy relationship between us and you."

A warm feeling began to fill Astrid. "You guys are manipulating me?"

"Of course! That's what friends are for!" Clare pulled out a bag of ground coffee. "Now, this is only for your caffeine fix when Wright's isn't open. If the store is open, you have to go there to get your food, see the peeps in the town, and remember that you are hopelessly and completely entwined with all of us and couldn't possibly survive on your own."

"Exactly." Emma pulled out a beautiful, antique lamp with a hand-crafted lampshade with colored tissue paper crafted into flowers pressed on the shade. "This is for your jewelry making area. Where are you setting up?"

Astrid's heart tightened at the sight of the beautiful lamp. The base was brushed brass, and there were beautiful engravings on it. "Can I see?" she whispered, almost afraid to touch it. She'd never owned anything so beautiful in her life.

Emma grinned and held it out. "Clare said it was too old-fashioned, but I knew you would appreciate it."

"It's beautiful." Astrid took it carefully in her hands, running her hand over the cool metal. The engravings were black in the crevices, and the brass needed a good polishing, but the artistry was incredible. There were dozens of different kinds of flowers, with their stems and leaves twisting together in a symphony of nature and beauty. In the center of some of the flowers were glass stones, covered in dust, but still evident in their beauty. There was a deep crimson one, several blue ones, and three yellow ones. There were numerous empty crevices where more stones had once resided, and Astrid ran her fingers over them, almost feeling the power of the stones that had once been there. "I've never seen anything so beautiful."

Emma grinned, and Astrid knew that Emma, with her artist's eye, had seen the same beauty that Astrid saw. "Look on the bottom," she said. "That's the best part."

"Better than the rest of it?" Mystified, Astrid flipped it over. Engraved on the bottom, in what clearly was done by hand, was a note in beautiful, curly script. "May you always see the angels guiding you," she read aloud. "May you always feel the warmth of the sun. May you always hear the beauty of nature. Love transcends it all. For my dearest May, with my love for all eternity. Hammond." And after Hammond's signature was a symbol with two intertwined hearts, incredibly similar to the double-hearts that Astrid had designed for her own jewelry.

"It's a love lamp," Emma said with a grin. "Hammond and May."

Astrid hugged the lamp to her chest. "It's so beautiful."

Emma smiled. "Isn't it? I knew you had to have it."

"Thank you," she whispered, too emotional to say anymore. She just held out her arms and Emma immediately hugged her, a fierce hug between two women who had seen the darkest sides of life.

"Oh, I want in on that," Clare announced as she ran across the room and flung her arms around them both. "You have to stay, Astrid," she said fiercely. "We need to stick together."

Astrid's throat tightened as she pulled back, looking at the two women who'd thrust themselves into her life. "I don't know what to say."

"Say you'll stay," Clare urged. "Why do you have to leave?"

"It's complicated."

"Great. We have no plans, so feel free to take as long as you need to fill us in on all the sordid details," Emma said, grabbing a third floor pillow out of a bag and setting it beside the others. This one was covered in hearts and peace signs, and it was sparkling, as if little crystals had been woven into the threads.

"Our only mission today is to help you unpack and to turn your home into something so cozy that you can never leave it behind," Clare said as she pulled a bottle of champagne out of one of the grocery bags, and began to untwist the wire. "We're completely capable of listening to you spill all your secrets while we're working, so start talking, girl."

"Champagne?" Astrid glanced between the two women. "It's only eight in the morning."

"So? We're celebrating you being in town." There was a loud pop as the cork shot out. Astrid and Emma both ducked as it shot past them. "Sorry!" Clare said with a grin. "These things have a mind of their own." She filled several plastic cups she'd apparently brought in with the champagne, then carried them over to Emma and Astrid. "Let's have a toast, girls."

Astrid's fingers closed around the cold plastic. "You guys are crazy."

"Yes, we are," Clare agreed. "That's why we're going to stay all day and help you unpack."

"I'm not staying long enough. I'm not going to unpack—"

"Yes you are," Emma said. "If you make this like home, then you'll never leave."

Astrid thought of Jason in the house with his parents, and her grip tightened on the champagne cup. "Even if I stay in town, and I'm not saying I am—" But it was the first time she'd even voiced the possibility, and the thought both terrified her and gave her chills of joy. "But on the slight chance that I do, I'm not staying *here* any longer than I have to."

Clare frowned as she opened the fridge and began loading it with fruits, vegetables and Birch's Best beer, the local brew. Two packages of local organic chicken and some fresh corn also made it into Astrid's fridge. "Why not? This is your dream house. Why would you want to leave?"

"Because—"Astrid stopped. How was she supposed to explain? "The rent," she said lamely, her cheeks flaming at the lie. How could she lie to these women? It felt so wrong, so horribly wrong. "It's too high," she mumbled. "Jason's just letting me stay here for a couple weeks, but I have to start paying rent after that."

Emma raised her cup. "Then sleep with the man. Men will do anything for sex. He'd let you stay indefinitely if he were getting a little nookie."

Astrid nearly choked as Clare tapped her cup against Emma's. "I have to concur. Now that Griffin has ignited that spark in my life, I can see that I missed out on a lot of fun times for the last fifteen years. Jason's hot. Do it with him. Repeatedly."

"Do it," Emma agreed. "It's worth it for this beautiful place." She beamed at Astrid and tapped her cup against Astrid's. "Cheers, girlfriend."

"Cheers, but I'm not having sex with him. Ever." Astrid tapped her cup against theirs and pretended to take a drink when the others did. She hadn't even taken the rim from her lips when Clare's eyes widened at her. "What?"

"Oh my God," she said, staring at Astrid. "You already slept with him. That's why he's letting you stay here for free. Dammit. I would have slept with you if I'd known that was what it would take!"

Astrid started to laugh at the absurd comment. "Sorry, Clare, but you're not my type."

"But Jason is?" Emma had almost dropped her cup in shock. "I can't believe you had sex with Jason Sarantos? When?"

Astrid stared in growing horror as her friends waited expectantly for her answer. She realized that they weren't going to let it go. They'd seen right through her façade. How had they figured it out? "I didn't—"

"Was he amazing? He looks like he'd be a fantastic lover. His shoulders are to die for, and he has great hands." Clare sank down on the peace and heart pillow and hugged the corner of it to her chest. "I so have to hear this. Astrid Monroe finally got seduced! I can't believe it!"

Astrid was too shocked to deny it, too horrified to know what to say. She was an expert on keeping her secrets private, but she had no experience in lying to people she cared about. She couldn't lie. But she couldn't tell the truth. "I—" She what? What could she say?

Emma's smile faded as she looked at Astrid's stunned face. "Oh my God, Astrid," she said quietly. "What happened? Did he hit you?"

"No, no, no, nothing like that." Astrid's hand began to shake, and she set the drink on a box. "I just—" God, she couldn't say it. What would they think?

"What?" Clare stood back up, her eyes blazing. "What did he do to you? What's wrong? We aren't just talking about sex, are we? Something else happened. Tell us. Now!"

For a long moment, Astrid stared into the worried faces of the two women who had somehow become her friends.

She looked past them at the roses, and the groceries, and she hugged the lamp she was still holding.

"Astrid," Emma touched her arm, her fingers brushing lightly. "Sometimes it helps to talk. What's going on?"

Clare put her arm around Astrid's shoulder and squeezed. "Was he bad in bed? Was that it? A waste of your time and energy?" Her voice was gentle but teasing, making Astrid smile slightly.

"No, he was great," she admitted. "Really kind of fantastic, actually."

Clare raised her brows. "So, what's wrong, then? He's a great lover. He's letting you live in your dream house for free. He seems like a good guy. So...?"

Astrid grimaced. Was she really going to tell them everything? "So..." A door slammed at the main house, making Astrid jump. She quickly glanced out the window and saw Jason guiding his parents down the walkway in the direction of the carriage house. Her heart began to race. Was he really going to bring them over to meet her? "Wait a second." She hurried to the front door, her hands sweating as she looked out the window just in time to see Jason get into his Mercedes while his parents got into a silver sedan.

Shocked, she watched as he started the engine. He was leaving? Taking his parents off the premises before they could stumble onto her? Anger and outrage burned through her, but also humiliation. How could she have been so wrong about him? She'd believed him last night. She'd believed *in* him. And now he was driving away, while the comforter on the floor was still warm from the heat of his body. She clenched her fists. "Bastard," she whispered.

"What?" Emma was leaning over her shoulder to look out the window. "Is he having an affair with that woman? She's not nearly as pretty as you are, and she's a little old. I think you'll win."

"No," Astrid said, tearing herself away from the door as Jason began to drive out, followed by his parents. "That's his mother."

Clare frowned. "So...he's a jerk for having a mother?"

"No, forget it." Astrid walked across the room to set the lamp by the windows that looked out onto the lake, where she was already starting to set up her work area. "So, anyway, I don't need to unpack. I'm not staying." She positioned the lamp on the corner of her table, and then turned back toward her friends.

Emma and Clare were standing side by side, arms folded across their chests. "You have three seconds to tell us what is going on with Mr. Hot Stuff from New York," Clare said. "Or I'm getting in my car and chasing him down and asking him why you called him a bastard." She held up her index finger and started the countdown. "One."

"Clare, don't—"

"Two." Anger blazed in Clare's eyes, and Astrid suddenly realized that Clare was really planning to do it, in her defense.

"No—"

"Three!" Clare turned toward the door as Emma pulled it open.

Dear God, she was really going! Astrid panicked and lunged for the door, horrified at the idea of Clare chasing Jason down. "Stop! I'm mad he didn't introduce me to his parents," Astrid blurted out, immediately feeling stupid. Hello? She was a little old to be feeling slighted by a lack of parent-intro, wasn't she?

Her friends turned back toward her. "Seriously?" Clare's brow wrinkled in confusion. "That's why you're upset? Why does it matter? It's not like you're dating yet."

"And God help you if you want to meet his parents because you plan to marry him," Emma agreed. "You're way smarter than to do something like get married. I know that. So what's really going on?"

The gravel crunched under Jason's tires. As he drove away in his Mercedes, Astrid couldn't help but remember what it had been like before his parents had arrived. It had been magical, perfect, and beautiful. And now it was gone, stripped out from under her just like how it had happened with Paul.

Suddenly, the world seemed too heavy to bear. With a sigh, she sank down onto the pillows and pressed her face into her palms. "I slept with him twice," she said. "Once the day he arrived, and then again last night."

"And how was it?" Emma asked cautiously as she settled next to Astrid. "Just as good the second time?"

"Amazing." Astrid shifted nervously as Clare joined them on the pillows, aware that the two women were entirely focused on her, and wanting to know everything. It was out of caring, though, so that was okay, right? It made it safe to tell them, didn't it? She needed to tell them. She needed to trust them. It was too much to handle on her own. "And it wasn't simply the sex. We connected. It was beautiful."

Clare's face lit up. "Oh, sweetie, I'm so happy for you. You deserve it!"

Emma didn't smile. "So, what happened then? Why are you so upset?"

Astrid swallowed hard and fiddled with the tassel on the pillow, but she knew she was going to come clean. She'd been alone for too long, and she needed to confide in someone. These two women who had showed up at her house with so many gifts...if she couldn't trust them, who could she trust? "We didn't use birth control the first time," she admitted, stumbling over the words as she rushed through them.

Emma's eyes widened, and Clare sucked in her breath. "You think you're—"

"You gave me a pregnancy test, remember? I used it."

Clare was on her knees now. "And?"

Astrid looked at her. "And?" she repeated. "What do you think the result was? Seriously."

"Holy crapoly," Clare whispered, her face lighting up. "You're going to have a baby!" She screamed and hugged Astrid, but Emma still didn't move.

"No," Astrid pulled free of Clare's grasp. "I'm pregnant. That's not the same thing."

Emma's face paled. "You're going to abort it?"

"No, no, no. God, no." Astrid looked at her friends, and the truth finally spilled out. "Three years ago, I was pregnant and the baby was stillborn at eight months. Being pregnant doesn't always mean you're going to have a baby."

"Oh, Astrid." Clare hugged her. "It'll be okay..."

Emma was still watching her intently. "Do you want the baby?"

"I—" Astrid hesitated, trying to figure out how to answer the question. She'd never even thought about it, but as she did, a strong sense of rightness came over her. "Yes," she whispered. "More than anything. But I'm terrified."

This time, finally, Emma smiled, and so did Clare. "We'll help you though it," Emma said. "It's so awesome. You'll be the best mom."

"But what if—"

"No." Clare put her fingers over Astrid's lips. "None of that, Astrid. It's going to be fine. And we're going to help you, every step of the way."

Emma nodded. "There's no way you can leave town now," she said. "That would be crazy. You can't do this alone. Clare never would have managed with Katie if she hadn't had help from the town."

Astrid sighed. "I know, but—"

"But Jason," Clare interrupted. "Does he know?"

"That's why he offered to have me live here," Astrid admitted.

"And? He's happy about it?" Clare pressed.

"He wants another child, and I'm the way to make it happen," Astrid said, not quite able to keep the hurt out of her voice. "I thought there was more between us, but..." Her voice trailed off.

Emma's eyes narrowed. "But he didn't introduce you to his parents."

"Nope."

"Bastard," Emma snapped, her voice thick with loathing.

Astrid started to laugh at Emma's vehemence. "See? I told you."

"Don't worry, girlfriend, you have a posse now," Clare said. "This is your town, and you've got a team supporting you. We'll kick Jason's ass if he doesn't shape up. Just think what Eppie will do to him—"

Astrid grabbed Clare's arm. "God, no, don't tell anyone. I'm only a month along. Anything could happen over the next eight months." She hesitated. "I don't fit in here already, Clare. What if people find out I slept with Jason the day I met him and got knocked up? What will they think of me?"

Clare smiled and patted her arm. "Oh, sweetie, you have no idea what this town is really like, do you?"

Astrid hesitated. "I know that they think I'm different than everyone else. Like I don't fit in—"

"And that makes you a perfect fit," Clare declared. "Or haven't you noticed that this town is a bunch of eclectic personalities? You are loved, by everyone. It was automatic the moment you moved here. It's what the people here do."

Astrid's throat tightened even as she refused to let herself believe that or trust it. "That's not true—'

"Seriously, Astrid, you don't need to worry that the town will judge you." Emma grinned cheerfully. "Jason is the one who should be worried. Very, very worried..." Her smile widened. "I'm really looking forward to people finding out, actually. Jason is going to have to man up."

Clare started laughing. "God, yes, that's an understatement."

"No, don't tell anyone—" Astrid began, then she heard a low snort from behind her.

Her stomach dropping to her knees, she turned around and saw Eppie standing in the open door, carrying a huge casserole dish and a pair of fuzzy loon slippers. Beside her stood Eppie's best friend, Judith Bittner, whose gray hair was still rolled up in curlers. Judith's gold rimmed glasses were perched on the end of her nose, and the gold chain swung gently against her sea-foam green blouse. In Judith's arms was a box filled with china.

"Dammit," Eppie said. "I knew the loon slippers weren't going to be a good housewarming gift. Who the hell knew I should have brought a baby blanket?"

"Oh, God," Astrid whispered, feeling faint as the two older women beamed at her. "Eppie—"

"And to think that Eppie said your greatest need was a set of nice china to woo the men with," Judith said, marching into the carriage house, her leather boots thumping forcefully on the wood. "Astrid, I've packed up my great grandmother's china for you, but from the sounds of it, Jason Sarantos doesn't deserve to be eating on it."

Astrid scrambled to her feet. "No, please don't say anything—"

"Say anything? You don't want us to say anything, even though some out-of-town bastard isn't doing right by you?" Eppie gawked at her. "You think it's better just to sit back and let him go on his penis-waving way without calling him on it? Is that all the self-esteem you have, girl?"

Emma started to laugh, and a giggle ripped through Astrid. "His penis-waving way?"

"Everyone in this room knows about penis-waving, so let's not pretend we're a bunch of virgins in here." Eppie dropped the loon slippers on the floor. "Lordy, girl, you need a protector, and damn lucky for you, Judith and I are available. We're the best there is in a hundred miles in any direction."

"A hundred miles?" Judith snorted. "Try the whole damn world." She pulled a beautiful crystal champagne flute out of her box. "Come on girls, we need to celebrate this properly. Our Astrid is going to be a mama, and we've got ourselves another grandbaby coming to our town."

Everyone ignored Astrid's protests, and within moments, five women were armed with the most beautiful champagne flutes Astrid had ever seen, glasses that Judith had declared were now Astrid's. Amber liquid bubbled in all five glasses, but Astrid's was a concoction of apple juice and sparkling water, whipped up by Eppie. As the quintet raised their glasses in honor of Astrid, she felt the strangest sensation settle on her. Warmth. Belonging. Contentment. Safety. And utter bewilderment. "I don't know what to say," she said.

"Say you'll stay in town," Eppie said.

"Not that it matters," Judith said. "We'll just track you down, hogtie you to the bumper and haul your ass back here if you try to take off."

"No more being nice," Eppie agreed. "It's too late for nice." She leveled her champagne glass at Astrid. "Girl, you've just become a ward of the town. Don't mess with us."

Emma grinned and slung her arm over Astrid's shoulder. "Amen, sistah," she said, tapping her glass against Eppie's. "Astrid belongs to us now. Screw Jason. She's ours."

Tears began to burn in Astrid's eyes as Clare beamed at her. "Welcome to Birch Crossing, sweetie. I think you finally belong."

CHAPTER THIRTEEN

"THESE OVENS LOOK GOOD." Mack Sarantos, Jason's dad and the owner of the very first pizza store in Munson, Minnesota, peered intently into the ovens Jason had installed. "I like them. Nice work."

"Thanks." Jason glanced over at his mother and Noah, who were huddled up at one of the new tables, reading one of the books that his mother had brought Noah. He swore, watching them together. After not seeing his parents for so long, it felt surreal to see his mom hanging out with Noah. But it was good. Really good. He had his memories of sitting in his parents' pizza shop doing homework, and there was something so satisfying about seeing Noah beginning on that same path. "Shit, Dad. It's been a long time." Since he'd seen them. Since he'd talked pizza with his dad. Since there'd been any real sense of family in his life.

But as much as he was being affected by the sudden reappearance of his family, he was restless as hell being with them, when all he could think of was the way he'd ditched Astrid. It had been the perfect night, far beyond what he ever would have expected, even in his fantasies. The sex had been great, yeah, no doubt about that. But it had been more than that. It was the first time in years that his mind had quieted enough to let him sleep. When he'd woken up wrapped around Astrid... yeah... it had been right. So right.

Until he'd heard his damn parents outside. He almost laughed at the memory of how fast he'd hauled ass outside, all his adrenaline gushing on full cylinders. The moment he'd realized his parents were there, he'd been able to think of nothing but protecting Astrid from them.

The first thing he'd thought of when he'd realized his parents were there was how they would treat Astrid. He'd been through their judgments once with Kate, and he knew how brutal they could be if they found his choice lacking, which they always had with every woman he'd dated. Part of the reason he'd stayed away from them for so long was because of his loyalty to Kate. His parents had been brutal to her, judging her as superficial and cold, and unworthy of being their son's wife or their grandsons' mother. No woman he'd ever dated had met their standards, and Kate was no exception.

This morning, still basking in the glow of Astrid's warmth and confessions of the night before, his first instinct had been to protect her. He wanted his parents to stay far away from Astrid. He'd seen too much of her vulnerability to think that she could withstand what his parents might throw at her.

"Yeah, it has been a long time." Mack closed the oven door and leaned against the counter. "Looks like you have a lot in place," he said, the pride evident in his voice. "But you're going to be hard pressed to be ready to open in four days."

"I know." Jason rubbed his hand over the back of his neck, still trying to process the appearance of his parents.

"Why are you here?" He'd seen them only twice in the last thirteen years, and not since Noah's birth. He'd been in touch with them more since Kate's death, but he still hadn't seen them. He hadn't gone home, and he'd never invited them to New York.

Mack leaned against the counter and eyed his son. "I told you. We wanted to see our grandkid. We haven't seen him in too long."

Jason shook his head. It didn't ring true, not at all. There had to be more. He hadn't seen his parents in too damn long for them to simply show up unannounced after six years to see Noah. "What's the truth, Dad?"

Mack glanced over at his wife, and then back at Jason. He laughed softly. "You're still a stubborn cuss, aren't you?"

"Dad." Jason needed to find out their agenda. The last two times they'd visited, the purpose had been to undermine his marriage and try to get Jason to walk out on Kate and move back to Minnesota. It was all done out of love, in their opinion, but it had cut deep into Jason's ability to trust them.

Mack picked up a pizza cutter and examined it. "Nice choice, son. You did good."

Jason couldn't help the slight swell of pride at his father's words. His parents hadn't been proud of him much during his life, and he was well aware of it. Jason had chosen not to sacrifice his desires just to make them happy, so he'd chosen med school and New York instead of staying in town and making pizza. He was used to living without their approval, but to have his dad beaming with satisfaction over what Jason was doing felt surprisingly good. When he'd graduated from med school and decided to stay in New York, they'd thought he was selling out for money when he should have moved back to Minnesota to hang up a shingle in their small town. Not a moment of pride. Just insult. "But what's up with the visit?"

Mack finally met his gaze. "Jason, you walked away from the family thirteen years ago. You rejected every value that we'd raised you and your sisters to believe in and went off with that woman who had no values at all."

Jason ground his jaw, unwilling to listen to the lectures that had created the rift between them. "Dad, let it go. I'm in Maine, now. I quit my job. You should be happy about that. All the other crap is in the past."

"Yeah, it is." Mack eyed him. "It's been breaking your mother's heart, watching you and Noah suffer for so long, but we didn't know how to reach out to you. You seemed so far away and disconnected. We felt like we didn't know you anymore."

Jason narrowed his eyes, already resenting the guilt trip. "So, why now? What changed?"

"When you emailed us three weeks ago that you had a new address because you were moving to Maine to open a pizza store..." Mack shrugged. "It seemed to us like you were finally on a good path, and we wanted to help. Opening a pizza store is tough, and you have to get it right."

Jason blinked in surprise at his father's confession. "You came out here to help me with the store?" Not to give him grief for his choice, or to tell him to move back to Minnesota and do pizza there?

"Yeah." Pride gleamed in Mack's eyes. "You finally came into the family business, Jason. Do you know how happy that makes me? I brought all my recipes. Every damn one of them. They're yours."

Jason stared at his father. "You did?" He still remembered the day his father had quit his job as an appliance salesman to open a pizza store using old family recipes. His parents had stopped being around the house after that, spending every hour at the store, so Jason and his sisters had grown up at Mack's, behind the counters, in the kitchen and socializing with everyone who came into the store. By the time Jason was in high school, Mack's Pizza was *the* place to hang out in town. He and his sisters were substantially elevated in status because they were members of the inner circle at Mack's.

Today, his parents had seven stores in Munson and the surrounding towns, and had even managed to get their pizzas into the frozen food section of three local grocery store chains. It had been hard work, but there was no doubt that their pizzas were a cut above their competition.

His parents had never let anyone, even the kids in the family, know the specific ingredients of the crusts, the sauces and the cheese blends. His parents would always mix things up after hours, and then the workers simply assembled.

Mack and Henrietta had kept the recipes a secret even from their family because they didn't want their kids to be put in the uncomfortable position of being pressured to turn them over to someone who might want them.

And now..."You brought the actual recipes? For me?" Jason still couldn't believe it. It was a gift. Having Mack's pizza in his store would be a sure-fire winner.

"Damn right I did." Mack grinned. "Your mom and I talked about it, and we like the idea of our pizza making it all the way to the east coast."

Jason was stunned by the offer. The recipes were the financial basis of the chain. The implications were enormous if he used them.

"So, yeah, a Mack's Pizza starting in Maine," his dad said, beaming. "It's good shit."

Jason's smile faded. "Mack's Pizza? You want my store to be a Mack's Pizza?" He'd already ordered the sign for it. Luc's Pizza, in honor of his son.

"Damn right. We can't have Mack's recipes in a store that doesn't have the same name." Mack turned away and walked over to the freezer. He pulled open the door and walked inside. "We're going to have to order some new ingredients," he said. "You won't believe what's in my sauces."

Jason leaned against the counter, and suddenly all his old emotions came back. He remembered why he'd left town at age seventeen and never gone back. His parents wanted him to be like them, to follow the path they wanted for him, no matter whether it was right for him or not. "Dad. I'm naming it after Luc."

There was no sound from the freezer for a moment, and then Mack reappeared. The wrinkles on his face seemed deeper than they had been a moment before, and there was deep regret in his eyes. "Naming the store after your son won't change the fact he's dead, Jason," he said quietly.

Jason stiffened. "I know that—"

Mack held up his hand to cut Jason off. "Living in the past makes it impossible for the future to give you life," he added.

Jason's eyes narrowed. "You want me to forget my son?"

"Shit no. But I want you to start living again. You've been destroying yourself for over a decade, Jason. After all that crap, you've given yourself a chance. Take it."

"I am. That's why I dragged Noah up here—"

"You dragged all your baggage up here too," Mack said. "I can see it in your eyes. You're tired, you're exhausted, and you're going to break if you don't cut yourself some slack. Name the place Mack's. Make some money. You were a fool when you married Kate. Don't keep living that same life."

Anger rolled through Jason, and he shook his head. He had failed Kate and Lucas, and the answer wasn't to kick up his heels and gallivant through life just because their death had freed him to move to Maine. "I appreciate you coming out here," he said, unable to keep the edge out of his voice, "and you are welcome to stay as long as you want. But I'm naming the store after my son, and I'll use my own recipes."

He didn't miss the flash of pain on his father's face, but he steeled himself to it as he turned away. He needed space. He needed to get away. "I'm going to get coffee," he said to his mother as he passed her table. "Do you want anything?"

Henrietta looked up, and her face fell when she saw his expression. She looked between him and Mack, and she sighed. "Oh, Jason. We're just trying to help."

"By telling me to forget Luc?" he bit out. "Is that what you think I'm supposed to do?"

Noah looked up. "Luc? Who's Luc?"

Jason felt like his heart had just been stabbed. Noah didn't remember his own brother? "Lucas," he said, barely able to keep the anguish out of his voice. "I was talking about Lucas. Your brother."

"Oh, right." Noah shrugged carelessly. "Why'd you call him Luc?"

"Because that was his nickname," Jason said, as gently as he could, fighting not to explode at his son. It wasn't Noah's fault that he didn't remember his brother, but *hell*, it was devastating to be around three people who weren't trying to hold the memory of his son in their hearts. "You used to call him Luc because you couldn't say his full name when he was born."

"Oh." Noah frowned, and looked down at his book again, dismissing Jason and the discussion. "Grandma, what's this word?"

She put her hand around the back of Noah's chair and looked at Jason. "Your heart can take only so much before it breaks," she said softly. "You have to let go, Jason. You have to let yourself heal."

"I'm fine. I just need a pizza shop." Jason turned away, his fists clenched as he headed toward the door, guilt pouring through him. How could his parents tell him to forget his son? How could his father insult Kate? Wasn't her death enough to satisfy him?

His emotions burning, Jason strode toward the door and then his heart jumped when it opened. For a split second, his mind flashed back to that moment the first day he'd arrived, when Astrid had flounced into his store. Suddenly, he was consumed with the need to see her. To connect with her. To bury himself in the respite that she offered—

The door flew open, and a large man filled the doorway. His shoulders were as wide as the door, his dark brown hair ragged, and his tee shirt had sawdust on it. A half-grown beard darkened his jaw, and his bright blue eyes were flashing with fury.

Jason stopped immediately, his adrenaline igniting instantly at the challenge in his visitor's hostile stance. "Can I help you?" He gestured to his mom to take Noah out the back. He had no clue who this guy was, but the man had come looking for a fight, and Jason didn't want his parents or son involved.

"I'm Harlan Shea," he said with a snarl.

This was his real estate agent? He looked more like a wild animal ready to attack. Jason gave the man a polite smile. "Thanks for stopping by. I have a couple questions—"

"You fucking bastard." Harlan's fists bunched, and his body vibrated with tension.

Jason instinctively moved into a defensive position, fire racing through him. "What's your problem, Harlan?"

"You knocked up my sister, you bastard."

Jason felt his jaw drop as his mom gasped. "What?" How in hell's name had Harlan found out about that already? But even before he'd finished the thought, Jason knew the answer. It was a small town. That's what had happened.

"Oh, so you don't remember?" Harlan advanced across the wood floor, anger dripping from every pore of his body. "Astrid Monroe, remember? The woman you set up in your carriage house so she'd be there for you to use whenever you wanted."

"Shit," Jason held up his hands, trying to calm the irate man. "It's not like that—"

"You stupid bastard." Harlan fisted his hand and swung.

Jason saw it coming, and for a split second, he considered defending himself...but was he really going to punch Astrid's brother for the mere fact he was being protective of her? He *was* a bastard. In more ways than Harlan even knew.

So, he dropped his hands and let the behemoth make contact.

ASTRID LEANED BACK on her new couch, surveying her newly furnished apartment. Her friends had stayed all day helping her, and every box was unpacked. Pictures were hung. The new dishes were put away.

It turned out that Judith had an extra couch in her basement, so she'd recruited Griffin to go get it. He'd come back with not only the couch, but a table and four chairs that had been in the back room at Wright's. Clare had added a bookcase from her garage and Emma had contributed a carpet.

And now, Astrid had a place to live that looked pretty damn close to a real home. It looked like it belonged to someone who was going to stay for a long while, and she loved it. She really did. Which, of course, meant that her friends were in trouble, because that wasn't supposed to happen. At the same time, she couldn't stop the swell of warmth that spread through her at the thought of the people who had spent the day making sure she had a home.

She smiled and clasped her hands behind her head, her feet propped up on one of the floor pillows that Emma had brought her. The afternoon sun was stretching across the rose and light yellow carpet, making it feel even cozier.

Her orchid was sitting on the corner of her worktable, basking in the sun's rays, breathing in air that wasn't tainted with the smell of gasoline. All that was left was to organize her work station. The apothecary cabinet she used for beads was in place against the wall, and she had her new lamp set up.

But as Astrid looked at the place where creative genius was supposed to take place, a weight began to settle in her belly. It didn't matter how many hours she spent with her friends, or how organized her home was, or even how beautiful. The most idyllic setting in the world couldn't change the reality of her life, including the fact that her business was failing.

And the fact that she was pregnant with Jason's child. She couldn't afford to be creatively-drained now. She had a child to support... oh, God. How was she going to manage this? With a groan, she leaned her head back against the wall. What was she going to do? She—

A loud knock sounded on the door, and Astrid sat up, her breath catching. Was it Jason? "Who's there?"

"Harlan." He sounded tired, and Astrid hurried to let him in, surprised by his visit. In the two years that she'd lived in Birch Crossing, Harlan had stopped by her house maybe a total of five times. Why today?

When she opened the door, he was leaning against the doorframe, his arm propped above his head. He looked gaunt and worried. No, not worried. He looked like he'd seen a ghost, and the demons were haunting him.

She didn't know her brother well, but she'd never seen that expression on his face before. It scared her. "What's wrong?"

Harlan shook his head in a silent refusal to answer her question. "Can I come in?"

"Yes, sure." Tentatively, Astrid stepped back and admitted him. She'd forgotten how huge he was, how he filled the room with his massive size. He was solid muscle, so strong that his jacket bunched over his shoulders, barely able to contain him. "Can I get you something?"

"Water." He walked across the room and sank down on the couch. He braced his forearms across his thighs and bent forward, resting his forehead in his palms.

Frowning, Astrid fetched the drink and set it on a box she was using as a coffee table. "Um, is everything okay?" Silly question, because she knew it wasn't, but she had never felt that comfortable around him and never quite knew how to get personal with him.

He finally lifted his head to look at her. "Why didn't you come to me?"

She straightened the peace floor pillow, propping it against the wall. "About what?"

"Your pregnancy."

"Oh..." Astrid felt her cheeks heat up, and she retreated back toward the kitchen. Damn Eppie and the small town gossip chain. "I just found out. I'm still processing."

Harlan leaned back, and he looked exhausted. "You almost died last time, Astrid."

"I know." She swallowed, feeling very uncomfortable talking about this with her brother. The day she'd called him from the hospital to ask him for help was the first time she'd spoken with him in over ten years, but he hadn't hesitated. He'd driven down to New York that night, walked into her hospital room, and rescued her, taking her out of that hell and bringing her up to Birch Crossing, the place where he'd made his own home.

She'd never been to Maine before that night, but the

moment Harlan had driven her into the town center, she'd known it was the right place for her to be. Birch Crossing comforted her, despite the awkward silence between herself and the brother she barely knew.

She hadn't grown up with Harlan. His dad had split with their mother when Harlan was two, and he'd gone to live with his father. She'd never even communicated with Harlan until she was ten. She'd found his address in her mother's belongings. She'd been fascinated by the idea of a brother she'd never met, a gallant hero who could rescue her from her life, and she'd immediately written him. At the time, Harlan had been sixteen, and, according to him, totally fucked up, but he'd written back. After that, the two siblings had kept in touch, albeit somewhat sporadically.

They'd met twice before that night in the hospital three years ago. Once, when she was sixteen and she and her mom had passed through the town Harlan was living in. And then again when she was eighteen and she was on her own for the first time.

He was all she had, her dream of having a safety net. He was the one she'd called from the hospital to help her, and he'd come. She'd never given him the details of what had happened, and all he knew was that she'd been pregnant, lost the child and almost died.

She'd never forget that he'd come to help her, but at the same time, her hopes of becoming close to him had faded when she'd gotten to Birch Crossing. Upon arrival, she'd discovered she was related to a man who was so reclusive that she knew she'd never find out who he really was, or what his life had been like before he'd walked into her room that night. Harlan was an enigma, even more of an outsider than she was. He would often dump his real estate clients on another agent and then disappear into the woods for weeks at a time. No one knew where he went or what he did.

"I'm here for you, Astrid," he said, leaning forward to look at her. "Anything you need."

She smiled, her throat tightening. "We don't even know each other," she said softly. "How is that possible?"

Harlan let out a small grunt. "I haven't done right by you," he said. Regret flickered in his eyes, and secrets, dark ones, ones that he was hiding not only from her, but from the world. "But you need to know that I'm always here for you. Always."

She nodded, and let her breath out. Maybe her being pregnant would bring them together. Maybe she would finally start to connect with her brother. "I know that."

"Good." Harlan leaned back on the couch, and she noticed he was rubbing the knuckles of his right hand, as if they hurt. "Listen, I want you to move into my place."

Astrid sat up in surprise. "What?"

Harlan nodded as he ran his fingers through his hair. "It's yours. I need to take off for a while anyway." He shrugged. "I don't know how to do family, but when Eppie showed up at my place and told me what was going on... Shit." He looked at her. "This kid of yours, we have to do right by it. We were both screwed over by our mom. You got lucky not having a dad, because mine was from hell. Take my cabin. It's not much, but the roof doesn't leak and the heat works. Do your thing. Protect the baby from all the shit that goes down around us."

She leaned forward to listen, shocked by how much he was sharing. Harlan had never told her anything about what had happened to him after he'd moved out. "What was your dad like?"

Harlan shook his head. "He's dead, so he doesn't matter." Intensity burned in his gaze. "But by my soul, I swear that I won't let any kid I'm related to suffer what we did. Take my place. I'll take off and give you space. That child will never have to go through what we went through."

Astrid frowned. "Why would you leave? Why can't you stay?"

Something flashed in Harlan's eyes, something so lethal and scary that chills ran down her spine. "I will never subject a child to what I am," he said, his voice lethally quiet. "No fucking chance."

She stiffened, unnerved by the roiling darkness in his eyes. "What are you talking about?"

He shook his head and touched her face. "I wish I could be more for you, little sister, but it's not safe."

"Safe?" she echoed. "Safe for who?"

"You. And the baby."

"But why—" Tires crunched in the driveway, and Astrid's heart jumped. Was Jason back?

Harlan swore and stood up. "This baby will never have to know what it's like to have a bastard father who will hurt him."

The intensity of Harlan's voice hit Astrid hard. She realized he meant it. He would do whatever it took to protect her. After a lifetime of being on her own, even when she was living with her mom, she finally had family. A brother. A brother who sort of terrified her, but that was a start. "Thank you."

The smallest hint of a smile flickered across his face as footsteps thudded on her walkway. "I mean it, Astrid. The kid is going to have a home and security, and I'll make sure it happens." Shadows were dark in his eyes. "But I need to take off for a while." He wiped the back of his hand over his brow, and she saw a bead of sweat on his forehead.

"Harlan?" She frowned. "What's wrong?"

But her brother simply shook his head. "I'm leaving in the morning." He fished a key out of his pocket and dropped it in her hand. "Live there. I don't know when I'll be back. I wish I could do more, but the safest place for you both is to not be near me."

Grim resolution darkened Harlan's face, and Astrid shivered, realizing that something very dangerous lurked inside her brother. Suddenly, his retreat to Birch Crossing didn't seem like the actions of a man following his heart.

It seemed like the actions of a man trying to outrun the devil.

CHAPTER FOURTEEN

BEFORE SHE COULD ASK Harlan for more details, there was a firm knock at the door. Astrid jumped. Dear God. Was it Jason? Harlan spun toward the door, his fists bunching as if he were ready to strike first at the intrusion, but she leapt to her feet and held out her hand to stay him. "I'll get it," she said, trying to keep the tension out of her voice as she walked over to the door, forcing herself not to sprint over there and fling it open.

She pulled it open and was startled to see a woman with curly, gray-streaked hair, faded jeans, perfectly applied makeup, and fairly significant diamond stud earrings standing on her step. Astrid managed a brief smile. The woman looked familiar, but she couldn't place her. "Can I help you?"

The woman smiled, but her eyes were so full of such intense scrutiny that Astrid stood taller and pulled her shoulders back, wishing she'd brushed her hair before answering the door.

"My name is Henrietta Sarantos," the woman announced. "I'm Jason's mother."

Jason's mom. Of course that's who it was. Why was she at

the door? Astrid's heart began to race. Had Jason told his parents about her? "It's nice to meet you," she managed. What did Henrietta know?

Jason's mom gave her a cursory nod, as if she could barely be bothered with pleasantries. "Won't you come to dinner at the main house tonight? We brought takeout. We'd love to have company."

There was no warmth in Henrietta's voice, and a cold chill slithered down Astrid's spine. She looked past Henrietta and saw Noah and Jason's dad walking into the house carrying two shopping bags from Wright's. Where was Jason? Why wasn't he the one inviting her? Sudden resolution coursed through her, and she shook her head. She did not need to go where she wasn't welcome. She wasn't that desperate anymore. "Thank you, but I'm having dinner with my brother, Harlan."

Henrietta looked past her, and her eyes widened noticeably. "So, he really is your brother?"

Harlan walked up beside Astrid and set his hand on her shoulder. His fingers dug in, and she could sense the tension roiling off him. "Of course I am."

"Well." Henrietta looked back and forth between them. "Then I suppose you both should come."

Astrid gritted her teeth at the coolness of the reception. "Thank you, but—"

"Sure, we'll be there. Give us five minutes." Harlan reached past Astrid, extending his hand. "Harlan Shea. Nice to meet you, Henrietta. Sorry we didn't get properly introduced before."

Henrietta narrowed her eyes as she shook Harlan's hand. "Yes, well, then we will see you both in a few minutes."

She excused herself and scurried down the pathway toward the house, not even looking back as she ducked inside.

Astrid glared at Harlan. "Why did you accept? Didn't you see her hostility? I don't need that—"

"No, you don't," Harlan agreed. "But that woman is going to be the grandmother of your child. I'd rather find out what kind of world my nephew or niece is coming into than leave it to chance." His eyes flashed. "If you need to disappear, I'll help you. I can make you vanish."

Astrid stared at Harlan as the meaning of his words sank in. She didn't know which was more terrifying, the idea that her brother knew how to make her vanish, or the idea of Jason's parents trying to take her child. "You think they'll try to take the baby from me?"

"They have money. You don't. The playing field isn't even, and I want to know what we're dealing with." He took her hand and gave it a squeeze. "Come on, sis, let's go meet the rest of the family. I need to know that you're safe before I leave town."

Holy cow. She was supposed to go to dinner with Jason's parents so she and Harlan could assess whether they were going to try to take the baby? Terror licked at her heart, and she gritted her teeth. She was tired of being afraid that someone would find her inadequate and unworthy. So damn tired of it.

"Wait." She let go of Harlan and ran back into her bedroom. "Just a sec." She yanked open her closet and grabbed her favorite skirt, a shimmery ankle length skirt that flowed around her legs like the softest caress. It was black-based, with intense color swirls of blues and greens, and it always reminded her of the ocean, of the freedom that the huge expanse of water could offer. She quickly pulled it on, and then donned a cream-colored tank top that hugged her curves and always made her feel beautiful and strong. She quickly touched up her makeup, checked her hair, and then grabbed her favorite pair of earrings, the ones that were two intertwined hearts. One for her, one for the baby.

She paused to inspect herself in the mirror, and smiled at what she saw. Yes, there were still bags under her eyes from so many days of not sleeping and all the stress, but she looked like a woman who deserved to be listened to. She didn't look like a homeless waif who didn't deserve to be noticed. Astrid smiled and nodded. "Okay, then," she whispered. "Bring it on."

As she hurried out of the room, she saw the man's bracelet on her table that she'd started to design for Jason. The word *FIRE* blazed up at her. Fire. Dammit. She was tired of being ignored and underestimated. She grabbed the bracelet and fastened it around her wrist as she headed out into the living room.

Harlan let out a low whistle the moment he saw her. "Hell, Astrid. When did you grow up?"

She lifted her chin. "I grew up the day Mom brought her first boyfriend home when I was five. He passed out in the living room half-naked, with Mom on top of him."

Harlan's face darkened, and anger flashed across it. "Shit, Astrid. I'm sorry. I should have been there for you."

Astrid's throat tightened, and she pulled her shoulders back. "You're here now," she said softly. "And I appreciate it."

Harlan nodded. "You ready?"

She nodded, wishing that Jason was going to be there. Or maybe not. Would he make it better or worse? Not that she needed him. She'd relied on Paul to shield her from his parents, and he'd failed. No more relying on anyone else. She thought of Emma and Clare, and even Eppie and Judith, and how they'd stood by her even when they'd learned the truth about her. Harlan was there, too. She had her team now, for the first time in her life, and people like Henrietta Sarantos couldn't hurt her anymore. This was her life, and she was taking control. Confidence suddenly rushed through her. "Let's do it."

Harlan grinned. "Damn, sis, you're a knockout when you're pissed."

Astrid burst out laughing as she headed toward the door. "Thanks, I think."

"Anytime," Harlan said, pulling the door shut behind them. "You'll bring Sarantos to his knees, and that's the way it should be."

She was still smiling as she walked up the pathway to the house whose windows she'd peered into a thousand times, longing for it. And now, it was occupied by a woman ready to reject her.

Screw the house. It was just a house.

It was she who mattered. The only way anyone could take away her self-respect was if she let them, and damn, she was tired of that.

She fisted her hands, ran her finger over the inscription on her bracelet, and then went into the lion's den.

JASON SPED DOWN HIS DRIVEWAY, the gravel spinning up from his tires. His jaw was still aching from where Harlan had hit him, and he was frustrated as hell that he'd been tied up with contractors when his parents had decided to take Noah home.

To say his parents had been shocked by Harlan's revelation about Astrid's pregnancy was an understatement, but with Noah listening, they hadn't been able to corner Jason on it. Which was good. It gave him time to figure out how to handle it to best protect Astrid.

He slammed his palm on his steering wheel as he pulled up behind his parents' rental car. Shit. He'd wanted more time before exposing Astrid to his parents. How the hell was he going to deal with this?

Scowling, he climbed out of his car. He didn't bother to go to the main house. He just strode up to Astrid's door and thudded his fist on it. He didn't even know what he was going to say to her. He just needed to touch base and connect with her. He knew that simply being in her presence would settle him and help him figure out the best way to handle it.

She didn't answer the door.

He knocked again. "Astrid! It's Jason. I need to talk with you."

Again, no answer. Was she ignoring him, or not home?

Jason strode over to the window and peered inside. It was dark, without a single light on. Astrid wasn't there. For a split second, trepidation rocked through him, but then he saw the outlines of her furniture. She hadn't moved out. Swearing, he leaned his forehead against the window frame, shocked by the intensity of his reaction when he'd thought she might have left.

Shit. He was in over his head. Astrid was like a river, running freely. There was no way to grab onto her and hold her, and the notion of her slipping through his grasp sent panic racing through him.

Scowling, Jason turned away and pulled out his phone. He dialed Astrid's number as he headed across the grass toward his house.

Her phone went right into voicemail.

Tension ran through him as he jammed the phone in his pocket. Why would she have her phone off? What if something happened to her? Sweat broke out on his temple as he remembered that she lost her baby last time. What if something was wrong, and she couldn't call for help because her phone wasn't on?

Almost frantic, he slammed open his front door, then

froze when he heard Astrid's voice coming from his living room. Shock rippled through him, then the most intense relief he'd ever felt. *She was safe.* He tore down the hall, desperate to see her, to know that she was really okay. His whole body shuddered with relief and need as her voice continued to roll through him.

When he reached the doorway to the living room, and saw her sitting on the couch, he actually had to grasp the doorframe for a second to keep his balance, his relief was so great. Astrid's hair was untamed and wild around her shoulders, and she looked truly breathtaking in her rainbow-colored skirt and sexy-as-hell top. Her eyes were a vivid brown, deep with passion and fire. Jesus. He'd forgotten the sheer depth of his response to her, and his whole body surged with adrenaline at the sight of her. Jesus. She was like an angel brought down to earth.

"So, Astrid, why don't you tell us a little about yourself." He heard the cold tone of his mother, and looked sharply around the rest of the room. He'd been so infatuated with Astrid that he hadn't noticed anything else.

His parents had taken control of the armchairs on either side of the fireplace. Belatedly, Jason noticed that Harlan was sitting beside Astrid. He saw now how stiffly Astrid was sitting, with her shoulders erect and tense. A plate of Ophelia's lasagna sat in her lap, along with some salad, but her meal was untouched. Her chin was up, and her body language was one of battle.

He could see Noah in the next room, playing Wii, having clearly been excused so the adults could have private time. The atmosphere in the room was intense, so sharp the air almost bit his lungs when he breathed.

Shit. His mother had gone after Astrid. Fierce protectiveness surged through Jason, and he strode into the room. Without even pausing to consider his actions, Jason headed right for Astrid and sat down beside her, shoving himself between Astrid and her brother. He threw his arm across the couch behind her shoulders and leaned toward her, using his body to show they were on the same team.

Astrid stiffened and threw him a confused look.

He ignored it and gave his attention fully to her. "Are you okay?" he asked softly. "My parents can be a real nightmare."

"I heard that," his mother said.

"I figured you could." Jason didn't look away from Astrid, his heart tightening when he saw the outrage blazing in her eyes. "You okay?"

"Sit somewhere else, Sarantos." Harlan's voice was low and threatening.

Fuck that. This was his home, and Astrid was under his protection. Jason shot Harlan a hard look. "You had your one free punch," he said quietly. "You don't get another, so back off."

Astrid's eyes widened, and her gaze dropped to his jaw. "Harlan did that?"

"Yeah."

She looked past Jason at her brother, and he saw the flash of surprise in her eyes. Surprise that someone had defended her? Outrage rocked Jason, and he swore. How could she have been taught that no one would stand up for her? She deserved so much more.

"Jason," Henrietta said with overstated warmth. "You're just in time for dinner." She loaded up a plate from the casserole dish that was on a tray in the middle of his coffee table. "I was just asking Astrid about her parents. I was curious to know what they do."

Jason set the plate down on the coffee table, not interested in eating. He remembered all too well how they'd grilled Kate for her pedigree, and he wouldn't let them do it to Astrid. He had to set the standard that this was different.

That it would not be allowed. "It doesn't matter what they do—"

"No, it's okay, Jason." Astrid touched his arm to halt his protest, and electricity leapt between them at the touch. Jason put his hand over hers to keep her touching him, but she pulled her hand away and turned toward his parents. "I don't know what my father does. My mother divorced him before I was born, and I never met him."

Henrietta's eyes widened, and Jason swore at the hint of vulnerability in Astrid's voice. "So, who raised you, then?"

"Mom, let it go." Jason's voice was sharp. He could tell they were treading on dangerous ground for Astrid. "Why don't you ask Astrid about her jewelry-making business? She does incredible designs. Really amazing stuff."

"No." Astrid stood up, walking to the end of the table. "I want to answer this." Defiance flared in her eyes, courage so strong it made his heart stop. "By the time I turned seventeen, my mother had been married eight times. Harlan and I have different fathers, and we weren't even raised together. The longest I lived in any house was six months, because my mother moved us all around to try to find the next man she was going to marry and get some money off of."

Jason's heart tightened as he watched Astrid talk. There was so much hurt in her eyes, but her shoulders were back, daring his mother to judge her. "There were times we lived in our car for weeks and weeks. I never graduated from high school because I never stayed in a school long enough to finish an academic year. We had no money, except for what my mother stole from her boyfriends before we would skip town. She never had a job that I knew of."

Henrietta's eyes were hard, her face unreadable. "So, where is she now?"

Real pain flashed across Astrid's face, so intense Jason's

own heart ached for her. "I don't know. I haven't spoken to her in several years. We had a falling out."

Son of a bitch. Jason was shocked by her revelations, by the childhood Astrid had survived. She had no home. No roots. No foundation.

"Have *you* been married?" Henrietta asked, but there was a strange softness to her voice, that caught Jason's attention. Did his mother actually feel sympathy for Astrid?

"No." Astrid's answer was simple, but Jason heard the wealth of emotion beneath that one word. There was so much she wasn't sharing.

Henrietta leaned forward, watching Astrid intently. "Are you really pregnant with my son's child?"

Harlan growled and moved to stand up, but Jason was faster. Much faster.

"Enough." Jason vaulted to his feet and strode over to Astrid, stepping in front of her. He didn't care if Astrid wanted to keep it going. There were lines he could not allow his mother to cross. "Mom, you're stepping over the line—"

"I am not." Henrietta didn't bother to stand up. She just gazed calmly at Jason, her face the epitome of self-confidence. "You're my son. Any child of yours is my grandchild. It's my right to be involved."

It was exactly the same attitude as when she'd come after Kate. From the first meeting, Henrietta had judged Kate as inadequate. She'd spent the rest of his marriage trying to eat away at his belief in his wife and his marriage. "Let it go, Mom," he said, his voice edged like flint. "Now." He took Astrid's arm. "Come on. Let's leave. I'll walk you home."

"No." Astrid pushed past him, pulling out of his grasp. "Let me answer." She surveyed the room, her small hands clenched in fists as she looked at his father and mother. Mack had stayed silent the whole time, but he was leaning forward in his chair, listening intently.

"Yes, I am pregnant. But it is my child, not yours." Her words were fierce and strong, directed right at Henrietta. "You will *never* interfere in its life, and I will defend it against every threat with my entire soul. You may judge me as inferior because of my mother, but you know what? Your opinion doesn't have anything to do with the truth."

Pride swelled through Jason, and he grinned at Astrid. *You go, sweetheart.* Hell, she didn't need him to protect her. She had it handled all by herself.

A small grin played at the corner of Mack's mouth, and Henrietta sat up. "Are you threatening to keep me away from my grandchild?" She sounded shocked and a little incredulous.

Astrid's eyes blazed. "I'll do it if I have to."

Slowly, ever so slowly, Henrietta rose to her feet, and Jason saw the fury in his mother's eyes. Shit! This was completely spiraling.

"Astrid." Harlan stood up. "I think it's time to go."

"Yes, I agree." She lifted her chin, and turned away as Jason caught her hand.

He was startled to feel how cold her fingers were and how badly her hand was trembling. "Astrid," he said quietly. "I—"

"You will not keep my grandchild from me," Henrietta snapped. "And—"

"Mom!" Jason spun toward her, anger flaring deep inside him as Harlan hustled Astrid out the door. "What the hell is wrong with you?"

Henrietta's eyes flashed. "What are you doing, Jason? Can't you see that she's like Kate? She has no sense of family or how to be a parent. She was practically raised on the streets! You're a family man, Jason. You can't be with another woman who can't understand how to be a family."

"She's not like Kate," he snapped. "Kate was cold and cared only about her career. Astrid is the most emotionally alive and vulnerable woman I've ever met. Her heart is so full of hope and pain that it makes my soul hurt just to feel it."

"There's no love in Astrid," Henrietta interrupted. "Can't you see how aloof she is? She's not looking for a marriage or a family. She's planning to raise that child on her own. Can't you tell that? She didn't even once look at you for support when you came in." His mom's voice softened. "Jason, you don't need another cold, independent woman. It'll break you. You need someone who is so full of warmth and love, who will fill your home and your life with real love."

Her accusation burned through Jason, and he fisted his hands to keep his emotions in check. "For your information," he said, his voice steely with the effort of staying calm. "Astrid's had a fucking brutal life, and she has no reason to trust me or anyone else. Yeah, to you she may seem aloof at times, but she's simply protecting herself. She has the capacity to love deeply. I know she does."

"Do you?" His mom looked at him, and suddenly Jason didn't see the hostile woman trying to destroy his hope at a future. He saw an old, tired soul who wanted the best for her son. Some of his anger faded. "Jason, you made the same claim about Kate, and you were wrong. You and the boys suffered for it. Don't make the same mistake again. Can she really love? Or are you going down the same path you went down before?"

Jason swore. "Astrid's got a beautiful soul—"

"She might," Henrietta said. "But is it too damaged?"

"Jason." Mack finally spoke, his low voice rich with calmness and wisdom. "Before you go running off after this woman that you barely know, I want you to ask yourself something."

Jason ground his jaw but nodded. "What is it?'

"Is Astrid really all these things you're claiming, or are you just so desperate for another chance at a family and a child that you've convinced yourself that she's the right one because she's carrying your baby?"

Jason met his father's gaze. "Astrid asked me the same thing."

"Then she's a smart woman." Mack sighed. "You had the wife and kids once, and it didn't end well. Just think about it, is all I'm saying. The fact she's pregnant doesn't make her the right woman for you..." He looked over at the television room. "Or for Noah."

"What kind of a mother could she possibly be having been raised the way she was?" Henrietta asked gently. "Where would she have learned how to be a good mother? Or have acquired the kind of family values you want?"

Jason closed his eyes, his parents' words sinking in. They were absolutely correct that he'd believed in Kate. He'd been egregiously wrong, and Lucas had died for it. How badly did he want another chance? Badly enough to see hope where there wasn't any? Or badly enough to help the right woman find her way to love? Which was it?

His gut said the latter, that this incredible woman who'd sashayed into his life was the answer to everything he wanted.

But his gut had been wrong before. Dead wrong. Dead times two. Two graves, including that of an innocent child.

CHAPTER FIFTEEN

I'm impressed.

Harlan's words rang through Astrid's mind as she sat out on the deck, wrapped in a light blanket. She hugged herself tighter, her emotions warring between pride for how she'd stood up for herself to Jason's mother, and sadness for the realization that she'd lost her chance with Jason by being so defiant with his mother.

Not that Jason was the right man for her, if he ended up judging her unworthy based on her childhood, but a part of her still wished she hadn't been so forthright. Maybe it had been too soon. Maybe she should have waited until she and Jason had more of a foundation before exposing herself to him so completely.

No. She could have no regrets.

It was too late to change what she'd done. Plus, it was better to know now that he couldn't handle her past, than to have him leave at the last moment, like Paul had done. Better to know she couldn't count on him before she was foolish enough to actually do so.

She didn't need Jason Sarantos. She really didn't, no

matter how much he seemed to touch her heart. She lifted her chin and gazed out across the lake, watching the play of the moon on the water.

She forced herself to calm her frantic mind and to focus on the moment. On the setting. On the magic of the evening. It was beautiful here. So beautiful it made her heart cry, because she knew it was fleeting. Just like every home she'd had, it would slip out of her fingers. There was no way she could afford the rent to live here, and she would not live on the charity of a man who wanted her baby.

Her fingers brushed against the cold metal of her bracelet, and she looked down at the piece she'd started to make for Jason. *Fire.* Maybe fire didn't mean igniting her dreams. Maybe fire meant giving up her dreams for some stability. Maybe that was what took the real courage, that moment of deciding to walk away from her dreams and accept a life of less to take care of her child. Astrid fingered the cool metal. Maybe it was time to give up on the jewelry. Maybe it was time to get a job. Health insurance. A steady paycheck, even if it was small.

A small part of her rippled with relief at the idea of having a steady paycheck, of not having to panic about her fluctuating and dwindling income from her jewelry. But at the same time, the most immense sense of loss assailed her. Her jewelry had been her one constant for all these years. She'd been able to pack her jewelry-making supplies with her each time she'd started anew. The jewelry had always been there for her. A sanctuary into which she could retreat. How many hours had she gone into the corner and huddled up with her designs and her beads, lost in a world that made her surroundings and dingy motel rooms disappear? If she took a full-time job, what time would she have left for her jewelry-making? Especially when the baby came?

That dream would die.

Tears began to trickle down Astrid's cheeks as she stared at the beautiful scenery. She hugged her belly. "What am I supposed to do?" she whispered. "I don't know what to do."

For once, just once, she wanted someone to take her hand and show her the way. She was so tired of trying to figure it out on her own, of trying to hold up the world by herself. And now she was supposed to guide a child, too? Even Harlan would be gone in the morning, their fragile connection too fleeting. "It's too much," she whispered. "I don't know how to do this—"

"Astrid?" Jason's low voice drifted around the side of the house, and she heard his feet crunching on the gravel pathway.

She hurriedly wiped her cheeks and took a deep breath as Jason walked around the corner. Her breath caught as he came into view. He looked like a gallant knight, come to her rescue. His hair was disheveled. His tee shirt was loose, his jeans low on his hips. The moonlight cast his face into a mixture of silver light and dark shadows, like he was emerging from the darkness to help her. Dammit. He was beautiful.

Agonized by how tempting he was, she tore her gaze away from him and looked out across the lake.

"Can we talk?" he asked.

She bit her lip, her emotions warring within her. Why had he come after her? Why hadn't he been so disgusted so as to let her go? She didn't want to have hope. Hope was cruel. Hope caused pain and agony. "I'm kind of tired," she said softly.

"That's okay. I am too." He grabbed the railing with both hands and then vaulted easily over it, the muscles in his arms and shoulders flexing as he hoisted himself up. Dammit. She remembered how strong his muscles were. She was vividly aware of what his body felt like beneath her hands. And now, she was viscerally conscious of the close distance between them on the tiny deck.

"Jason—"

"Hi." He sat down next to her on the narrow bench, his shoulder pressed up against hers. Astrid caught her breath, her heart racing at the feel of his warmth and strength so close.

"I'm sorry about my mother," he said.

Astrid swallowed, trying to calm the frenzied pace of her heart. For a moment, she wanted to retreat into the old Astrid, and tell him that it was okay, that he didn't need to apologize, but then she thought of Harlan, and his belief in her worthiness. She didn't deserve to be treated like the enemy, no matter what his mother's motivation had been. It wasn't okay, and it was a lie to politely say that it was. So, she nodded slightly, and simply said, "Thank you."

"Tell me about your mom."

She glanced over at him. "I already—"

"No." He propped his feet up on the railing and clasped his hands behind his head, as if he wasn't even paying attention to her. "Tell me about who she was. Tell me something you admired about her."

"Something I admired about my mother?" Astrid stared at him. "But she was a mess."

"She raised a daughter who is courageous, strong, and incredibly passionate about herself and living. I think she did something right. Tell me." He closed his eyes and leaned his head back against the house, waiting.

Fresh tears began to burn in Astrid's eyes. No one, not even herself, had ever suggested she look at the good side of her mother.

"There has to be something good," Jason said, his voice a low rumble in the dark night. "Everyone has something good about them."

"I don't know—"

Jason turned his head slightly to look at her. "My former wife was a workaholic," he said. "She was obsessed with money and fame. Anything that got in her way was an irritation, including me and our boys. My parents hated her from the first moment."

Astrid bit her lips. "I know what that's like." She would never forget how Paul's parents had made their disapproval of her so obvious when she'd met them. She'd been so ashamed of who she was. Looking back, it made her want to cry for how much she'd let them bother her. Today, she wouldn't be that victim again. She simply wouldn't.

"But you know what?" Jason continued. "Even though Kate was cold as hell to us, three times a year, she went to South America on a trip to bring medical care to people who had none. I thought she did it for the fame and to be able to put a check box on her resume, but one day, she got a letter from someone in the program. They told her that a young girl who she'd treated for a brutal infection had survived. When Kate heard that the little girl was going to live, she cried. She was alone in our den, and she didn't know I was watching. She didn't cry to impress anyone. She cried because that little girl had another chance to live." Jason closed his eyes again. "Maybe Kate didn't have space in her heart for us, but I realized that night that she went to South America for the sole reason that she cared. She helped a lot of people over the years."

Astrid rubbed the back of her neck, thinking about the story. Not just that Kate maybe had more depth than people thought, but more importantly, the fact that despite all he'd been through, Jason was still able and willing to see the good in her. He hadn't judged her on her flaws, and had kept his heart open to see what beauty there was in her soul.

Maybe he wasn't like Paul.

Maybe Jason was different.

"Your turn," he said. "What's good about your mom? About your childhood?"

Astrid took a deep breath and for the first time in her life, tried to think of her mother and her childhood without being embarrassed by it. "She always protected me," she said quietly. "Some of her boyfriends thought that they could jerk me around, and every time it happened, she took me and left him within a half hour. No one ever got to mess with me. Ever."

Jason smiled. "That's a good mom, right there, protecting her kid. I like that."

Something warm began to build inside her at his words, at his support of her mother. Something so beautiful she didn't even have the ability to name it. Emotions whirling inside her, Astrid hugged the blanket tighter around her. "I hated being on the move all the time, but one of my favorite memories was driving down the highway with her on the way to our next destination. She would crank the radio to an oldies station, and we would belt out the lyrics, going totally crazy. I loved that. Singing with my mom always made things seem better."

Jason shifted so he was facing her. He slid his arm along the back of the bench, tucking it behind her head. His eyes were dark in the night, but he was watching her intently. "She sounds like a real character, living her own life no matter what anyone said. Like her daughter does."

Astrid's pulse hummed at his nearness, at the intensity of his gaze. She tried to hold her head up so it didn't rest on his arm, but his shoulder was too strong, too tempting, and she slowly relaxed against him. "That's for sure," she said. "My mom never did anything because it would make others happy. She lived for herself...and for me." Looking back, Astrid had to admit that they'd always had enough food, enough money for a roof over their heads, even if it was just the car. Was that why her mom had always chosen men with money? To make sure her daughter was taken care of in that unconventional lifestyle?

Jason's fingers rubbed along her upper arm, a seductively tempting touch that was more than sensual. It was emotional, dragging her right down into his world, and she didn't want to resist it. It just felt too good to connect with him like this.

"Why haven't you talked to her in years?" he asked. "What happened?"

Astrid's good feeling fled, replaced with the bitterness and anger she'd associated with her mother for so long. She looked down at her hands and began to fiddle with her bracelets. "When I started to date Paul, she was furious with me. She didn't want me to get married. Now that I was old enough to date men and toy with them, along with her, she wanted me to stay with her, so we could run around and be girls together. She wanted us to look for a father-son team to hook up with. But when I became pregnant..." Astrid thought back to her mother's reaction, her fury that Astrid would do something so foolish. "I was ecstatic. I thought it was my chance to have the family that I'd never had growing up. A mom, a dad, a daughter, a nice house. It was my dream."

Jason began to play with the hair at the nape of her neck. "She didn't want that for you?"

"She told me I was being a fool. That I wasn't cut out for that. She was so angry at me, and for the first time in my life, I refused to go along with her. I told her I was staying with Paul when she decided to leave town again. She said I was on my own and left." Astrid swallowed, fighting back the feelings of betrayal. "When I lost the baby, and Paul walked out, I tried to call her. I left a message on her voicemail, and she never called back. She never came back to help me. Only Harlan did." She would never forget that sense of abandonment when she'd realized her mother had cut her out. "She finally called me over a year later. I missed the call and she didn't leave a message. And that's the last I've heard from her."

"Shit, Astrid." Jason sighed, still watching her. "You've never had anyone stick by you, have you?"

Astrid sat up, pulling away from Jason. "I don't need anyone," she said tartly. "I can do it myself."

He didn't move. He just sat there watching her. "We all need someone," he said quietly. "It's human nature."

"It's dangerous."

He shrugged. "Yeah, it is." He moved his hand to cup the back of her neck. "I know that it fucking sucks to be wrong about someone. To trust them and then have them let you down. But you survive it. We all do. As humans, we always find a way to keep going." He tightened his grip on her neck, pulling her closer. "You're so courageous, Astrid. Don't let fear stop you from living, or from trying to make your dreams a reality."

Astrid tensed as he leaned forward to kiss her, and she blocked him with a hand on his chest. "Don't," she whispered. "Please don't."

He paused, but didn't retreat. "You have no sense of how amazing you are, do you? You have the most beautiful soul, and you have so much love in your heart. That little baby is going to be the luckiest kid around to have you for a mother."

"No." Panic clawed at her. "Don't lie to me, Jason. I'm so tired of being lied to. I know that I have no idea how to be a good mother. I have no money. I have no income. What do I have to offer a child?" As the words tumbled out, a grim reality came to light. "I'm going to be like my mother," she whispered in horror. "That's why she went from man to man. Not because she liked them, but because she had no other resources to provide for me—"

"That's bullshit," Jason snapped. "You're not going to be like your mother. There are always choices. There are a lot of ways to support a child, and she chose that because of her own needs or issues that had nothing to do with you. You're not like that, and you won't choose that life, because it's not what you want. You yearn for stability and you'll find a way to do it." His fingers tightened on the back of her neck. "I believe in you, Astrid, and I won't walk away—"

"What is wrong with you?" She stood up, needing to get away from him, freaking out at the way he kept saying all those magical things she wanted to believe, and making promises she knew he wouldn't keep. "Why do you see all these great things when you look at me?" She held out her arms. "Look at me, Jason! Really look at me! I'm not some angel who has swept in to bring light into your life! I'm a mess! I'm flawed! Don't you see? You think I'm this amazing creature, and I'm *not*. You've created this image in your head of how amazing I am! Am I really supposed to trust it? What's going to happen when you wake up one morning and realize that I'm just me? That this woman who you convinced yourself was an angel because she could give you a baby is just ordinary, or worse than ordinary?'

His face darkened in denial. "You're not ordinary," he growled.

"I am! Dammit, Jason, stop trying to seduce me with all these words." She thudded her palm against her chest. "See me for who I really am, Jason. Stop living in your world of fantasy, and stop thinking that I can sweep down and fix your life. I'm not that girl. I'm the one who will come in and bring turbulence and chaos. I'll push you away because I'm terrified of being hurt. I won't let you in my bed because I don't want to give up my space. I'm a mess, Jason! A mess!"

"I don't care!" Jason was on his feet now, fury boiling in

his eyes. "Shit, Astrid, why can't you see how amazing you are? I know what you're like, and I see the beauty in it—"

"What do you want in a woman, Jason?" His words were too beautiful, too tempting, and she could feel herself wanting to fall into them. "Tell me your dream. Don't talk about me. Tell me about the woman that you moved up here to find." She had to do something to make it clear to both of them that there was no fairytale romance developing between them. It was just cold, hard reality with no happy ending.

Jason paused before he answered. Had he heard the intensity of Astrid's voice, the plea for his honesty? He swore and ran his hand through his hair, and she could see him gathering himself, forcing himself to take a step back and answer her question. Her heart began to thud, because she sensed he was going to give her the truth. Did she want to hear it? Truly. Suddenly, she was terrified of what he was going to say, that he would prove her right that there was no hope for them together.

She didn't want to be right. She wanted to be *wrong*.

"I want a mother for Noah," he admitted. "I want a woman who will be warm and loving, who will adore him and make him feel like the most important thing in the world. He's never had that, and every kid deserves it."

Grim realization flickered through Astrid at his words, a sinking feeling because she knew she couldn't live up to that standard. "What else?"

"I want that for me, too. I want a partner who loves me beyond words, and who lets me love her beyond comprehension." He met her gaze. "I want the fairytale, Astrid. I want a wife who comes to the store with me every day. We spend all day together at the pizza shop making our dream come true, and then we come home at night to a family. Yeah, we might argue or disagree, and I'm sure we'd drive each other mad sometimes, but in the end, we'll all know that the love that binds us is so unconditional that we go to bed at night feeling like each other's arms is the safest damn place in the world."

Astrid stared at him, overwhelmed by his vision. Yearning pulsed through her, a sense of longing so strong she felt her entire heart ache. It was beautiful and perfect. In a few short sentences, he'd articulated every dream she'd had her whole life, starting from when she was a little girl and she'd wanted that family from a child's perspective, all the way through to this very moment, when she wanted it as a woman and a future mother.

"Yeah, I know, babe. It would be amazing, wouldn't it? You want it, too. I can see it in your eyes." Jason took her hand, and pressed it to his chest, over his heart. "See, Astrid? We're not so different, are we? Neither of us are teenagers anymore, sweetheart. We've both been through hell, and we know what we want, and we know when we find it. We've found it with each other. Stop fighting it, Astrid, and let it happen. Give us a chance."

Longing burned through her so intensely that her chest actually hurt. For a split second, she imagined saying 'yes' to him. To trusting him. To letting him into her heart. And the moment she did, she was hit with raw fear, an absolute terror of being wrong. "And what if I do, Jason? What if I let down my guard and allow myself to believe in your beautiful words of forever, and then I lose the baby?"

Shock flashed over his face. "Don't say that—"

"But what if it happens? What if I lose the baby, stripping you of your dream that I can give you a family? And then you run across some woman who fits your vision? A woman with a couple kids. She's domestic. She bakes cookies. She knows how to decorate a home." Astrid's throat burned as she spoke, as the truth of her shortcomings became more and more glaring. "A woman who is everything you want?"

"Hell, Astrid, you're everything I want—"

"Am I?" She forced herself to speak the truth, knowing that she had to say it. "I don't want to bake pizza, Jason. I want to design jewelry."

Regret flashed over his face, but then he shrugged. "We can work with that—"

"I don't know if I can love someone else's child the way he would deserve. I don't know how to bake cookies." She met his gaze, and her heart broke at the disappointment in his eyes. "And I will run away if I think you're going to hurt me. I don't know how to stay, Jason. In my fantasies, I want to be the woman you yearn for, but I'm not."

"You could be—"

"I'm not. That's why I was leaving Birch Crossing, Jason. I have all these friends here, and I was still leaving. I don't know how to stay." Her heart aching, she peeled the fire bracelet off her wrist and handed it to him. "I made this for you, and I can't even get this right. How could I get a partnership with you right? I can't do it, and I won't lie to myself or you that I can. Paul was right. I'm not that woman."

"Dammit, Astrid—"

"No." She held up her hand as she pulled open the window to go inside the house. "If you are the good guy you say you are, you won't let the baby trick you into making promises that neither of us can keep. I've been through it once. I won't do it again." Then, before he could reply, she stepped over the window frame into the house and pulled the glass shut.

As she reached for the shade to close it, Jason set his palm on the window. She knew he was asking her to reconsider, to give them a chance. For a split second, she placed her hand over his, and the cool glass burned her skin, reminding her of the reality of how different they were. "I can't," she whispered, and then she closed the shade, blocking him from her life.

CHAPTER SIXTEEN

JASON WIPED the sweat from his brow, surveying his cafe. He'd left his parents at home to watch Noah, and he hadn't invited them to the store to help him or hang out while he organized.

He was doing it himself, and he was doing it in time for the Fourth of July grand opening. He'd been working his ass off for almost three days straight, and the place was looking damned good. He had only thirty-six hours until opening. It wasn't much time, but hell, he was going to make it.

But even as his vision came into shape, Jason was grimly aware that not a single person from town had stopped in to see him in the last week. When he'd gone into Wright's, conversation had stopped and silence had greeted him. A few people had even suggested that he move back to New York and find a woman there, which told him that the town had taken up arms to protect Astrid from him. No small town hospitality was being extended in his direction, that was for certain.

Granted, Jason liked the fact Astrid had an entire town supporting her. It told him it was exactly the kind of town he'd hoped it was, but at the same time, being ostracized by the entire community had not been a part of his vision. He was becoming increasingly aware that unless something changed, not a damn soul would darken his threshold and patronize his store once he opened.

He had no idea what the hell to do about it. He'd stopped by to see Astrid three times, but she had never been there. He'd called her, but she never answered her phone or returned his messages. He knew she was still living there because all her belongings were still inside, but she might as well have left, given how inaccessible she was.

He didn't know where she was going all the time, and it was starting to get to him. He needed to see her, to talk to her, to be in her presence. Hell, last night, he'd spent ten minutes staring at the carriage house when he'd gotten home, hoping for some sign of activity from within, but there'd been nothing. Her car had been there, but the lights had been off. Since it was three in the morning, he couldn't bring himself to wake her up, but man, how he'd waited for some sign that she was still awake.

Nothing. So, he'd gone to bed without talking to her yet again.

As hard as he'd been working, it hadn't been enough to take his mind off Astrid. He kept thinking of her past, of the yearning in her voice. He *knew* she wanted what he did, but at the same time... Shit. He couldn't handle another woman who didn't want to be a part of his life. Running a pizza store was long hours, and if his wife refused to be a part of it, it would be the same kind of marriage he'd had before. Two separate lives.

And Noah. His son deserved a real mother. Jason couldn't get entangled with a woman who wouldn't love his son, like Astrid had claimed. But even as he thought it, anger roiled through him. He didn't believe that she didn't have the capacity to love. He just didn't. It made no sense! He slammed the hammer down on his thumb, missing the nail, and pain shot through his hand. "Shit!"

"Lovely language for a father," Eppie said as she strode into the cafe. "What kind of example are you setting for your son?"

Jason groaned at the interruption. "Listen, Eppie—"

"The store looks much improved," she said as she walked briskly across the newly finished floorboards. Eppie was wearing a wide-brimmed violet hat with yellow pom-poms hanging from the brim. They swung about like minia-ture lemons taunting him as she moved her head. "I didn't think a city slicker would have a vision that fit with this town, but I was wrong." She tilted the hat back. "Nice work, Doc."

Jason grinned, then cocked his head to study her as a sudden idea popped into his mind. Eppie was connected to the community more than anyone he'd met. She could reach people. "I don't suppose I could hire you to be my marketing guru? You'd be in charge of spreading the word and getting people to come here."

Eppie's gray eyebrows shot up so high they disappeared under the brim of her hat. "Son, I haven't sold my services for money in forty years. You can't pay me for that kind of thing. The value I bring to this world far exceeds any translation to monetary value."

He leaned on the counter, suddenly feeling weary. "Well, then, what would it take to get your help? The whole damn town hates me."

"Well of course they do." She folded her arms across her chest. "You deserve it."

Anger rippled through Jason, the same anger that had festered inside him for all the years of his marriage, when Kate had lashed out at him each time he'd dared to ask that she be present for some aspect of their children's lives or their partnership. "Is that right? And why is that?"

Eppie wandered over to the refrigerated glass case that was already holding an assortment of drinks, plus a few beers for his own consumption. "Really, Jason? You have to ask why?" She pulled open the door and helped herself to a beer, selecting the most expensive beer he had in there: a German microbrew that he'd brought up from New York.

"Yeah, I do." He couldn't keep the irritation out of his voice. "And those aren't for sale. I don't have a liquor license."

She popped the top. "I wasn't offering to buy it, so we're all good there." She took a long drink, and then sighed with contentment. "I have to admit, that I love Birch's Best. It's the best local brew in the state. But there is just something satisfying about a good German ale." She pulled a bag of chips off the display rack and opened it. "You really should buy local with the chips, Jason. Who in town wants to buy chips made in Minnesota?"

"They're the best damn chips made," he scowled. "What do you want, Eppie?" Piles of supplies were stacked on the counter behind her. He still had so many things still to set up. He didn't have time and he wasn't in the mood to take grief from Eppie.

She stuck her nose into the bag and inhaled deeply. "Damn, Doc, those do smell good."

"Of course they do." He gave up trying to get anything useful out of her and strode across the store. He ripped open a box of paper plates and began unloading them to the shelves beneath the front counter.

"Astrid went to the doctor," Eppie said.

Jason whirled around, his heart leaping. "She did? Is everything okay?"

"Yep. Just fine." Eppie took a chip out of the bag and

peered at it. "What are the red specks? It looks like cayenne pepper. Who in God's name wants to eat a chip with cayenne pepper on it?"

"Is she healthy? The baby's fine?" He set the plates on the counter, leaning forward to study Eppie, to search her face for secrets she might not be telling him. "Did Astrid tell the doctor what had happened before? What's the name of the doctor?" He pulled out his phone. "I'm going to look him up. I'll make some calls to ensure he's legit."

Eppie raised her brows. "You know, I think I agree with the rest of the town. You are indeed a bastard." Then she popped the chip in her mouth, and her eyes widened with surprise. "Holy crap. These are incredible. Where in God's green earth did you find these?"

"I grew up with them. My aunt and uncle make them." He was barely paying attention to the chip discussion. "What the fuck is going on with Astrid, Eppie? Tell me everything. I need to know."

"If you were a real man, you'd ask her yourself."

Jason stared at her, outrage boiling through him. Son of a bitch. He was so tired of being accused of not being enough. He'd tried so fucking hard with Kate. He'd moved his life up north for his son. He'd moved Astrid into his damn carriage house and tried repeatedly to contact her. What the hell else was he supposed to do? "I think you should leave," he said, unable to keep the bitterness out of his voice. "I'm done with this conversation."

"I'm not." Eppie ate another chip and sat down at one of the tables. "See, here's the way I see it, Jason. Astrid is a treasure, a real treasure, but she doesn't trust anyone. Not even me, or Clare, not really."

"I know that," he said tightly. "I have work to do. You can leave." He strode across the room and ripped open another box. Flour. Great. Some dead weight was exactly what he needed. He shouldered the cartons into the back room, relishing how fucking heavy they were.

"No one has ever believed in her," Eppie called out. "Even Astrid doesn't believe in herself."

Jason ignored her as he began to set the bags on the shelves. How in the hell did the fact Astrid had problems make him the bad guy? He'd fucking tried.

"She can't even design jewelry anymore," Eppie said, her voice carrying into the rear of the store with surprising ease. "Her spirit is broken."

Jason rested his forehead against the cool metal of the shelves, too drained to keep working. "So, what's your point?"

Eppie walked into the back room, still munching on the chips. "My point, Jason, is that you're a bastard because you gave up on her."

"I didn't—"

"Just like you gave up on your marriage."

Jason scowled. "I didn't give up on my marriage," he snapped. "Don't go there, Eppie. I've had enough of this conversation."

"Even though you went through the actions of trying, you gave up in your heart. That's where it counts. All the words and actions in the world can't make up for a lack of faith." She raised her brows. "It's not the marriage that was the problem, Jason. It's not Astrid. It's you. You have no heart left. You have nothing to give Astrid, or your son, or even this store. You just want to bleed it all dry and use it to hold you up because you can't hold yourself up anymore."

Jason stared at her. "Fuck that," he snapped. "I've been holding up the damn world. I've given it everything I have."

Eppie raised her brows, raised the empty bag of chips and let the crumbs drop all over his new floor. "No, you haven't. You've got shit, Jason Sarantos, and until you figure that out, you'll never have anything more. Including Astrid." Then she dropped the bag and walked out.

Jason stared after her, fury roiling inside him. How dare she accuse him of giving up? She had no idea about his marriage, or Lucas, or anything.

She was wrong.

She was so damn wrong.

But he didn't move. He didn't unpack another box. He didn't make any plans for his grand opening.

He just stood there in his back room, alone.

Always alone.

Even in his marriage, he'd been alone.

And in this store...he looked around at the dream he'd worked so hard to achieve, at the polished wood, the shiny fixtures, the well-organized shelves of ingredients and supplies, and suddenly, it didn't look like the key to a new life, a new future.

It looked like nothing.

~

"What are you doing?"

Astrid jumped at the small voice right behind her. She spun around to see Noah standing in her living room. The boy's blond hair was sticking out from under a Yankees cap, and he was wearing a New York Jets football jersey. His blue eyes were fixed on hers without reservation, with the unabashed curiosity of a six year old.

She glanced at the moving box she was filling up. "I'm...um...rearranging."

Noah looked around the room. "It looks like you're moving. We had boxes like that when we moved up here."

She thought of Noah tattling to Jason, and quickly shook her head. "Oh, no, I'm unpacking." She took her new lamp from Emma out of the quilt she'd wrapped it in so carefully. "See?" She set it on the kitchen counter. "What do you think? Does it look good there?"

Noah tilted his head to study it. "No. It looks too fancy for a kitchen. A kitchen should be stainless steel so you can keep it clean."

Astrid stifled a smile. "Stainless steel, huh? Is that what you had in New York?"

"Yep." Noah eyed the fridge. "I'm thirsty. Do you have any juice?"

"Um, sure." Astrid hurried over to the fridge and peered inside to see what Clare and Emma had left her. "I have ice tea and orange juice."

"Orange, please." Noah perched on a kitchen chair while she poured it. "My mom liked stainless steel."

"Did she?" Astrid set the juice in front of him, suddenly feeling awkward. What did one say to a child who had lost a parent? "I bet she loved you a lot."

Noah studied her. "Maria loves me a lot," he said. "She cried when we left."

"Maria?" Astrid glanced restlessly at the boxes she still needed to pack. She had to get the open ones out of sight before Jason came home, in case he came in. He hadn't yet, but he'd waited in the driveway last night for what felt like forever. He'd sat there watching her house, no doubt waiting for a sign that she was still awake. She'd barely gotten her light out in time after she'd heard his car arriving, and she'd sat in the darkness for so long, waiting for him to give up.

It had taken him a long time, and she'd wanted desperately to open the door and invite him in. She'd wanted to stop fighting her need to see him. To stop trying to be smart and practical by keeping her heart protected from him. "Who's Maria?'

"My nanny." Noah took a gulp of the orange juice. "We

used to go to the movies every Friday, and she let me order the big popcorn." He sighed, a big shaky sigh that made Astrid's heart tighten. "I miss Maria," he said softly.

"Oh, sweetie." Astrid sat down at the table, her heart aching for the tears brimming in his eyes. She remembered so clearly what it was like to be six and trying to find her way in a new place. She'd moved to Kansas City on her sixth birthday, moving into an apartment that didn't allow animals. "I had a kitten when I was five," she said. "Her name was Chocolate Chip. I had to leave her behind when I moved, and I missed her so much."

Noah studied her. "Was she black?"

"She was white with black spots. She used to sleep on my bed."

"My mom is allergic to cats and dogs," Noah said.

Astrid nodded. "Some people are—"

"She's dead, you know," Noah said. "She's in the spirit world. She's not coming back."

Astrid's throat tightened. As hard as her life had been, she'd always had her mother. "I'm sure she visits you from heaven," she said. "Angels do that."

"My mom wouldn't do that," Noah said matter-of-factly. "She's too busy. I'm sure she's working in heaven. People need her help. She's important."

Astrid was suddenly filled with sadness for Noah, for a child who was taught that kind of lesson. She thought of her mother, and all the hours they'd spent together. Men had come and gone, but in the end, it had always been Astrid and her mom in the car, onto their next destination. "Yes, she was busy, but that doesn't change how much she loves you. Parents can be a little crazy, but they always love their children more than anything. It's how they are."

Astrid had a sudden memory of her mother buying her a Dairy Queen blizzard on her tenth birthday to celebrate her turning to double digits. She still remembered so clearly her mom counting out the exact change, the way the sunlight had sparkled on the coins that her mom had saved up so carefully for Astrid's birthday. She would never forget the delight of ordering her first Blizzard, the pride she felt as she carried it outside to the picnic table to eat, all by herself. Her own Blizzard, on her birthday.

Noah studied her thoughtfully. "That's what my dad says. That parents always love their kids, even if they forget to show it."

"It's true."

"Are you a mom?"

A lump settled in Astrid's throat. "Sort of."

Noah nodded, apparently not concerned about her half-answer. "Is your mom dead, too?"

Sudden fear leapt through her at his question. "I don't think so." But even as she said it, she realized she didn't know. Would anyone contact her if her mother had died? Or would her mom have simply passed away with no one caring, and no one noticing?

He looked at her. "How come you don't know? Shouldn't you know?"

"Well, I haven't seen her for a while."

"Oh." He nodded. "Like when my mom went to South America to help people."

Astrid laughed softly, trying to imagine her flighty mom injecting people with medicine. "Yes, exactly like that."

Noah nodded sagely. "I'm going to hunt dragonflies," he said, changing the subject with the alacrity of a child. "Do you want to come?"

She raised her brows. "Dragonflies? Where?"

"On the dock. There are like a billion of them down by the lake. I'm going to catch a bunch and then let them go in my bedroom so I have company when I go to bed. Don't you think that would be awesome?"

Astrid laughed, remembering the first time she'd seen dragonflies. "Did you ever look at their wings? They're really beautiful."

He held up his hands so his palms were about six inches apart. "And they're huge! I've never seen such massive bugs!" He jumped up, getting excited. "You have to come. My dad won't let me go down by the water without a grownup, but grandma is making curtains for dad's shop. My grandpa is in the kitchen making pizza sauce, and Dad's at the store." He grabbed her hand. "Come on! You have to!"

Astrid hesitated. "I really need to unpack—" Then she saw Noah's crestfallen look, and sudden resolution surged through her. She'd spent too many lonely nights as a kid while her mom had gone out on dates. Screw that. If she could give back what she'd wanted, she was doing it right now. "We're going to need jars to keep the dragonflies in once we catch them—"

"I have some in the shed! Let's go!" Noah raced to the door, shrieking with delight.

Astrid couldn't help but chuckle as she followed him out, her heart lifted by the exuberance of youth. And as she stepped outside into the beautiful afternoon, she knew playing with Noah was the right choice. It would be her final salute to her dream home, a final afternoon at the lake before she left. A memory she could hold with her. It was good. It was how it was supposed to be.

IT WAS ALMOST nine o'clock by the time Jason jogged up the stairs to his son's bedroom, swearing at himself. Once again, he'd gotten home later than he'd planned, too late to put

Noah to bed. Was it too late to talk to him? Would Noah be asleep already?

He quietly pushed the door open. "Noah? You still up?"

There was no reply, and regret coursed through Jason. He stepped inside and shut the door. He could see his son sleeping in the moonlight. Another day had passed without him seeing his son. It wasn't supposed to be like this in Maine. Noah was supposed to love the pizza store and want to hang around with his dad. But the youth had no interest. Instead, he had wanted to go to camp and hang out with his newly discovered grandparents.

Alone with his work, Jason had driven himself hard all day, unable to get Eppie's accusations out of his head. What did she mean by them? He still didn't understand it. With a weary sigh, Jason started to sit down on the bed, then leapt up when Noah erupted from the blankets with a shriek of outrage. "Dad! Watch out!"

"What is it?" Jason whirled around, his adrenaline jacked as he searched for the threat.

"You might squish the dragonflies."

"The what?" Jason stared at his son. "What are you talking about?"

"They're sleeping." Noah's hair was askew as he stared accusingly at Jason. "Did you know dragonflies sleep at night?"

"No, I didn't." Jason stared suspiciously at his son. "Are there real dragonflies in your room?"

"Of course there are." Noah ran his hand over the blanket where Jason had been about to sit, and then nodded. "There aren't any right there. You can sit on that spot."

"Well, good to know." Jason eased himself carefully down, waiting for another screech of outrage, but Noah just curled up happily under the blankets. "How many dragonflies are in your room?"

"Fifty-six," Noah said proudly. "That's a lot, isn't it?"

"Fifty-six? It's a ton. I'm so impressed." Jason looked around the room, wondering what the place would be like in the morning when all the dragonflies started flying around. He grinned, thinking about how much he would have loved that at Noah's age. "How on earth did you catch fifty-six dragonflies?

"Astrid helped me catch them. She's nice."

Something shifted inside Jason. "Astrid helped you?"

"Yeah." Noah beamed at him. "Everyone else was too busy, so Astrid went with me." His lower lip went out in a pout. "She wouldn't let me fall in the water. I tried six times, and each time she stopped me." Then he brightened. "I got wet in the marshes though. That was cool."

Jason raised his brows. "Astrid took you into the marshes? We have a marsh near here?"

"Yeah, there are frogs in there, and even turtles. And we saw a snake!" Noah held out his hands so they were as far apart as he could reach. "It was like that long! Maybe fifty feet!"

Jason laughed at his son's exuberance. "I used to trap snakes when I was little."

"You did? No way." Noah sat up in bed, his eyes wide. "Can you show me how? Can we keep them? I could get a box for my room and they could live in there." He swung his feet out from under the covers. "Let's go now. Can we? I don't have camp tomorrow. It's Saturday, right?"

Jason ruffled his son's hair. "It's nighttime, Noah, and I have to go back to the store."

"No, come on. You can't go back. There are bats in these woods. Bats! Astrid showed me some of them where they were sleeping under the eaves of the garage. They look like little black fur balls tucked up there."

"Astrid showed you *bats?*" Jason glanced in the direction

of the carriage house. Astrid had actually taken his son into the marshes and hunted for frogs, snakes and *bats*? He almost started laughing at the image of Astrid traipsing around after rodents, with her colorful scarves, hand-crafted jewelry and audacious smile. Then his amusement faded as he thought of Eppie's claims, of Astrid's rejection, of the whole town condemning him. Astrid was so far out of his reach, and he had no idea how to change that.

"Oh, yeah." Noah leapt out of bed and grabbed his shoes off the floor. "Come on, Dad. I'll show you. Maybe we'll see the bats flying around. Can we go now? Can we?"

For a moment, Jason hesitated, thinking of all the work he had to do to fix the store...and suddenly, he didn't want to go back there tonight. He had left his medical practice for a reason, and that reason was sitting on the bed in front of him. "Yeah, sure, Noah. Let's go find some bats."

Noah shrieked with delight, making Jason grin as his son yanked on sneakers and raced into the hall. As he followed his son out the door, he couldn't help but feel he was still missing something. But what?

But he knew what it was.

He was missing Astrid. She was supposed to be there with them.

CHAPTER SEVENTEEN

ASTRID HUMMED to herself as she sketched another dragonfly, trying to replicate the shimmering iridescence of their wings. She'd been so inspired by the dragonflies today while she'd been hunting them with Noah. She shaded in some pink and some blue, with a faint hint of yellow. She felt alive and excited, rejuvenated by the creatures she'd helped Noah find earlier. They were so bold and daring as they flew around, streaking through the air as if they owned it, their wings so beautiful.

She'd never used dragonflies in her jewelry before, but after seeing them, she wanted desperately to try to capture their beauty and bring it to life. She felt like she could channel their elusive confidence and beauty into her own being, if she could figure out how to make them come alive in her art.

She finished her sketch and sat back, inspecting it. But even as she studied it, her excitement began to fade. It was just a flat, two-dimensional image. She hadn't done it justice. She hadn't brought the magic to life. She could already tell that if she tried to make earrings from her sketch, they wouldn't be good enough.

"Crap!" Frustrated, she shoved back from the table and walked out onto the deck. The sun was setting and it was getting dark. How many days had it been since she'd moved into the carriage house? Long enough to find her muse in the idyllic setting, and yet she hadn't accomplished anything. She'd come no further on her jewelry. She had no leads on a job. She hadn't found any affordable housing that was decent enough to raise a child in.

She still had Harlan's key, but she felt weird moving in there. She'd stopped by once to check it out, and it had felt really empty and depressing, almost as if a dark shadow haunted the place. It was a tiny cabin on the lake, hidden in the darkness of trees, isolated from anything else. Harlan's presence was all over it, with his belongings silently waiting for his return from who knew where. She knew she couldn't make her home there. It wasn't the answer for her.

She'd sent out ten resumes to places in Maine, New Hampshire and Vermont. She'd called sixteen art galleries and none of them had openings. Three jewelry stores. No one had been impressed with what she had to offer.

A part of her had been relieved that she couldn't get a job and be forced to give up her dream.

And another part of her had been terrified at the prospect of continuing to rely on her dying business.

"What do I do now?" she asked the night.

There was no answer except the forest and lake sounds. The croak of bullfrogs from the marsh. The hoot of an owl. The call of a loon. Astrid closed her eyes and listened. A cold chill crept up her arms as the loon switched to its call that sounded like a dying woman, a female screaming as she was brutally killed.

Astrid's eyes snapped open as goose bumps slithered down her spine. She knew the haunting scream was simply the loon. Not a woman. But it made her think of her mother. Where was she? What was happening? What if she had died, and Astrid had never heard about it, leaving her to die alone? Her mother had no one besides Astrid, which meant that now she was alone.

Noah had lost his mother so bravely. Astrid still had hers, and yet she'd blown her off. Would she want her child to do that? To give up on her? She knew she wouldn't be perfect as a mother, probably no better than her mother was. Did she want her child to ditch her?

God, no. She would love that child, with everything she had.

A sweat broke out on her brow as she pressed her hand to her belly. What did she have to offer this baby? Herself? And what else? What family? All she had was Jason's judgmental parents. What kind of life was that for her child? Astrid's mom was a mess, sure, but in her own way, she'd loved Astrid so unconditionally. Astrid suddenly thought of what her mom must have felt like the day she'd realized she was pregnant with Astrid, and realized she was going to have to raise her daughter by herself. It had been hard, yes, Astrid knew that. And yet, Astrid had never felt alone or abandoned, or worried she wasn't loved. Wasn't that the message she wanted her child to have?

Suddenly, Astrid missed her mother with such aching fierceness she couldn't even think. She rushed back into the house and grabbed her phone. Her fingers shaking, she looked up her mom's phone number and pressed 'Send.' "I can't believe I'm doing this," she muttered as her hands shook. The loon called again, and Astrid shivered, desperate to hear her mother's voice and to know she was all right.

The phone beeped twice, and a recording told her that the number she'd dialed was no longer in service. Disappointment raged through her, a raw, stark loss that crumbled her to the couch. She pressed her forehead to her hands at the sudden gaping loneliness. How would she find her mother? *How?* All she had was her brother and... Harlan! He might be gone, but he did have a cell phone. Astrid quickly called her brother, who picked up on the first ring. His voice was rough and raw, as if he'd been in a fight. "You okay?" he asked bluntly, without preamble, and she knew he had answered the phone only out of concern for her.

"Yes, fine, but I want to find Mom. Do you know where she is?" Astrid held her breath after she blurted out the question.

There was a long silence. "Why do you want to know?"

"Because I want to see her. Do you know?"

Another long silence. So long that she began to think he'd hung up on her, or walked away from the phone. "Harlan?"

"She's sick, Astrid."

Astrid gripped the phone. "Sick? What do you mean sick?"

"She's in a hospital in Portland."

"What?" That was so close. Portland was only an hour away. "How do you know? Why didn't you tell me?"

"I've kept track of her," he said. "But I haven't spoken to her since I was about ten. I just like to know where she is."

"What's the name of the hospital?"

Again, silence. "Why don't I go with you?" He made a growling noise of anger and tension. "I can try to be back in a week. We can go then."

"No. I have to do this for me. I want to do it." She grabbed a pen. "Where is she, Harlan? Tell me now!"

"Shit, Astrid. You sure?"

"Yes! I need to see her."

"Fine, but don't invest in her. She will always be who she is."

"I know that," she said. But for the first time in her life, she was okay with it. "Tell me where she is, Harlan."

The moment he gave her the name, she grabbed her keys and sprinted for the door.

~

"ROOM THREE-FOURTEEN," the receptionist at the front desk told Astrid. "Take the elevators at the end of the hall."

"Great! Thanks!" Her palms sweating, Astrid hurried down the white corridor, squinting against the bright lights of the hospital. It was almost midnight, but she'd managed to convince the nurse to let her visit her mom. She hadn't had to fake her desperation or tears, and she was frantic now to see her. How sick was her mom? How much time had she missed with her mother?

Astrid pounded at the elevator button, tapping her feet restlessly as the elevator slowly dinged its way down to her. After what felt like an eternity, the doors finally opened and she leapt inside and punched the button for the third floor.

Another agonizingly slow ride, during which Astrid got more and more nervous. What would she say? It had been so long, and the words they had exchanged before were so harsh. Such a judgment on each other and their lives.

The doors finally slid open, and for a long moment, Astrid didn't move. She just stared at the off-white hallway with its polished floors. Several medical students hurried by, looking exhausted, but thrilled and excited, as if someone had just come in with some horrific injury that they were going to get to see.

The doors began to close, and Astrid leapt through them,

her sneakers squeaking on the tile. The arrows pointed right to room three-fourteen, and slowly she began to walk. Then faster. By the time she reached the room, Astrid was running. She raced into the room. "Mom!"

The room was silent and dark, and for a moment, Astrid couldn't see anything. Finally, her eyes adjusted and she saw two beds. An empty one by the window. A small figure in the one by the door.

Her heart racing, Astrid hurried over to the occupied bed and scooted a chair up to the edge of it. "Mom?" she whispered, leaning over to see the figure.

The light was dim, but she managed to make out the face. Astrid's throat tightened when she saw her mother's familiar features. "Mom," she whispered, unable to keep the tears out of her voice. "I'm here."

Her mother's face was pinched and wrinkled. Her hair was disheveled and messy, which was such a stark difference from the woman who had always looked her best, because people judged based on looks. It was important to be deemed worthy. Astrid touched her hand, and she was shocked to feel how cold her mother's skin was. "Mom? It's me. Astrid. Wake up."

There was no response.

Desperation began to course through her. "Mom," she said more urgently. "Wake up. It's me—"

"She isn't going to wake up."

Astrid jumped and then whirled around. Standing in the doorway was a man with gray hair, a paunch belly and saggy jowls. He was wearing an old sweatshirt and a pair of ratty sneakers, and he was holding a cup of coffee. "Who are you?" she asked.

"I'm Ralph. Rosie's husband. You must be Astrid?"

Astrid squinted as Ralph flicked on the lights. He wasn't polished. He clearly wasn't rich. And he wasn't some hotshot looker. He was ordinary and worn out, but she immediately noticed that his eyes were kind and gentle. "My mom's married?"

Ralph nodded. "It will be two years next week."

"Two years?" Astrid stared at him in shock. None of her mother's marriages had lasted more than six months. And never had she married a guy as ordinary as Ralph.

"Yep." Ralph walked into the room and sat in the chair on the other side of the bed. He set his coffee down and took Rosie's hand in his. "Rosie," he said softly. "Astrid's here to see you. Did you know that?"

Astrid was shocked by the tenderness in his voice, by the love pouring out of him. No man had ever spoken to her mother like that. No one had ever held Rosie's hand so gently. Stunned, she looked at her mother's face, and then her heart went still when she saw Rosie in the light. She looked a hundred years old, with wrinkles and sallow skin. She looked like she was dying. "What's wrong with her?"

He met her gaze. "She's almost out of time, Astrid. She went into a coma this morning, and she won't come out of it. She has maybe a few hours left."

"What?" Panic hammered at Astrid. "But she can't die. I need to talk to her."

Ralph's eyes narrowed, and she thought she saw a flash of bitterness. "For years, she's been waiting for you to call her. For years, I've been trying to talk her into calling you. Neither of you did a damn thing, and now it's too late."

"But—"

"Talk to her now. She'll hear you. I'll give you a few minutes. Call me if there's a change." Ralph pressed his lips to Rosie's forehead, then grabbed his coffee and walked out, leaving Astrid with her mother.

For a long moment, Astrid simply stared at Rosie. She didn't know what to say. How could she apologize for a lifetime of not appreciating her own mother in two minutes? Tears burned in her eyes, and she tentatively reached for her mother's hand again. "Mom." Her voice cracked and she had to clear her throat. "Mom," she tried again. "I just want you to know that I love you. I always did, and I know you did the best you could for me."

There was no response, and Astrid gripped the bony hand more tightly. Her mother was only forty-seven. *Forty-seven.* And her life was over? How was that possible? It was so unfair. Astrid swallowed. "So, Ralph seems nice. It seems like he loves you—" She paused when she saw the wedding ring on her mother's hand.

It had a tiny diamond, no bigger than the head of a pin, and a plain wedding band. Her mother had always had huge diamonds, even if they were low quality. Anything to parade around and show the world she belonged to someone. To have such a plain ring meant one thing: Ralph hadn't had money to offer her mother. He'd had only love, and that had been enough for Rosie.

After eight marriages, countless men and a lifetime of being on the run, her mother had finally married for love. "Mom," she whispered, her heart filling. "I'm happy you found him." But even as the words left her mouth, she realized the tragedy of it. Her mom had found love too late. Death had come just when she'd found her place. "Dammit," she said. "That's not fair!"

Tears burned in her eyes and she bowed her head, pressing her mom's palm to her forehead. God, to feel her mother's hand on her again, it was too much. It was like she was a child again, feeling sick, and her mom would test her for fever. "Don't die," she whispered. "Please don't die. I'm so sorry that I never appreciated you. I'm so sorry I got mad at you. You were right about Paul. I lost the baby, and he left me." The words began to tumble out, hundreds of confessions and emotions she'd held so tightly for so long. "I'm pregnant," she finally whispered. "If everything goes okay, you'll have a grandbaby." She started to cry. "I wish that it could meet you, and see what a brave woman its grandma is."

She realized then that her mom hadn't been crazy or irresponsible. Her mom truly had been brave, fighting the world for Astrid and for herself, trying to make a living as best she could. She'd managed to find her way in a world that didn't favor women who didn't have an education or a background or a family to help them. Astrid was the weak one. She was the one who had lived in constant fear of bad things, of the world disapproving, of someone rejecting her. She was the one who had hidden from life, while Rosie had embraced it and gallivanted through it, finding pleasure and happiness wherever she could. "Dammit," she said. "I love you, Mom. I'm not ready to do this alone."

Her mother suddenly sucked in a breath, and her body lurched. "Mom!"

Ralph rushed into the room, his coffee spilling on the floor. "What happened? What's going on?"

"I think she's waking up. She just took a deep breath." Astrid clenched her mom's hand. "Mom, come on."

"Rosie, baby." Ralph took her mom's other hand and bent his head, sinking into his chair. "I love you, sweet girl. I'll always love you. You wait for me in heaven, because I'll be coming for you."

Astrid grabbed Ralph. "What are you doing? Don't encourage her to die—"

He ignored her as her mother's body lurched again. "Have a safe journey, Rosie. I'll always be with you."

Astrid suddenly realized what was happening. Her mother wasn't waking up. Her mother was dying. Right then. Right there. In front of her. Her spirit was leaving her body. "Mom!"

Astrid threw her arms around her mother. "I love you! Please don't leave. You have to stay!"

Her mother's body lurched once more, and then she went still, and all the air seemed to leave her.

"She's gone," Ralph said softly, laying his hand over her heart. Tears were streaming down his face as he pressed his lips to Rosie's mouth. "Rest in peace, my love. You deserve it."

Astrid felt her soul crumble as she listened to Ralph's beautiful words. She realized then that there was no place for her in the room. Ralph deserved his moment with Rosie. He was the one who had clearly, finally, loved her mother for who she was.

She stumbled back from the bed. "I'll get a nurse," she whispered.

Ralph didn't look up from Rosie as he continued to sob for the loss of the woman he loved.

Astrid made her way to the door and then turned back as she reached it. Something sparkled around her mother's throat, and Astrid realized it was one of the necklaces she had designed. It was one that was two intertwined hearts. Her mother had died wearing Astrid's necklace. And suddenly she knew that her mother had forgiven her, that the love had not died, that their hearts had always been intertwined even when they'd been apart. Astrid pressed her hand to her heart. "I love you too, Mom. Rest in peace."

As she said the words, the room suddenly seemed to brighten. Just for a split second, and then the lights faded again. Her mom's final farewell.

Astrid made it out of the room, but before she reached the nurse's station, pain shot through her belly. Gasping, she pressed her hands to her stomach, and stumbled. She made it another two feet, and then she collapsed.

JASON LEANED against the door of his son's room, watching him sleep. They'd spent almost two hours in the night woods, and it had been the best two hours he'd spent in a long time. It had brought back memories of his own childhood, and he'd had the best damn time.

This was why he'd moved to Maine.

Shit, it felt good to get something right.

But as he turned away, the darkness of the hallway caught his attention. The other bedrooms were empty, his own room silent. The only activity was the hum of the television in the den downstairs where his parents were watching the news.

Shit.

It wasn't enough.

Jason jogged down the stairs and ducked out past the den. He loped across the lawn to the carriage house. The front door was ajar, and he pushed it open. "Astrid?"

There was no answer from within, and alarm shot through him. "Astrid!" He flicked on the light and walked inside.

Cardboard boxes were stacked against the corner. She was moving again. Son of a bitch. *She was leaving him.*

Shit. Why hadn't he been able to get her to stay? What the fuck was he doing wrong?

"She's leaving you."

Jason didn't turn around at the sound of his father's voice, somehow not surprised that his father had followed him out to the carriage house. "Apparently."

"I left your mom when you were two years old."

Jason turned sharply. His father was leaning against the door frame, his arms folded loosely over his chest. "What?"

"It was too much pressure to be a father and a husband. I bailed."

"That makes no sense." Jason stared at his father, trying to grasp the words. "You guys have the best marriage."

"Yeah, now we do." His dad walked in and sat down on the couch. "It wasn't easy, though. She wanted more from me than I knew how to give. I wasn't that different from Kate back then. That's why I reacted the way I did when you brought Kate home. I used to be the way she was, so I knew instantly what kind of person she was."

Jason studied his father. "So what changed? When did you get into the dad thing?"

"Your mom did it. She loved me anyway. She said I was okay the way I was, and I could be how I wanted to be. It took all the pressure off, so I came back." He grinned. "As it turned out, the family and dad thing was okay after all." He pointed at Jason. "You blew it with Kate, you know. Your mom blames her, but it was you."

Jason pulled his shoulders back. "I know that."

"Do you?" His dad raised his brows. "You didn't accept what she was able to give. You saw her as less because she didn't fit your ideal. She knew she fell short, and she retreated. The further she retreated, the more you pressured her and found her inadequate. You pushed her away because you couldn't accept her for who she was, and you couldn't take responsibility for your own vision."

Jason narrowed his eyes. "I never stopped loving her."

"That's not the same thing," his dad said. "You can love the hell out of someone, but not accept them. It's different, and it's brutal as hell to do that to someone."

Jason clenched his jaw. "What's your point?"

"You're doing the same thing with Astrid."

Fury poured through him. "No, I'm not. I think she's amazing the way she is."

"Do you? Or do you think she's amazing because you think she'll do something for you? She'll give you a kid. She'll bring love and passion into your life. She'll be a mother for Noah. That's why you like her, Jason."

Jason narrowed his eyes. "What the hell's wrong with that?"

"You should be thinking about what you can give to her, no matter who she turns out to be. That's when you have a chance."

"Of course I think about that. She deserves to feel safe and secure—"

"Then give it to her," Mack said. "Truly give it to her." He stood up. "Your mom and I have an early night planned. Do me a favor and don't come back in for an hour or so." He grinned. "You might be shocked at what you hear."

Jason started laughing at his dad's tone. "Jesus, Dad. I don't want to hear that."

"Then don't come back for a while." His dad raised his brows. "Or are you going back to the store tonight? How's that going?"

Jason ran his hand through his hair. "Not so well."

His dad nodded. "Let me know if you need help."

"I'm naming it after my son," Jason said softly. "I'm not calling it Mack's Pizza."

Mack raised his brows. "Instead of naming it after the child who died, why don't you name it after the one you still have left? The one who wants you to notice that he's still around? Ever think of that?" And with that, he walked out, slamming the door shut behind him.

"See him? Of course I see Noah—" But his dad was already gone, obviously not interested in Jason's reply.

Jason stared after him. Name the store after Noah? It made sense, but at the same time, how could he let go of Lucas? There was so little to hold the boy's spirit alive and he was slipping away day by day. Naming the store after him made sense.

But he could see the point in naming it after Noah as well. Shit.

He paced to the window and leaned his palms against the frame, moodily staring out at the lake. His fingers brushed against cool metal, and he looked down to see a wire twisted into the shape of a heart. Two hearts, intertwined. The work was delicate and intricate, but it had an unfinished quality to it.

He turned and saw Astrid's work station, the place that meant so much to her. Frowning, he walked over to it and sat at the table. On the desk were drawings of dragonflies, ones he was sure were from today with his son. He picked one up, and swore softly. Her talent was indescribable. The magic with which she brought the colors of its wings to life was extraordinary. Stunned, Jason began to sift through her other designs.

He found a page of baby charms: baby shoes, a rattle, a teddy bear. All of them were drawn with such warmth and love he felt his heart tighten. Astrid had poured every emotion she had into the drawings, and he could practically feel the page vibrating with them. This was the woman who thought she didn't have love to give?

Another page had drawings of a phoenix, a glorious red and gold bird with tremendous feathery plumes. His heart literally stopped for a split second when he saw it, he was so stunned by the intensity of it. A single, golden tear was falling from its eye, leaving a red trail over its golden feathers. Its feet were consumed with flames, and they were falling in black ash to the ground. The agony in the bird's face was evident, so stark and raw it was chilling. There was no triumph for the bird, no indication that it was ever going to rise from the ashes and be reborn.

This phoenix was dying, and anyone looking at it would know it.

That was how Astrid saw the phoenix? Not as rebirth, but as death?

Sadness coursed through him and he turned to the next page, where the phoenix had become nothing but a pile of ashes. A few feathers scattered about, drifting as if an arid breeze was trying to blow them away. On top of the pile sat a silver chain, two hearts entwined. Death to love? To a partnership? To her child? The page was so stark and bare. No hope. No life. Just the end. Just hopelessness. Just a lack of a future.

Mesmerized, Jason leaned back, studying the design. He felt the agony of the bird. He knew what it was like. He *knew* it. And suddenly, he understood what Eppie had been telling him, what his father had been trying to tell him.

He was so consumed with his failings, with the past that had destroyed his family, that he saw the future only as ashes.

He had to let go. Of Kate. Of Lucas. Of his guilt.

No wonder Astrid had bailed on him. She was the smart one, the one who knew that it wasn't her job to fill the wound in his heart.

It was his.

He took the picture of the dying phoenix and folded it up as he headed toward the door. He strode over to his car and climbed in. The engine revved smoothly as Jason peeled out of the driveway.

Ten minutes later he pulled up in front of his store, shining his lights on the sign above the door. "Lucas's Pizza." For a long moment, Jason stared at it, then he got out of the car and walked over to it. He grabbed a drill from inside the store, and then carefully began to remove the sign from the front of the building.

The heavy wood fell hard as the final screw came loose, and it crashed to the ground with a loud crack that split the sign in half, right through his son's name. Pain jabbed through his chest as he watched his son's legacy splinter into pieces, the golden letters torn apart by the force of the impact.

Jason went down on one knee and picked up the top left corner, which still had the L and part of the U. The wood was cold and sharp in his hand. Inanimate and dead, just as his son was. As he held that crappy piece of wood in his hand, he realized that it had done nothing to bring his son back, or to help him heal. He didn't need a sign to hold Lucas in his heart, but there was another child, a six-year-old boy, who might need a sign to make the place his.

His heart feeling lighter than it had in years, but also heavier, Jason stacked the wood on the curb for the garbage truck. He backed away from the pile and bowed his head. "Good-bye, Lucas. It's time for you to go." He blew his son a kiss, then turned and walked into his store.

He headed straight toward the back to where he knew he'd stashed an extra piece of plywood. He grabbed a Sharpie from the register as he passed by, and it took only a few minutes to make a new sign.

Noah's Place.

A sense of rightness filled him as he stepped back to look at it. It wasn't much, but it was a start. Noah would be psyched. It was right. Then, on a whim, Jason added a dragonfly in each corner. One for Noah, one for himself, one for Astrid and one for the baby. Yeah, that was good—

His phone buzzed in his pocket. Who would be calling him at this hour? He quickly pulled the phone out of his pocket and saw Astrid's name flashing on the display. His adrenaline leapt through him and he quickly answered. "Astrid! Where are you? You can't leave. We need to talk. I'm not giving up on us—"

"I lost the baby." Her voice was raw and harsh, as if she'd been crying, and his gut froze.

"What?" He gripped the phone, sinking back down into a chair.

"The baby. I lost it."

He bowed his head, and suddenly all the feelings of Lucas's death came surging back. The loss. The grief. The guilt. The helplessness. He'd fucked up. He hadn't supported Astrid enough. It was his fault. "Where are you?"

"In Portland." She sounded so exhausted and drained. "In a hospital."

"Where?" He leapt to his feet. "I'll come see you—"

"No, Jason. Don't. You don't have to anymore."

"Fuck that." He ran toward the door, his heart racing as he fished his keys out of his pocket. "I'm coming. Are you okay? Are you in danger?"

"I'm fine!" Tears thickened her voice. "Dammit, Jason, don't you get it? I'm not the answer to the family you want. I'm not pregnant, and I don't know that I'll ever carry a baby to term. So leave me alone!" And then she hung up on him.

What the hell? He leapt into his car and turned on the ignition as he redialed her.

It went straight to voicemail.

"Shit!" He slammed his fist on the steering wheel. "Astrid," he said into the message. "Don't shut me out. There's no fucking way I'm letting you go through this alone. Call me!" He then hung up and called her three more times, leaving a message each time.

He swore and backed up, swinging the car around to head to Portland while he dialed Harlan. Surely she would have called Harlan and told him where she was. Again, it went straight to voicemail.

"Shit!" He swore as he peeled out, dialing Information. The moment someone answered, he said, "Connect me with a hospital in Portland. I don't care which one." He was going to call them all until he found the one Astrid was in.

Anger and desperation tore through him as he sped down the road toward the highway. How could she shut him out like that? But even as he drove, he knew why. It was because she believed that their connection was about the baby, about his need to use her for healing.

Shit, he'd blown it. How was he going to fix it?

CHAPTER EIGHTEEN

"WHERE ARE YOU GOING TO GO?" Emma sat on the edge of Astrid's hospital bed while Astrid got dressed.

Her heart was so achy and empty. She felt so drained. Like she had nothing left. "I'm going to go to a town in northern Vermont. There's a seasonal art gallery there that needs someone to run the desk for the summer. It's a start." She managed a smile, trying to feel optimistic about the phone call she had received this morning, offering her a job for the summer. "They said that if I could get their business online, then I could potentially have a job there all winter too." Her experience with her own internet jewelry business had sealed the deal with the art gallery, because they wanted to expand into the online market. It felt good to know she had assets that others valued, but at the same time, she felt a strange emptiness at the idea of helping someone else's dreams come true.

Emma bit her lip. "Is that really what you want to do?"

Astrid had to lean on the bed for support, her legs were shaking so badly. "I need to make a place for myself," she said. "I need to start over." She managed to get her shirt on, and then sat down heavily beside Emma. She was so tired of feeling weak. Her doctor had said that she was fine, but she couldn't seem to find strength anymore. "Thanks for bringing my stuff."

At Astrid's request, Emma had brought a few of Astrid's most precious belongings with her: her lamp, her orchid and the clothes she'd already packed. She was leaving the jewelry supplies behind. It was time to move on.

"I put them in your car in the hospital garage," Emma sighed. "But you're not really welcome. I wish you'd stay. You have friends in Birch Crossing, you know. A lot of us."

Astrid looked at Emma. "Did you have friends in New York? From when you were married."

Emma bit her lip. "A few."

"So, why didn't you stay?" Astrid wanted Emma to understand, and to stop looking at Astrid like she was making the gravest mistake of her life. "Too many bad memories?"

Emma shook her head. "No. It wasn't that I didn't want to stay. It was that I wanted to come home."

Astrid shrugged. "See, that's what I want to do. I want to go to where I belong. Or, I want to find it."

"But you do belong here," Emma said. "Why don't you understand that?"

Astrid shook her head. "I need to find my space," she said quietly. "I just do." She now understood why her mother had kept them on the run. It was easier to forget when she wasn't surrounded by memories. It was easier to keep things bottled up if you never got close enough to anyone to feel things, or to experience emotions that hurt.

Like with Jason. Like those moments where she'd dreamed that maybe there was a way for the magic to come true—

"Astrid." His low voice broke through her thoughts, and she sucked in her breath, leaping to her feet.

There he was, in her doorway. He was unshaven, and he had dark circles beneath his eyes. His hair was a mess, and his tee shirt was half-tucked in. "Jason," she whispered, her heart leaping. "Why did you come? How did you find me?"

He didn't answer. He just searched her face and his gaze scanned her body, coming to a rest on her belly. She instinctively covered her stomach, feeling raw and exposed, as if the one thing of value she could bring was gone. His gaze returned to her face. "You look like hell," he said softly. "I don't like that. You should be in bed."

She swallowed and lifted her chin. "I'm fine. I'm actually leaving the hospital now." She gestured to Emma, who was still sitting beside her. "You remember Emma?"

"Yeah." He didn't move, his gaze riveted on her face. "I need a dollar, Astrid. Can you give me one?"

"A dollar?" She blinked. "Are you kidding?"

"No. I need one." His voice was urgent. "Give me a dollar. Now."

Astrid glanced at Emma, who shrugged. With a sigh, Astrid grabbed her wallet and handed him the dollar. His fingers brushed against hers, and electricity leapt through her. Dammit. How could she still be affected like that?

"I need you to sign something," he said, pulling a sheaf of papers from behind his back. He held out a pen. "Just sign at the tabs."

She frowned. "What is it?"

He shook his head. "Sign it."

"Oh, no." Emma stood up. "Don't sign anything from him."

"Take it," he said urgently. "Sign it. I already signed it."

Something in his eyes caught her attention, and Astrid took the papers. She glanced at them, and then her heart stuttered. "What is this?"

"I'm selling the carriage house to you for a dollar." He held out a pen. "It's yours, Astrid."

She stared at him. "But I'm not pregnant."

"I know that." Grief flickered in his eyes. "This isn't about the baby. It's about you. That place is your home and I don't want you to ever have to worry about losing it. Sign the paper, Astrid. It's yours."

Tears filled her eyes as she stared at him in disbelief. "I can't take charity. It's worth so much money."

"I don't need the money, and it's not charity." He walked over to her and set the pen in her hand, his eyes blazing. "I need to do it for you. No strings. I'm not asking for anything from you in return. This is something I need to do. Let me do this for you."

"I don't understand," she whispered, clutching the paper to her chest. Her heart was pounding so fiercely. "Why would you do this?"

"Because if you love something, you have to let it go. If it loves you, it will come back to you."

Her heart stopped. "What do you mean by that?" He couldn't love her. That wasn't what he meant. It couldn't be what he meant. She had nothing to offer him.

He touched her face. "I'm freeing you, Astrid. You don't need to rely on me or anyone else to have the home you deserve. You don't need to be on the run anymore. You have the house." He gestured at Emma. "You have the friends. You have the roots. You don't need me for anything." He smiled. "There's no out in that contract," he said. "There's no way I can take it back. I want you free to be who you want to be."

"But why?"

"Sign it." He held out his pen. "No conditions. Just take it."

"Take it." Emma nudged her. "Take the damn thing, Astrid. Don't look back."

Astrid closed her eyes, fighting against the tears. How could she take a house from him? "I don't understand."

"Sweetheart."

She opened her eyes to see Jason on one knee before her. Tears filled her eyes at the passion blazing in his eyes. "I'm doing this because I am hopelessly, desperately in love with you. I know you don't believe anyone could love you, and I know that you're afraid your need for a home and security will impair your ability to judge me objectively. So, I'm giving you that home, so that you can see me for who I am and not have it clouded with your dreams of the fairy tale." He smiled. "I hope you choose me, but if you don't, that's okay, because I'm doing this for you. Because sometimes, when you love something, the best thing you can do is offer them the world, without asking for anything back. I've never done that before, and I need to do it now. For you. For me."

Tears filled her eyes. "You love me," she whispered.

"Sign the damn paper," he said gruffly. "Just take it."

"Do it," Emma said.

Astrid stared into Jason's eyes, and in them, she saw something she'd never seen before. A fierce intensity and total confidence. Raw and untamed commitment to his choice. He was no longer the man who had fallen under the spell of a dream. He no longer simply saw her as a way to attain his fantasy. Now, there was hard reality in his eyes, but something else, too. Peace? Serenity? He had found his place.

"Astrid," he said. "I know you want a home. This is your chance. Are you too afraid to take it? Afraid that if you stay someplace long enough, that people will find out who you really are and then reject you?"

She stiffened at his accusation. "I'm not—"

"You don't hide yourself as well as you think," he said. "Stop running. Running is safe. The risky, bold move is to stay and admit you care, admit that people can hurt you, and give them the chance. Be brave, Astrid."

"Astrid?" The door opened and in walked Ralph. She hadn't seen him since she'd left him in her mother's room, crying by Rosie's side. He looked old and tired, and her heart tightened for him. "Your mother wanted you to have this. I was supposed to track you down even if you didn't want to be found, but you made it easy." He held out the twin heart necklace Rosie had been wearing. "It was good to meet you," he said quietly, touching her cheek. "You're just like her, aren't you? So beautiful. So scared."

"Scared?" Astrid stared at him in surprise. "My mother wasn't scared."

Ralph laughed softly. "She was the most skittish woman I've ever met. It was no easy task to win her over. I've been after her since we were both sixteen."

Astrid stared at Ralph. "You knew my mom when she was sixteen?"

"Damn straight. It took thirty years, but she finally got brave enough to let me catch her." He winked. "Stay in touch, Astrid. It's good to see her sparkle in your eyes." He nodded then at Emma and Jason, but slipped out before introductions could be made.

Astrid stared down at the necklace in her hand, and a sudden sense of determination swelled through her. Her mother had finally had the courage to stop running, and she'd found Ralph and true love. So maybe, it was time for Astrid to stop running as well, to accept all these olive branches offering her a home and friends and security.

It was what she wanted with every fiber of her being. Relief and excitement rushed through her, and she grinned. "Okay." Taking a deep breath, she took the pen and signed the documents. Her hand was shaking by the time she finished, but she couldn't keep the grin off her face. "Thank you," she said.

Jason's smile was even bigger. "No, thank you." Then he caught the back of her neck, pulled her toward him, and kissed her.

Before she could react, or kiss him back, he released her, took his set of copies, and walked out, leaving her behind.

Astrid sank back onto the bed, staring after him in surprise. "He left?"

"He sure did." Emma grinned. "That's the sign of true love, my friend!"

"True love?" The words made Astrid shiver, both with longing and fear. "Why would he leave if he loved me?"

Emma cocked her head. "Didn't you hear him? He set you free. It's up to you to come back to him. He's given you everything you want, so that the only reason you'd come to him was if you loved him. He's given you the chance to no longer look at him through the lens of fear."

"Oh. Wow." Astrid traced her fingers over the documents with her name on it, giving her the first home she'd ever had. Jason had done that for her? It was extraordinary.

"You do realize that you can't leave town now, don't you? Who will take care of your house?" Emma was beaming at her. "You're trapped here, Astrid. Your life as a nomad is over. How does it feel?"

Astrid looked down at the papers in her hand, still trying to grasp what had happened. "I'm not sure yet."

Emma raised her brows. "What are you going to do about Jason?"

She looked at her friend and held out her hand. They both could see her hand was trembling. "I'm terrified," she whispered.

Emma's face softened. "I know, babe. If anyone could understand how terrifying it would be to fall in love again, it's me." She put her arm around Astrid's shoulder and squeezed. "Take your time, sweetie, until you're sure. You owe that to yourself."

"I know." Astrid fisted the necklace from her mother and thought of Ralph's tears when he'd grieved the loss of her mother. "I know."

∾

SHE COULDN'T GET out of the car.

For twenty minutes after Astrid drove up to the carriage house, her car full of the items Emma had brought to the hospital, all Astrid could do was simply sit in the driver's seat and stare at the place that was hers.

Hers.

She sat in her car and looked at the red metal roof, designed to ensure the winter snow slid off it. She looked at the dark brown shingles, and how the rich colors varied according to how much sun and wind they'd gotten over the years. She basked in the overgrown gardens beneath the front windows, gardens that no one had tended to in far too long. They were her gardens. *Hers.* They needed love and care, which she could give to them.

The lawn...oh...the tremendous lawn with its bare spots and dandelions was so incredible. She could do yoga by the lake in the grass at sunset. She could have the windows open all year long, and learn the sounds that the lake made depending on the season.

She could become a horrible, evil person, and no one would ever be able to take it away from her. She could go completely broke, and no one would be able to take it away from her if she couldn't pay rent. She could have a dog. A cat. Fifteen children. They would all have a place to live, forever, and ever. No one who entrusted their life to her would ever, *ever,* have to sleep in a car.

"Oh, God." Tears blurred her vision, and suddenly she didn't want to be in her car anymore. She flung the door open, raced up the walkway and burst into the house. The sunlight drifted through the windows, making sunbeams across the living room. "I'm home," she shouted, throwing her arms up to the sky. "It's me!"

Her shouts echoed through the high ceilings, repeating her words back to her, like the heavens themselves were affirming her words. *It's me. It's me. It's me.*

"Holy cow." She flopped down on the living room carpet and stared up at the ceiling, awed by the beautiful wood beams crisscrossing the white plaster. "How can this be mine?"

No one answered her, but no one needed to.

It was hers because a beautiful, amazing man had given her the one gift he knew she craved beyond anything. Security. Safety. Freedom to never be reliant on anyone again. Roots.

Astrid closed her eyes, her heart filling with emotions at the thought of Jason. "Thank you," she whispered. "Thank you."

The house was silent, and as she lay there, the silence seemed to grow louder and louder. She heard the distant sound of Noah shouting, and the laugh of his grandmother. As she heard the sounds of family, a faint hint of loneliness began to squeeze into her sanctuary.

The losses of the last few days began to press at her, and Astrid sat up, draping her arms over her knees. Her second chance at a child was gone. Her mother was dead. Jason had set her free, and he had no reason to want her now that she wasn't pregnant. She bowed her head, the magnitude of her losses almost overwhelming.

She had a home, finally. She had stability. She had security. But there was still a growing emptiness inside her. A restlessness. A fire beginning to grow, pushing her for more.

A fire? The image of raging flames flashed through her mind, and she thought of the phoenix that she'd tried to draw so many times during her life, but had never been able to get right. She hadn't even tried to draw in in almost two years, although she kept her sketches handy, hoping that someday, sometime, things would come together for her. And there, with her chest aching with both loneliness and pride, she knew what the problem with the phoenix had been.

Energy surging through her, Astrid leapt to her feet and raced over to the table. This time, she didn't bother with drawing it first. She opened the drawer on her apothecary cabinet and began to rifle through it to find the right pieces for her project. She knew what she needed to do. The image was so clear in her mind.

She simply knew.

It had been a long, long time since her mind had felt this quiet and this clear, and it felt amazing. And she knew Jason Sarantos was the one responsible.

CHAPTER NINETEEN

HE COULDN'T CONCENTRATE. He just couldn't fucking concentrate. Oregano just didn't matter.

Jason braced his hands on the counter in his kitchen and took a deep breath. He'd been experimenting with pizza sauce recipes all evening, and he couldn't even focus long enough to notice how they tasted.

Ever since he'd heard Astrid's car drive up to her carriage house, he'd been on edge. His parents had taken Noah to the movies because they'd all agreed they needed to get away from "cranky dad." His solution had been to cook. Cooking was good. The store was opening in two days. But as hard as he tried, he couldn't fucking concentrate.

What was Astrid doing in there? Was she packing the rest of her boxes? Was she unpacking? Had it been the wrong move to leave the hospital and give her time to digest? It had been hell to walk out of her room, but he'd been so certain that he needed to give her the space to feel safe. Had he been wrong? Had she misinterpreted it when she'd thought he didn't care?

"Fuck!" He turned off the burners, threw down his spoon

and yanked off his apron. That was it. He couldn't wait any more. Restlessness and need burning through him, he sprinted through the house and yanked open the door— "Astrid!" He barely stopped in time to keep from plowing her off the front step, catching her by the upper arms to help her keep her balance.

Dear God almighty, he was stunned by how good it felt to touch her. He wanted to haul her against him and bury her against his body. For a moment, Astrid seemed to melt into him, and his heart leapt, then she stiffened and pulled back. "I made this," she said. "It's for you." She held out a small item wrapped in white tissue paper.

Frowning, Jason accepted it. "How are you doing? Do you feel okay?"

She nodded. "Open it."

He unwrapped it, and when he saw what it was, he caught his breath. It was a stained glass image of a phoenix. It was the same phoenix he'd seen in her sketches, but this one had orange and blue fire blazing in its eyes, instead of tears. Silver wire was delicately twisted into the design of the phoenix, and Astrid had filled the spaces with iridescent beads glittering like they themselves were on fire. There were flames around the bird's feet, but instead of the claws turning to ash, they were a vibrant gold. Sitting on each foot was a dragonfly, its colorful wings glittering like rainbows. The bird's wings were extended as if it were rising into the air. He could almost feel the feathers fluttering as it took flight.

This was a bird that was coming to life, not the one that was being pulled down by the ashes. It was pure magic. "It's incredible, Astrid."

She smiled, and her eyes lit up with more energy and fire than he'd ever seen before. Her eyes looked like those of the phoenix, alive and brimming with passion. It was the courage and zest he'd seen before, but this time, the shadows were quiet. The fear was at peace. All that was left was the woman he'd seen from that first moment. It was as if facing her worst fears had finally cleansed her soul and given her the freedom to move forward.

Or maybe his gift of the house had done it, or at least helped. Did her peace have anything to do with him? Hell, he hoped it did.

"I know," she said, elation filling her voice. "I haven't created anything truly beautiful in almost a year, and then this came to life for me. I want you to have it."

Warmth coursed through him, awe that she would offer him such an incredible gift, but he knew he couldn't take it from her. She needed it too much. "No." He tried to hand it back to her. "You need to sell this. You'll make a lot of money on it."

"It's for you." She folded his hand over it, her touch warm and gentle. "I can tell that my inspiration is back. I'll be okay. But this one was for you." She touched the dragonfly on the bird's claw. Her eyes were full of passion and warmth. "These dragonflies are helping the phoenix fly. They're giving the phoenix wings, in case she can't fly." She smiled at him. "That's you," she said quietly. "Thank you for being my dragonfly."

Jason's chest ached with words he was afraid to say, and he caught her wrist as she started to turn away. "Where are you going?"

She smiled. "Home." Then she pulled out of his grasp and hurried down the pathway.

Jason tightened his grip on the phoenix as he watched Astrid return to the carriage house. That was it? Was that her good-bye? Was that her way of saying thank you? And that was all?

No way. "Wait!" Jason leapt through his doorway and sprinted after her.

Astrid glanced back, and her eyes widened when she saw him running after her. For a split second, he wasn't sure if she was going to wait for him.

Then she turned toward him, and he knew she was.

~

ASTRID'S HEART was pounding as she watched Jason sprint toward her, her phoenix clenched in his hand. She hadn't known what else to say to him, how to let him know. She'd hoped he would understand what the phoenix meant without her having to tell him—

"Astrid." He caught up to her, stopping right in front of her. Almost touching, but not quite. They were so close, inches apart, but not yet together.

For a moment, neither of them spoke, the air heated between them. Astrid swallowed, knowing she had to say it. "I'm not sure if I can have children, Jason. I might never carry to term."

She waited for the regret or the anguish to flash over his face, a revealing expression that would tell her that it bothered him.

But he simply took her hand and pressed his lips to her palm. "I don't mind."

Hope leapt through her, but she quickly shoved it away, not daring to reach for the golden ring, for the fairytale that had failed her before. "But you want more children. You want a family."

"I have a family. I have an amazing son who is enough all by himself." He grinned. "I changed the name of the cafe to Noah's Place. He's so thrilled. He's been designing the new sign all day, and he's been naming each of the pizzas." He paused. "One of them is named 'Astrid's Adventure.'"

243

Astrid blinked, sudden tears filling her eyes. "He named one after me?"

"Yeah, he sure did. He thinks you're amazing."

Astrid swallowed, her throat tightening. "Really? But all I did was look for snakes and dragonflies with him."

"That was perfect." He ran his fingers through her hair, tucking it behind her ear. "I think you're amazing too, Astrid. Last night, my dad agreed to help me with the store, and to share some of his recipes. Eppie came by and announced that she was going to charge me a fortune, but that she'd decided she would be in charge of marketing. Noah loves it. The whole thing is coming together."

She smiled. "That's great—"

"No, it's not." His eyes darkened. "I have everything I want, but it isn't enough. All I can think about is that you should be a part of it—" He pressed his finger to her lips before she could protest. "I don't mean I want you to be making pizza sauce with me. I want you to be making your jewelry and doing your thing, whether it's jewelry or standing out on your deck or hanging with the girls, as long as you're a part of my life." He slipped his hands around her waist and pulled her up against him. "I want to crawl into bed at night with you. I want to call you up when I make my first sale and celebrate with you. I want to take you out for dinner when you hit your first threshold with your jewelry sales."

The most incredible sense of warmth and belonging began to fill her, swelling through her like a great burst of sunlight. "Jason—"

"No, that's not all." He got down on one knee and took her hand. "I want to be connected to you for the rest of my life. Say you'll marry me, Astrid. Even if it takes you a year or two or ten before you trust me enough to actually marry me, just tell me that someday you will. Will you marry me, Astrid? I love you, every last bit of you."

"Oh, Jason," she whispered, too stunned to answer. He knew everything about her. He knew about her mother. About her past. He had no reason to marry her, not even through some misguided sense of duty because she was pregnant. She had nothing to offer him except herself, and that was enough.

"Wait." He jammed his hand into his front pocket and pulled out a ring. "Marry me, Astrid." He held it up, and she saw that he hadn't honored her with the traditional diamond solitaire. It was two diamonds, cut into the shape of intertwining hearts, an almost perfect replica of her trademark pattern. She knew he must have had it created especially for her. For them. By choosing her signature design, she knew it was his way of promising that he honored and loved *her*, exactly as she truly was.

"Oh, Jason," she whispered. "It's beautiful."

"My heart hasn't beat on its own since I met you," he said. "It's a part of you, and yours is a part of mine." He smiled. "I had this ring designed right after I met you. I knew you were the one for me. Your soul has been open to me since we met, Astrid, and that's what I fell in love with. I love you, sweetheart. I love you exactly the way you are, and so does Noah."

Tears filled her eyes, and Astrid knew she'd come home, in every way. She then whispered the words she'd thought she'd never say again. "I love you, Jason, and yes, I'll marry you."

He let out a whoop and leapt to his feet, sweeping her up in a tremendous embrace. She laughed as he swung her around, unable to contain her joy.

Jason finally stopped the embrace, and he lifted her hand. Slowly, never breaking eye contact with her, he slid the beautiful ring onto her fourth finger. It fit perfectly, and the white diamonds sparkled like a waterfall in the morning sun.

"You're mine now," he growled, a mischievous light flashing in his eyes.

Her heart leapt, but before she could react, he swept her up in his arms and carried her across the threshold to her home. Her home. Her man. Her future.

JASON KICKED THE DOOR SHUT, his heart singing as he carried Astrid into the carriage house. He'd found his future, his life, his meaning. But he knew it wasn't enough. The ring was a symbol, but he needed her soul, as well. He needed to feel her commitment to him in the core of her body, in her very soul. "I need to make love to you."

She smiled, a heart-melting tenderness that went straight to his core. "Yes."

Desire leapt through him. He instantly pulled her tighter against him and caught her lips with his as he carried her across the floor. Her response was instant and electrifying, as full of fire and heat as he'd known it would be. The kiss was intoxicating, and he growled as he deepened it, needing more, needing to access all of her.

He reached the bed, and started to lower her to it, when he remembered her aversion to letting him into it. He paused to grab the comforter off the bed so he could toss it on the floor—

"It's okay, Jason." Astrid let go of him, dropping to her mattress. She held up her arms to him. "Be the first and only one to share my bed with me," she whispered. "I always swore that I would never share it, not unless I knew it was forever. Be my forever, Jason Sarantos, because I'm yours."

"You bet your ass this is forever," he said as he lowered himself on top of her. He moved slowly, giving Astrid the chance to change her mind, searching her face for fear or trepidation, but he saw only love and commitment. He saw trust, and that touched him the most deeply. Astrid had no reason to trust, and yet she'd given her heart to him.

Rightness surged through him, and he brushed his lips over hers. "I will never let you down," he whispered. "Never."

"I know." Astrid wrapped her arms around his neck. "Now kiss me, and make me yours forever."

Jason grinned. "I love it when you get demanding."

"I hope you love me no matter what I do." But there was a sparkle in her eyes that told him that she knew he would. There was no fear inside Astrid anymore. Hot damn. He'd finally done it right, and gotten her to trust him.

He laughed and kissed her hair. "You know I do." Then he kissed her again, and talking turned from words into touches, into kisses, into the kind of intimate communication that could happen only between lovers.

Jason reveled in the feel of her skin beneath his hands, in the look of desire in her eyes as he slid her shirt over her arms, and her jeans down her thighs. Her skin was hot, burning for him, and he felt equally on fire. His kisses turned deep and desperate, and Astrid was clinging to him just as desperately, as if she couldn't bear to let him go.

With a growl, he broke the kiss to tear off his shirt, but before he could do it, Astrid stopped him by grabbing his wrist. "No," she said. "Let me. I want to do it."

He sat back on his heels as she sat up. His body began to tremble as she gently grasped the hem of his shirt and tugged it up his body, sliding her lips over his stomach as she did so. Desire flamed deep and hot inside him, but it was also something more. Something so primal and powerful, driven by the fact that Astrid so clearly wanted him, by the way she ran her hands over his body as if she were savoring every touch, every inch, every curve of his flesh.

"No one has ever made me feel like you do," he whispered

as she unfastened his jeans. "Like you want this as much as I do."

Her smile faded as she raised herself onto her knees so her face was level with his. She laid her hands on either side of his face, and let him see into her soul. "I'm on fire with how much I want you to make love to me, Jason. You're the most incredible man, and you're mine, all mine, and that is the most amazing gift *ever.*" The sincerity of her words struck right to his core, and he felt the truth of her words.

This wasn't one sided. Not in any way. Not on any level.

Fierce desire rushed through him, an uncontainable urge to consume her and stake his claim on this incredible woman. He yanked his jeans off and took her to the bed beneath him, manipulating her with his kisses and his hands, pinning her where he wanted her.

"Yes," she whispered, writhing beneath him, her hips moving in desperate invitation. "Make love to me, Jason. Open your heart to me."

He pressed her hand to his chest as he moved between her legs. His heart was pounding so fiercely he felt like it was going to explode out of his ribs, and Astrid smiled when she felt it. "I love you," she whispered. "I'll love you until the end of time."

"And I'll love you to the end of time, and back again, my sweet Astrid." Then he sheathed himself inside her with one swift move, her body slick and welcoming as they became one.

For a moment, he didn't move, and they just stared at each other while their bodies adjusted to the awe of their connection with each other. Jason grasped Astrid's hand and lifted it to his lips. He pressed a kiss to her ring, to the symbol that would tell the world of their commitment to each other. "Forever," he said. "No matter what."

A slow, beautiful smile spread over Astrid's face, and she

pulled him down toward her. "Forever," she whispered. "Two hearts, intertwined, forever."

As the words filled his heart, Jason kissed her, pouring every ounce of his soul and love into it. She kissed him back, unleashing the desire that had been building so powerfully inside them. With a roar of possession, of lust, of desire, Jason plunged even deeper inside her. Astrid gasped as he began to move, clinging to him as they stoked the desire higher and higher, until they were at the precipice, consumed by it.

Jason entwined his fingers with hers, and then did one final plunge. Astrid screamed his name at the same moment he shouted hers, clinging to each other as the orgasm took them, catapulting them into a future of love, of connection, of finally finding their place.

CHAPTER TWENTY

ASTRID SMILED WITH CONTENTMENT, her heart filled with love as she trailed her fingers along Jason's spine. Her sheets were soft under her back, draped over them both, enveloping Jason into her most private world.

And it was perfect.

"I love you," Jason muttered into her neck, where his face was nestled. "Plus, you're great at sex."

She laughed, her heart almost exploding with joy. "Why thank you. I have to admit, you're really talented as well. I don't suppose you'd be willing to do it with me again sometime?"

He propped himself up on his elbow, staring down at her. His hair was rumpled, his eyes dark with the aftermath of their lovemaking. He looked rough and untamed, and her heart melted at the affection in his expression. "How about now?"

She grinned. "Now? Already?"

"Hell, yeah." He bent his head to kiss her, and then they heard the crunch of tires on the gravel. Jason broke the kiss and cocked his head to listen.

A car door slammed, and then they heard Noah's shout and Mack's low rumble. "It's my parents," Jason said. "Shit." He rolled off her and grabbed his jeans off the floor. "I gotta go."

"What?" A heavy weight slammed into Astrid's chest as Jason hurried to get his clothes on. She'd forgotten about his parents. Her heart aching, she watched him yank on his shirt. It was just like before. How could it be the same? She'd thought it was different. "Jason—"

"Get dressed." He leaned over to give her a quick kiss, then sprinted out of the bedroom. Her front door slammed, and she heard Jason shouting for his parents and Noah.

Humiliation burned through her as she quickly pulled her own clothes on. How could he leave her like that? How could—

"Astrid?" There was a light knock from the front of the house as Jason called her name. "You decent?"

"What?" She fastened her bra and yanked her shirt over her head, then hurried out of the bedroom. She froze when she saw that Jason, Noah and his parents were standing in her living room. "Oh."

Jason grinned when he saw her, a tremendous smile that made her heart flutter. "Astrid," he said softly as he left his parents and Noah and walked across the room toward her. He took her hand and kissed her lightly on the mouth before turning toward his parents and Noah. He slung his arm over her shoulder, tucking her tightly up against his side. "I would like you all to meet Astrid Monroe."

His dad raised his eyebrows. "We've already met her, Jason."

Jason grinned. "No, you haven't. I would like you to meet the woman who is crazy enough to love me to the ends of the earth, the woman I love with every bit of my soul."

Astrid felt her cheeks turn red as Jason's mother's

eyebrows shot up, but at the same time, she felt her chest swell with pride.

"Astrid has agreed to marry me," Jason said. "Mom, Dad, I want you to meet my future wife. And Noah..." Jason went down into a crouch so he was on his son's level. "How would you feel about Astrid being your mom?"

Astrid held her breath as the most enormous smile exploded on Noah's face. "That rocks!" He raced across the room and tackled Jason, nearly knocking him down. "Thanks for getting her, Dad! You're the best!"

Astrid's throat tightened as Jason broke the hug and held out an arm toward her, to bring her into the embrace. For a moment, she hesitated, then Noah looked up. "I'm going to name my snake after you," he said, "Queen Astrid."

Queen Astrid? Suddenly, all hesitation vanished and Astrid went down on her knees, letting Jason and Noah pull her into the hug. It was a fierce hug, as only two males would do, and it made her heart tremble with disbelief. Was this really her world? Was this really her life?

"Astrid," Jason's mom interrupted.

She tensed and looked up, noticing that Jason didn't loosen his embrace on her at all. Instead, he kept her tight against him, making his commitment to her clear. Warmth and strength burned through her, and suddenly Henrietta didn't feel like such a threat. Astrid knew that she was safe, and no one could take it away from her. "Yes?"

To her surprise, Henrietta was smiling, and tears were gleaming in her eyes. "Welcome to the family. It's about time you and Jason found your way to each other."

Astrid swallowed. "Really?"

Mack was the one who answered, as he put his arm around his wife's shoulders, a broad grin on his face. "Really."

$\sim$

"I THINK IT WENT UNDER HERE." Ten months later, Astrid stretched out on her belly to peer beneath the woodpile, a position she'd found herself in many times since she'd agreed to marry into the Sarantos family.

"Do you see it?" Noah hunkered down next to her, his frog-hunting net damp against Astrid's side.

"No." Astrid frowned. "We need a flashlight."

"We gotta catch it," Noah said. "If Dad finds out there's a mouse in the cafe, he's going to kill it."

"We'll catch it," Astrid said. "Don't worry."

Noah flashed a grin at her. "I love this cafe. We've caught six mice already and it's only the first week of May. How cool is that?"

Astrid grinned at him. "As long as they don't get inside the restaurant, it's cool—"

"Oh, there she is." The voice of the man her mother had finally found peace with broke into the mouse moment. "See, your mama is still here. No need to fuss."

Astrid looked up as Ralph came walking out of the back of the store, a tiny bundle cradled in his massive arms. Her heart filled with the joy that had been overwhelming her for months. Joy that had been mixed with terror, when she'd accidentally become pregnant so soon after her miscarriage. Without Jason's support and his reassuring medical scrutiny, she knew her stress would have taken another baby away from her. But instead, the nine months had built the most incredible bond between her and Jason as they leaned on each other for support and courage that everything would work out okay and they wouldn't lose another child. Together, they'd made it, and little Rosie had blessed them with all the joy and love that Astrid had never thought she'd have. "Is she awake?" Astrid asked.

"Waking up." Ralph nuzzled the baby, his weathered-face filled with such love. "Hi, little Rosie," he crooned. "You look just like your grandma. You are a lucky girl. She was the prettiest lady I've ever met, and you look just like her."

"Aw...not the baby again," Noah groaned. "She's so boring."

"Some girls don't like mice, so you're going to have to teach her to like them." Astrid smiled as she took the infant from her grandpa. Rosie's cheeks were flushed and her eyes were sleepy as she snuggled against Astrid. An overwhelming sense of love and wonder swelled as she looked down at her innocent, beautiful baby, who was growing up with a doting father, a mischievous brother and a home that was more beautiful than Astrid had ever imagined as a child.

"Can I really teach her to play with mice? Is that okay?" Noah grinned. "I have a fake rat inside. Can I get it for her?"

"Of course," Astrid grinned, happy that Rosie was going to grow up actually knowing her brother. The cycle had been broken...no, not broken. It had been healed, with love and courage, and all the things she never knew she was capable of.

"Great!" Noah raced inside, shouting for Jason.

Ralph smiled at Astrid. "You sure you don't mind me living in the carriage house?"

She laughed, delighted by the warmth and happiness in the older man's eyes. For months after Rosie's death, Ralph's spirit had been broken, but the moment they'd told him that their baby would carry Rosie's name, it was as if Ralph had finally come back to life. He'd taken on his role of doting grandpa with such vigor and excitement that his enthusiasm still made Astrid giggle with delight. "Of course not. You're family, Ralph. You belong with us. Besides, it is so wonderful to have your help with Rosie. I'd never be able to keep up with my orders if you weren't there to help me with the kids."

"Okay, then." The older man smiled. "I never thought I'd have grandkids. Rosie would be proud, wouldn't she?"

"She would—"

"Astrid!" Eppie came charging around the corner. "Jason needs some..." She paused, her eyes widening. "Oh, hello there, Ralph. I had *no* idea you were back here with Astrid." She gave him a wide smile, flipping back some of the beads that were hanging from the brim of her hat.

Ralph's cheeks turned red. "Oh, hello, Eppie. You look lovely today."

"Oh, this old thing?" Eppie smiled and fluffed the yellow flowers embroidered onto her fuchsia dress. "Why, I've had it for hours. Maybe even a full day. It's no big thing."

Astrid chuckled as she hugged Rosie to her chest. "I'm going to go inside and find Jason. I'll see you guys later." She ducked past them, grinning when neither of them even looked her way as she walked into the back of the store.

She pushed open the door just as Jason walked out. He was wearing a bright red tee shirt that proclaimed Noah's Place as the number one new pizza store in Maine, courtesy of Eppie personally filling the place every day for the first six months until it started to gain steam on its own. Eppie had even convinced Clare and Griffin to let Jason cater their wedding, filling the lakeside tent with more pizzas than Astrid had ever seen in her life. It had been so amazing to see Clare so happy, and to be experiencing those same emotions herself. Never again would Astrid stand outside a loving relationship like Clare and Griffin's, and wonder what it would be like. No, she knew what it was like, and it was the most incredible gift ever.

"Hey, gorgeous," her husband said with a mischievous glint in his eyes. There was flour on Jason's shoulder and smudged on his cheeks, and he looked radiantly happy. "How are my girls?"

"Perfect." Astrid smiled as Jason locked his arm around her waist and kissed her. "You'll squish Rosie," she laughed.

"Good. She needs to learn that her daddy can't keep his

hands off her mommy." Jason's face softened as he looked down at the infant. "One month old today. I can't even believe it."

"I know." Astrid sighed happily as she leaned her head against her husband's shoulder, utter contentment filling her. It amazed her she could feel so at peace, but with Jason and her family, she did. The only dark spots in her life were Harlan and Emma. She hadn't heard from her brother in almost six months, and he hadn't been back to his house. And Emma...poor Emma. She was getting too thin, and she looked like she wasn't sleeping at night. Astrid and Clare had taken Emma out to dinner so many times, but there was such weight in Emma's soul that it made Astrid want to cry for her, because she knew what that felt like. But Emma felt so out of reach, especially since Rosie had been born and Emma had retreated even more.

Rosie gurgled in Astrid's arms, drawing her attention back to the beautiful little girl who had been brave enough to be born into this family, and her heart filled once again. "She's perfect, isn't she?"

"Just like her mama." Jason kissed her again. "Ralph's going to babysit the kids tonight," he said. "We're going out to celebrate."

Her heart leapt at the love in his eyes. Would she ever get used to the way Jason looked at her? "What are we celebrating?"

"Us." He kissed her again. "I just want to celebrate that my wife loves me as much as I love her. Isn't that a good enough reason to celebrate?"

She smiled. "It is."

And it was. It definitely was.

~

What's Harlan's secret? Can he heal Emma's broken heart and teach her to trust again? Can she erase the shadows from his past? After a midnight tryst results in a marriage-of-convenience, hearts ignite and chaos ensues when they must unexpectedly make their fake marriage real in a way they never intended. Find out more by grabbing your copy of Unintentionally Mine, and fill your heart with this wonderful story of love that was always meant to be.

"One of the best books of the year! I was absolutely blown away." -Tapnchica (Amazon Review)

Get your copy now!

~

Or are cowboys your thing? The Stockton brothers are a fiercely loyal family of cowboy hotness. When Chase decides that a marriage of convenience is the only way to protect the secret baby of his late best friend, his bachelor days are seriously numbered. Check out A Real Cowboy Never Says No for more!

Get your copy now!

"Tender, loving, and exquisite!" -*Emris L (Amazon Review)*

~

SNEAK PEEK: UNINTENTIONALLY MINE

"One of the best books of the year! I was absolutely blown away." ~Tapnchica (Amazon Review)

After a midnight tryst results in a marriage-of-convenience, hearts ignite and chaos ensues when Harlan and Emma must unexpectedly make their fake marriage real in a way they never intended.

~

SHE WAS LIKE an angel in the night.

Harlan couldn't take his gaze off Emma as he cut the engine, letting his boat drift in toward her dock. He'd been out for one last tour of the lake, one last night to remember the town that he'd made his home for the last five years. He'd expected to feel relief, but he hadn't. He'd felt strangely melancholy, as if he was leaving before he was supposed to. Instinct had taken him past Emma's small cabin, as he'd done on so many other sleepless nights.

This time, for the first time in two years, she'd been outside, even though it was past midnight. The way she'd been huddled up in that huge blanket had caught his attention, as if she were a broken bird stranded on land. He hadn't intended to approach. Hadn't planned to say anything. But the boat had drifted right toward her anyway.

"Harlan?" She grabbed the bow of his boat as it bumped her dock, jerking him back to the present.

He caught one of the pilings on her dock, anchoring the boat as the blanket slid off her shoulders. In the moonlight, he could tell she was wearing a white tank top with straps so thin they looked like they would snap under the faintest breeze. Her black shorts were boldly short, revealing so much more leg than he'd ever seen from the woman who wore long skirts and blue jeans every day of her life, or at least on every day that he'd seen her. Her hair was down, tangled around her shoulders, as if it were caressing the skin she'd so carelessly exposed to the night.

"What are you doing here?" she asked. Her voice was throaty and raw, and he realized she'd been crying.

"Couldn't sleep." He leaned on the piling, not daring to get out of the boat, not when the need to play the hero was pulsing through him so strongly. All he could think of was folding her into his arms and chasing away the demons haunting her. "You?"

"Same." She hugged herself, her huge eyes searching his. The moonlight cast dark shadows on her face, hollowing out her eyes and her cheeks.

"Want a ride?" He asked the question without intending to, but found himself holding his breath while it sat in the air, waiting for her response.

"To where?"

He shrugged. "Nowhere. I'm just driving."

She looked back at her cabin. "I was just—"

"Crying. I know. Going back inside will help, do you think? Or maybe getting the hell away from life for twenty minutes would be better?"

Defiance flared in her eyes, and her shoulders seemed to lift. Without a word, she grabbed the corner of his windshield and set her bare foot on the edge of his boat. Silently, he held out his hand to the woman he'd never touched in all the years he'd known her, except for last night. She met his gaze, and then set her hand in his.

Jesus. Her skin was like the softest silk, decadent in its fragility, tempting in its strength. He closed his fingers around hers and helped her into his boat. Her hip slid against his side as she stepped in, and electricity sizzled through him.

She caught her breath, glancing at him as she moved away to sit in the passenger seat.

Harlan said nothing. He had no idea what to say. Not to her. Not to this woman. Not in this moment. So, instead, he restarted the boat, backed up until he was clear of her dock, and then unleashed the throttle. The boat leapt forward, slicing through the water with a boldness that was probably irresponsible in the dark.

But he knew the lake, every inch of it, and the moonlight was bright enough to guide him.

He didn't feel like being careful. Not tonight. Tonight he wanted wind. He wanted water. He wanted freedom.

And he wanted the woman sitting in his boat.

A woman he had no right to want.

A woman who had haunted his dreams since the moment he'd first met her.

As if feeling the intensity of his gaze, Emma glanced over at him. The moment she saw the expression on his face, her face paled in the moonlight, and she sucked in her breath.

Shit. She knew now how much he burned for her. His face had given it away.

She jerked her gaze off his and stared across the lake, not acknowledging what had just happened.

But she knew. Son of a bitch, *she knew*.

The boat ride had just changed irrevocably.

Like it? Get it now!

SNEAK PEEK: A REAL COWBOY NEVER WALKS AWAY

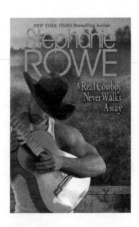

"Beautiful story full of emotion and depth, and wonderfully written." ~Amber S.
(Amazon Review)

When a single mom enlists the help of a handsome stranger during a busy lunch at her Wyoming café, she has no idea she's just conscripted a world-famous country music star to be her busboy.

~

She tried.

She *really* tried not to be so aware of him.

But there was no way for Lissa McIntyre to ignore the man sitting at her counter.

When he'd first walked into the café, she'd been a little unnerved by the sheer size of him. He was tall, broad-shouldered, and wore his leather duster as if he were an outlaw from the Old West, owning every joint he walked into. His dark brown hat was low over his eyes, casting his face into shadows, and he moved as if every muscle in his body was primed and ready to pounce...on her.

She never dated. She was careful not to even look at a man in a way that might make him think an overture would be welcome, especially not when she was working and had a café full of cowboys. Men were trouble, dangerous, and a threat to everything that mattered to her, which was a very short list.

And yet, the moment he'd raised his head and looked at her, she'd felt herself falling into the depths of his steely blue eyes. He was pure male, loaded with testosterone. His clothes were old and worn. He was soaking wet. And...God...she couldn't lie. He was insanely, irresistibly sexy. Sensual. Tempting. Every word she would never dare apply to a man had been rushing through her mind for the last hour.

He hadn't said much, except to ask for a refill on his coffee and to thank her each time she refilled his water, but the way he spoke made chills rush down her spine. His voice was deep, almost melodic, filling her with a longing so intense that she wanted to sit down on the stool next to him, prop her chin up on her hands, and ask him to just talk for a while so she could lose herself in the magic of his voice.

Before he'd arrived, she'd been feeling sorry for herself,

dreading festival week, and all the chaos and long hours it brought with it. If she didn't need the money, she would shut down for the week and take Bridgette to all the events. Instead, she'd had to pawn her daughter off on her amazing neighbor, Martha Keller, who had become the grandmother that Bridgette would never have. Martha was the one taking Bridgette to all the events of festival week, while Lissa worked. Of course, it would be worth it when her bank account had enough money in it to make it through another slow winter, but on the first night, she always felt cranky, wondering how she'd ended up with this as her life.

But when her counter cowboy had shown up, he'd been a welcome distraction, drawing her out of her negative thinking and into the present. He made her think of a time when she'd thought life was full of opportunity and sunshine, before everything had crashed down around her. Plus, a little eye candy always made a girl's day brighter, right?

The door jangled again, and she grimaced when she saw another group of competitors from the rodeo walk in. She was already at max capacity, and the crowd was getting boisterous and impatient with the slow service. Even if Katie was here, it would have been tough to keep up, but alone? It was impossible, and she knew it. It wouldn't take much for word to get out about the *Wildflower Café* to the rest of the tourists and competitors. If tonight was a bust, no one would be coming back this week. Fear rippled through her at the thought of losing all that income. She desperately needed a profitable week. *Desperately.*

"Hey." Her counter cowboy waved at her.

She hurried over to him, grabbing her water pitcher as she went. Sweat was trickling down her spine, but she knew she had to find a way to go even faster. "What's up?"

"You got anyone in the kitchen watching those burgers while you're out here?"

She spun around. "Why? Are they burning?" She couldn't afford to burn them. Her customers had already been waiting too long. "I'll go check--"

He stopped her with a hand on her forearm.

She froze, her belly flipping over. His hand wrapped all the way around her arm easily, but his touch was gentle, so gentle that she knew he wasn't trying to trap her. She could pull away if she wanted...but she didn't want to. "What?"

He gestured at the café. "There's no way you can handle this alone. Want help?"

"Help?" She blinked at him. "Who? You?"

"Yeah. I can cook." He still had his hand on her arm. "I'm too antisocial and bitter to socialize with the public, so I'm not waiting on tables, but I'll flip some burgers."

God, she needed help. There was no way she could manage both the customers and the cooking by herself tonight. A part of her wanted to throw herself over the counter, hug him fiercely, and then put him to work....but there was no way. "I really appreciate the offer, but I don't even know you. I can't have a stranger in my kitchen, but thanks." She started to turn away, but he tightened his grip on her arm.

Her breath caught, and she looked at him. "Yes?"

He hesitated, emotions warring on his face. For a long moment, he said nothing, and she frowned, turning back to face him. "What is it?"

He flexed his jaw, his blue eyes fixed on her face. "You're new to town, right?" he finally said. "You didn't grow up here, did you?"

She blinked at the random question. "I've been here eight years. Why?"

Again, a long moment of silence, as if he were waging some massive internal debate about whether to speak. She leaned forward, her curiosity piqued while she waited.

Finally, he met her gaze. "You know Chase Stockton?" His voice was low, as if he didn't want anyone else to hear.

"Chase?" He was all worked up about Chase? "Of course. He comes in here once a week. He supplies my pies when I don't have time to bake them. Why?" But even as she asked it, his penetrating blue eyes took on new meaning. She'd seen eyes like his before. Exactly like them...on Chase. "You're related to him, aren't you? One of his brothers? Aren't there like nine of you or something?"

His face became shuttered, but he didn't pull away. "Yeah." He said nothing else, waiting, watching her face.

"Oh, wow." Relief rushed through her. Chase was one of the nicest guys she'd ever met. Yes, he was intimidating, but there was a kindness beneath the surface that was true and honorable. He'd helped her out on more than one occasion, and she adored his wife, Mira. She'd met his brothers, Steen and Zane, a couple times, and the loyalty between the brothers was amazing. Everyone in the family was incredibly kind, despite the fact that the men were tall, broad-shouldered, and more than a little intimidating when they walked into a room. "Which brother are you?"

He raised his eyebrows, still watching her warily. "Travis."

"Travis Stockton." She frowned, trying to remember if she'd heard anything about him, but she didn't think she had. No matter. The fact he was Chase's brother was enough, given the level of her desperation right now. "Well, if you're as good a guy as Chase, then I trust you in my kitchen."

Surprise flashed across his face. "Really?"

She hesitated. "Why? Is there something about you I shouldn't trust?"

He paused, looking hard at her. "I'm completely fucked up in a lot of ways," he said, his voice hard, almost warning her. "People in this town don't like me."

She raised her brows at his defensiveness. His face was

dark and almost angry, and his fingers had tightened around her arm. Her heart turned over, and she wanted to hug him, because she knew what it felt like to suffer under a town's disdain. It was a brutal, horrible way for a child to grow up, and the scars never went away, no matter how hard one tried. "Well, townspeople suck sometimes."

He blinked. "What?"

She shrugged. "Does the fact that they don't like you mean I can't trust you in my kitchen?"

He stared at her for a long moment, then shook his head once. "No. It doesn't."

Of course it didn't. "Then please, please, please help me out tonight. I'm desperate."

A grin flashed across his face then, a smile that was so genuine that her chest tightened. "I'm on it." He slid off the stool. "Give me the ninety second tour, and then I'll be good."

As he stood up, she realized how tall he really was. He towered over her, taller, wider, and so much stronger than she was. He was gritty and tough, a man who wouldn't stand down from anything. She hesitated for a split second, suddenly nervous. Her kitchen was her sanctuary, her world, the only thing that had saved her eight years ago. Having Travis in there felt dangerous, like she was turning over her foundation to someone she barely knew--

He shoved open the kitchen door and disappeared inside, not waiting for a second invitation.

Like it? Get it now!

STAY IN THE KNOW!

I write my books from the soul, and live that way as well. I've received so much help over the years from amazing people to help me live my best life, and I am always looking to pay it forward, including to my readers.

One of the ways I love to do this is through my mailing list, where I often send out life tips I've picked up, post readers surveys, give away Advance Review Copies, and provide insider scoop on my books, my writing, and life in general. And, of course, I always make sure my readers on my list know when the next book is coming out!

If this sounds interesting to you, I would love to have you join us! You can always unsubscribe at any time! I'll never spam you or share your data. I just want to provide value!

Sign up at www.stephanierowe.com to keep in touch!

Much love,

Stephanie

A QUICK FAVOR

Did you enjoy Jason and Astrid's story?

People are often hesitant to try new books or new authors. A few reviews can encourage them to make that leap and give it a try. If you enjoyed Accidentally Mine *and think others will as well, please consider taking a moment and writing one or two sentences on the eTailer and/or Goodreads. to help this story find the readers who would enjoy it. Even the short reviews really make an impact!*

Thank you a million times for reading my books! I love writing for you and sharing the journeys of these beautiful characters with you. I hope you find inspiration from their stories in your own life!

Love,
Stephanie

BOOKS BY STEPHANIE ROWE

Do you know why I love to write?

Because I love to reach deep inside the soul, both mine and yours, and awaken the spirit that gives us life. I want to write books that make you feel, that touch your heart, and inspire you to whatever dreams you hold in your heart.

"This book has the capacity to touch 90% of the women's lives. I went through all the fears and anguish of the characters with them and came out the other side feeling the hope and love. I would even say I experienced some healing of my own." -cyinca (Amazon Review)

All my stories take the reader on that same emotional journey, whether it's in a small Maine town, rugged cowboy country, or the magical world of immortal warriors. Some of my books are funnier, some are darker, but they all give the deep sense of emotional fulfillment.

"I adore this family! ...[Wyoming Rebels] is definitely one of

my favorite series and since paranormal is my usual interest, that's saying something." -Laura B (Amazon Review)

Take a look below. See what might strike your fancy. Give one of them a try. You might fall in love with a genre you don't expect!

CONTEMPORARY ROMANCE

WYOMING REBELS SERIES
(CONTEMPORARY WESTERN ROMANCE)
A Real Cowboy Never Says No
A Real Cowboy Knows How to Kiss
A Real Cowboy Rides a Motorcycle
A Real Cowboy Never Walks Away
A Real Cowboy Loves Forever
A Real Cowboy for Christmas
A Real Cowboy Always Trusts His Heart (Sept 2019!)

A ROGUE COWBOY SERIES
(CONTEMPORARY WESTERN ROMANCE)
A Rogue Cowboy for Her, featuring Brody Hart
(Coming Soon!)

LINKED TO A ROGUE COWBOY SERIES
(CONTEMPORARY WESTERN ROMANCE)
Her Rebel Cowboy

BIRCH CROSSING SERIES
(SMALL-TOWN CONTEMPORARY ROMANCE)
Unexpectedly Mine
Accidentally Mine

Unintentionally Mine
Irresistibly Mine
Mistakenly Mine (Coming Soon!)

MYSTIC ISLAND SERIES
(SMALL-TOWN CONTEMPORARY ROMANCE)
Wrapped Up in You (A Christmas novella)

CANINE CUPIDS SERIES
(ROMANTIC COMEDY)
Paws for a Kiss
Pawfectly in Love
Paws Up for Love

PARANORMAL

ORDER OF THE BLADE SERIES
(DARK PARANORMAL ROMANCE)
Darkness Awakened
Darkness Seduced
Darkness Surrendered
Forever in Darkness
Darkness Reborn
Darkness Arisen
Darkness Unleashed
Inferno of Darkness
Darkness Possessed
Shadows of Darkness
Hunt the Darkness
Awaken the Darkness (Oct 2019)

ORDER OF THE NIGHT
(AN ORDER OF THE BLADE SPINOFF SERIES)
(DARK PARANORMAL ROMANCE)

Edge of Midnight, featuring Thano Savakis
(Coming Soon!)

HEART OF THE SHIFTER SERIES
(DARK PARANORMAL ROMANCE)
Dark Wolf Rising
Dark Wolf Unbound
Dark Wolf Untamed (Coming Soon!)

SHADOW GUARDIANS SERIES
(DARK PARANORMAL ROMANCE)
Leopard's Kiss

NIGHTHUNTER SERIES
(DARK PARANORMAL ROMANCE)
Not Quite Dead

Writing as S.A. Bayne

NOBLE AS HELL SERIES
(FUNNY URBAN FANTASY)
Rock Your Evil

IMMORTALLY CURSED SERIES
(FUNNY PARANORMAL ROMANCE)
Immortally Cursed
Curse of the Dragon
Devil's Curse (Dec 2019)

THE MAGICAL ELITE SERIES
(FUNNY PARANORMAL ROMANCE)
The Demon You Trust

DEVILISHLY SEXY SERIES

For a complete list of Stephanie's books, click here.

ABOUT THE AUTHOR

NEW YORK TIMES AND *USA TODAY* bestselling author Stephanie Rowe is the author of more than fifty novels. She's a 2018 winner and a five-time nominee for the RITA® award, the highest award in romance fiction. Stephanie also writes high-octane, irreverent paranormals as S.A. Bayne.

For the latest info on Stephanie and her books, connect with her on the web at:
www.stephanierowe.com
www.sabayne.com

ACKNOWLEDGMENTS

Special thanks to my core team of amazing people, without whom I would never have been able to create this book. Each of you is so important, and your contribution was exactly what I needed. I'm so grateful to all of you! Your emails of support, or yelling at me because I hadn't sent you more of the book yet, or just your advice on covers, back cover copy and all things needed to whip this book into shape—every last one of them made a difference to me. I appreciate each one of you so much! I want to give a huge shout out to all my beta readers, whose eagle eyes and late night reading helped whip this book into shape. You guys are the BEST! Special thanks also to: Carla Gallway, Jeanne Hunter, Jan Leyh, Sharon Stogner, Summer Steelman, Teresa Gabelman, Holly Collins, Janet Juengling-Snell, and Phyllis Marshall. There are so many people I want to thank, but the people who simply must be called out are: Denise Fluhr, Dottie Jones, Alencia Bates, Emily Recchia, Rebecca Johnson, Nicole Telhiard, Mary Lynn Ostrum, Denise Whelan, Tamara Hoffa, Jean Bowden, and Ashley Cuesta. Thank you also to the following for all their amazing help: Judi Pflughoeft, Deb Julienne, Julie

Simpson, and Shell Bryce. You guys are the best! Thanks so much to Pete Davis for such an amazing cover, and for all his hard work on the technical side to make this book come to life. Special thanks also to my amazing daughter, who I love more than words could ever express. You are my world, sweet girl, in all ways.

For all those who love pizza. 'Nuff said.

Made in the USA
Columbia, SC
04 September 2021